WELCOME TO WRIGHTSBRIDGE

In the flickering candlelight over dinner, Kate marveled at how handsome Russell looked. How in love she felt sipping a glass of wine, listening to her husband regale her with the history of Wrightsbridge. It had been built by his great-grandfather, and four generations of Wrights had lived and died in this house.

After dinner, Kate cleared the dishes off the table and stacked them in the sink. She'd just rinse them off now and leave them for tomorrow. She had other things to attend to. Russell had winked at her and told her he'd meet her upstairs. She smiled broadly. They would make love, this first night in the old family home. Maybe even conceive an heir.

She giggled at how grand she was sounding to herself. Oh, how she loved Russell . . .

She felt his hand on her shoulder. "Yes, darling, I'll be there in a second," she promised. But the hand felt odd. . . . She looked over at it. She reached up and touched it. It was ice-cold.

She spun around. Behind her stood a man she had never seen, a man so horrible she was struck momentarily mute. His eyes were bulging from his face, his skin was black and blue, and his neck was twisted at an odd angle, as if he'd been hanged. He *was*, Kate realized as her horror mounted. The torn noose still dangled from around his neck.

Kate screamed. . . .

BOOK YOUR PLACE ON OUR WEBSITE AND MAKE THE READING CONNECTION!

We've created a customized website just for our very special readers, where you can get the inside scoop on everything that's going on with Zebra, Pinnacle and Kensington books.

When you come online, you'll have the exciting opportunity to:

- View covers of upcoming books
- Read sample chapters
- Learn about our future publishing schedule (listed by publication month *and author*)
- Find out when your favorite authors will be visiting a city near you
- Search for and order backlist books from our online catalog
- Check out author bios and background information
- Send e-mail to your favorite authors
- Meet the Kensington staff online
- Join us in weekly chats with authors, readers and other guests
- Get writing guidelines
- AND MUCH MORE!

Visit our website at
http://www.kensingtonbooks.com

WHERE DARKNESS LIVES

Robert Ross

PINNACLE BOOKS
Kensington Publishing Corp.
http://www.kensingtonbooks.com

PINNACLE BOOKS are published by

Kensington Publishing Corp.
850 Third Avenue
New York, NY 10022

All Kensington Titles, Imprints, and Distributed Lines are available at special quantity discounts for bulk purchases for sales promotions, premiums, fund-raising, and educational or institutional use. Special book excerpts or customized printings can also be created to fit specific needs. For details, write or phone the office of the Kensington special sales manager: Kensington Publishing Corp., 850 Third Avenue, New York, NY 10022, attn: Special Sales Department, Phone: 1-800-221-2647.

Pinnacle and the P logo Reg. U.S. Pat. & TM Off.

First Printing: July 2002
10 9 8 7 6 5 4 3 2 1

Printed in the United States of America

Kate and the Dead Girl

She first saw the dead girl on her wedding night.

No more than fourteen, her face was blue, as she'd suffocated to death. Her dark hair was pulled back into a ponytail, and there was spittle at the corners of her mouth. She was staring at Kate with her dead dull eyes, and in her arms she held a Raggedy Ann doll. One of the doll's legs was missing.

The dead girl was sitting in a rocking chair, watching as Kate and her new husband Russell entered the little cottage. Kate gasped when she saw her, but just a little. She said nothing. She'd learned that was best.

They were spending their honeymoon in the cottage of Kate's friend Erik, not six yards from the shore. It was little more than a shack, really, battered and bruised by the wind and the sea. A cold steady rain had fallen all day, and it chilled Kate to the bone. She stood now in the center of the living room, still in her overcoat, her arms wrapped around herself, watching Russell attempt to build a fire in the little stone hearth. The flame wouldn't hold and he cursed several times, making Kate afraid. Outside a shutter had fallen loose in the wind. It banged over and over again against the side of the cottage.

Kate turned her face toward the dead girl in a rocking chair. Sometimes they just went away, these ghosts that she had seen all her life. But sometimes they remained, just sitting there, as the girl was doing now. Kate looked away, keeping her eyes on the hearth. The flame caught, finally, after Russell had crumpled some old newspapers and placed them under the logs.

"There," he said, standing, clapping his hands together to clean them. "That should do it."

Kate looked up at him. Her husband. How handsome he was. Dark and brooding, like the heroes of the romantic novels she'd read as a girl. Her husband. And she'd known him barely three months.

Suddenly she heard a creak. Her eyes moved back over to the girl in the chair. She had started to rock now, and her lips were moving. Her eyes were intent on Kate.

"Kate?"

Russell took her in his arms.

"You're so cold."

Over his shoulder she could still see the girl. She seemed to react to Russell's embrace, as if it enraged her, offended her. Her mouth opened. Her hands lifted off the arms of the chair and clenched into little blue fists. The misshapen Raggedy Ann slid off her lap and fell to the floor.

Kate made a little sound of fear and buried her face in Russell's chest.

"Are you all right, darling? What's the matter?"

"I don't want to stay here," she said in a small voice.

"You don't want to stay here?" He sounded incredulous. He pulled back to look her in the eyes. "What do you mean? It's our honeymoon."

"Not here," she said weakly, not daring to look again over at the girl.

Russell stiffened. "You're being absurd, darling. There's nowhere else around for miles and it's late." He tried to smile, reason with her. "*You* found this place, after all, darling. It's *your* friend's. It was *your* idea to come here."

"Let's go back to New York," she pleaded.

"Now stop this, Kate. Stop this right now." He let her go, moving impatiently across the room to the couch where they'd set their suitcases. He popped his open, withdrawing a bottle of champagne. "We are on our honeymoon, and we will celebrate."

She forced her eyes to look again at the rocking chair. It was empty. She permitted herself a tiny sigh of relief.

But she knew she wasn't gone. Indeed, Kate would spend her entire wedding night with the little dead girl watching from the foot of the bed, snarling and gnashing her teeth like some crazed rabid animal, pulling first the other leg off her doll and then each of its arms. Once Russell had rolled off of Kate and fallen fast asleep, his snoring the sound of a hibernating bear, the girl seemed to calm a little, retreating into a corner. But still Kate lay awake all night, her eyes never moving from the little blue face that glared out at her from the dark.

Kate and Erik

"I can't imagine who she could be," Erik said, rubbing his chin. "I never knew the people I bought the cottage from. And I've never felt any presence there. Never."

"Well, whoever she was, she didn't like us there." Kate tore open a Sweet 'N Low and shook it into her coffee. "Especially when Russell and I got affectionate."

Erik's eyes sparkled over his menu. "But it was your wedding night."

She smiled wanly. "And there she was, watching us the whole time."

She took a sip of coffee. Thank God for Erik. He was the only one who knew about the things she saw. Not even Russell had any idea. Ever since her parents had had her committed at age twelve, she'd learned the wisdom of keeping such things to herself. Better to remain silent than be locked away.

But Erik believed her. He was a writer of books on the paranormal, and had witnessed everything from exorcisms to apparitions. His latest book, *How to Make Friends with Ghosts,* had received considerable attention in the press. He'd made several appearances on television to promote it, with people calling in to tell him about the forces—good, bad, or simply neutral—that lived in their homes or haunted their office buildings. Erik explained how ghosts weren't usually dangerous, merely confused about how to move on to the other side. Many of the experiences he discussed in his book were, in fact, based on conversations he'd had with Kate, who'd long ago made peace—if not friends—with her plethora of ghosts.

"What was so odd," she told him as he set down his menu, "is that the girl seemed so *angry.* As if we were doing something to spite her." Kate shivered. "She really frightened me. It's been a long time since anything I've seen frightened me so."

Erik considered this. "If the cottage was her home at some point, maybe she felt you were defiling it in some way."

Kate shrugged. "Maybe. But it's a one-room beach cottage. It couldn't have been her *home.*"

"It doesn't matter, Kate. If the place mattered to her, and then you come along and start gettin' down and dirty in it, she may have felt violated in some way."

Kate smirked. "Yet it's *your* place, Erik. I don't suppose that when *you* take your latest boyfriend up there, the two of you live like monks."

Erik laughed. "No. That's for sure. But then again, I can't *see* ghosts the way you do, Kate." He paused. "But I *can* usually *feel* them, and I've never felt any hostile presence there at all. Curious!"

The waitress had arrived. They each ordered cheeseburgers with fries, the same meal they'd ordered together ever since they first became best friends, nearly three years ago now. Kate had just arrived in New York, fresh out of college, hoping to find a job as a writer at a magazine. She'd had to settle for working in a video store on the Lower East Side. But she remained determined to become a successful writer, and sought out opportunities to practice her craft. She'd met Erik at a Tuesday night writers' group. He was almost ten years older than she was, but still had a youthful energy and vibrant spirit. He was handsome, if a bit overweight, with dancing blue eyes and deep dimples in his cheeks when he smiled. When Kate realized his interest in the paranormal, she made it a point to ask him out for coffee. When she then realized they shared *another* interest—men—she was only a little disappointed. More important to her than finding a lover was finding a *friend,* someone with whom she could finally talk to about what she *saw.*

Her parents had never understood. The first ghost she could remember seeing was a man in a black tuxedo, wandering around her bedroom. She was three. Her parents had been alarmed when she told them, thinking a prowler or a kidnapper had invaded their home. But after hearing about him over and over but never seeing him, they chalked him up as one of Kate's imaginary friends. The first of many.

The man in the tuxedo hadn't frightened her; he was just lost, aimless, sad. But when she was five she'd seen a woman in her kindergarten class covered with blood. That had caused her to scream, to throw a fit in the middle of story time, and so began her long history in and out of psychiatrists' offices. Her parents had just never believed her. Never.

"You've *got* to tell Russell at some point, sweetheart," Erik was saying to her.

She sighed, running her hand through her long red hair. "I don't know. Russell is such a rational, logical kind of person."

"Ain't *that* the truth." Erik made a face. "I still can't see what attracted you to him."

"He's my husband now, Erik," she scolded. "You can't talk bad about him."

"I'm not talking bad about him. I'm just saying that I never would have picked him out as the one for you." He sat back in the booth as the waitress delivered their burgers and fries. "It just all happened so fast, Kate. Just a few months ago we sat here like we always have, with no sign of Russell on the horizon."

It *had* happened very quickly, Kate couldn't deny that. Sometimes that made Kate scared, as if she wasn't sure what she'd gotten herself into. Up until meeting Russell, she'd always been such a careful person, a trait she learned early. She had to be on her guard, always on the alert, ever vigilant, to escape the men with the nets and straitjackets. She laughed to herself thinking of the image, but it was true: before she'd learned to control herself, keep her truth hidden, there were always well-meaning but ultimately ineffectual doctors and therapists ready to lock her up or give her drugs. Yes, she had learned to be careful, not to let down her guard.

But she had with Russell. And how wonderful that felt. For the first time in her life, she had allowed herself to fall in love and to be loved back. Thinking of Russell made her very happy. It had been out of character for him, too, he said, to propose so suddenly. Which was precisely why she had accepted, trusting the Fates.

"You'll like him when you get to know him better," she told Erik.

He took a bite of his burger and rolled his eyes. "For you, I'll try, sweetheart."

Kate laughed. "I know he can be a little stodgy. He's from an old New England family. Isn't that the way they come out of the mold up there? All levelheaded and rational and stoic. Maybe I need a little bit of that in my life.''

"Hopefully not too much," Erik said.

Kate smiled. She dipped a french fry into a little bowl of ketchup. There wasn't much chance of her getting too levelheaded and rational—not with dead folks regularly crossing her path and popping around corners to say "Boo!" She didn't see them as often these days, not every day as she had when she was a girl. Or maybe she *did* still see them, except they had become merely part of the fabric. Usually they were just there, walking along, sitting on a bench waiting for the bus. Sometimes they smiled at her; sometimes they were crying; sometimes they tried to scare her, but she didn't scare easily anymore. When she'd been a kid, of course, just their sheer presence had been enough to terrify her, causing her to be sent to all those shrinks and therapists. Finally her parents committed her to an institution, the Institute for Living Well. She had been just twelve. When she was released, three years later, the doctors gave her a clean bill of emotional health. Yet all that was different was that she had learned not to speak about what she saw.

Ever since that time, her relationship with her parents had been strained. Her younger self had grown up into the daughter they wanted: calm, not excitable, unimaginative to the core. After college in the Midwest, Kate decided not to return to Sacramento, where she'd grown up. She would go to New York, where she could pursue her dream of becoming a writer. Gradually she stopped all communication with her family. She hadn't even informed them yet of her marriage.

It had been a small ceremony. Russell's parents were both dead—killed, he explained, in a car accident when he was just seven—and his sister was traveling in Europe. So it had just been the two of them before the justice of the peace, with Erik as witness. Afterward the three of them had dinner at a small French restaurant in the East Village, and then she and Russell had set out on the long trek to Montauk in the driving rain.

"Have you met any of his friends yet?" Erik asked.

Kate shook her head. "No. But we haven't even been married a week. I'm sure I will."

"Why are you so sure? You didn't meet any of them in the three months prior to the wedding." He made a face. "Strange, isn't it, how he had no one to stand up for him?"

"You only need one witness," Kate said defensively. "Still . . ."

Kate laughed, wanting to brush aside any feelings of unease. She didn't want to consider the possibility that Russell didn't actually *have* any friends. "I think you're jealous of Russell," she teased. "Even if you are gay! You're afraid I won't see you anymore. Well, there's no need to worry, Erik. You'll always be my best friend!"

He smiled back at her. "So where is Prince Charming today?"

"He had some business. With the stock market in such a flux these days, he's all over the place."

Russell was an investments counselor. He worked from home mostly, trading on his computer. He came from money, so he had money to start with, but Kate had the impression he'd made bundles more—even if his apartment was just a small, sparsely furnished two-bedroom walk-up on Fiftieth Street at Ninth Avenue. Kate had been out this afternoon buying some new curtains and cleaning out her stuff from her old place on Avenue B. Her roommate had already found a replacement for her, and she needed to clear out her old room.

"Aren't you going to miss the old neighborhood at all?" Erik asked.

She considered the question. "Well, I'll miss seeing you all the time, of course, but I'm sure we'll still get together a couple times a week. I won't miss that job at the video store though. All those drunks renting porn and making eyes at me."

Part of her liked the fact that Russell was old-fashioned enough to insist she quit her job and let him support her. It would give her time to write, which Russell encouraged. Her dream was to write a beautiful gothic love story like the kind they just didn't write anymore. Of course, it would have its resident ghost. Kate figured she knew enough about ghosts to write a good one.

"Oh, God, Erik, I need to get moving," Kate said suddenly, looking at her watch. "I want to finish my errands and have Russell's dinner started before he gets home."

Erik shook his head. "Don't be turning into Laura Petrie now."

"Oh, pooh."

She pulled her wallet out of her purse but Erik shook his head. "Consider it a belated wedding present."

"Your present was letting us use your cottage."

He waved his hand at her. "You know, I'm going up there next week. I think I'll do a séance. Maybe the girl will talk to me and tell me who she is."

"Well, tell her hello from me," Kate said, "and tell her I didn't mean any harm."

"I'll do that."

She stood and walked over to Erik. They embraced firmly. "I love you, Erik," she said.

"Me, too, sweetie. You call me if ever he doesn't treat you right."

She promised. But she thought there was little chance of that.

Russell and Rosalind

Something dead was floating in his coffee cup.

Whether it was a fly or a cockroach Russell couldn't tell, as it had shriveled up into a tiny ball of string. It did not occur to him that it might indeed be a ball of string, a minuscule wad of dust, a speck of lint. No, it was something dead, there was no question about it, and it had fallen into his coffee while he had gone to pull on his sweater, and it had died there.

"Damn," he said, and tossed the coffee, still hot, with a side-handed splash into the sink. It had gotten so cold in his apartment—unusually cold for April—and now he'd have to put on another pot, make another cup.

That's when he felt her—Rosalind—the way he always felt her before he saw her. His sister was coming up the stairs, he knew, and would, at any moment, be knocking on his door.

"Rosalind," he said softly to himself, and decided the coffee would do no good.

The knock came just as he expected.

"Well," she said, standing there, appraising him, "you don't look so worse for the wear."

He shrugged a laugh. "I told you. Marriage has done me good."

"This apartment is freezing," she complained, hugging herself. She wore nothing more than a black blazer over a red satin lace blouse, tucked into snug black jeans. She smelled of thick Indian perfume, heavy and fragrant. She looked around the cramped apartment, surveying it the way she had the last time she was there—except last time it had been Theresa he'd been married to, and not Kate. "It's colder in here than it is outside."

"That's what happens in these old New York apartments," he offered, wishing for his coffee. "They seem to retain the cold."

Rosalind shivered. "I don't know why you stay here."

He sighed. Somewhere in his mind he saw the dead bug in the sink—a spider, he thought now—slowly stretching its curled-up legs, opening itself the way a flower blossoms, gingerly tapping against the porcelain to find its way back.

"So," he said finally, looking at her, "Rosalind."

"Russell," she replied.

Their mother had named them—twins, the girl seven minutes older than the boy—Rosalind and Russell, after seeing the movie *Auntie Mame*. It was the only story he liked about his mother, the only one he would tell. But, as Grandmother always said, it was such a white trash kind of thing to do.

"We were very disappointed you didn't make it back for the wedding," he said quietly, aware he hadn't asked her to sit down.

"I was in Paris, Russell. It's not like I was around the corner."

He held firm. "I let you know in enough time."

She only smiled. She moved carefully, gliding easily

into the living room, around the ottoman and the piles
of floppy disks on the floor, her long legs almost rhyth-
mic in their precision, her long, shiny, ebony-black hair
moving as one solid mass down her back. She took a
seat on the white leather couch, a study in contrasts,
black and white. She crossed her legs and folded her
hands—tipped with scarlet nails—over her knee.

Looking up at him, she said plainly: "I think you
should come home, Russell."

· Home. He knew what she meant. Home was that old
house in Connecticut with bats hanging from its eaves,
with no one living there now except old Auntie Cee.
He hadn't been back in many years, and neither had
Rosalind. Yet still the place always followed them
around, no matter where they went. Home.

"Rosalind, I am *married* now. I can't just—"

"You've been married before."

"And I didn't go home then either!" He felt himself
growing angry at the reference to Theresa. "Even
though you wanted me to go home then too. Well, I'm
not, Rosalind. I'm not going home."

"Now, don't go upsetting yourself, baby brother."

"I'm not upset."

Rosalind laughed. "You have every right to be,
remembering that whore."

"Don't call her that."

"She cheated on you! I call things as I see them."

Russell let out a long breath. "Maybe that's true, but
she was my wife and now she's dead, and we shouldn't
speak ill of her."

She shook her head in amusement. "Have it your
way, baby brother."

Remembering Theresa *did* make him upset. So many
conflicting emotions. She had died in this very room.
Here, on the couch where Rosalind now sat. Russell
would never—*could* never—forget her hands, clawing

the air, beckoning up at him, drawing him down closer to her face with its sunken eyes and protruding teeth. Here Russell had kissed his wife, horrifyingly beautiful in the hour of her death, and here their twenty months together had come to an end.

Twenty months Russell had discovered were filled with lies and treachery.

"You always fell in love far too easily," Rosalind said. "Remember that foolish Amy Duggerman in fifth grade? She let you carry her books so she could flirt with Bobby Shortridge. Well, we took care of *them*, didn't we, Russell?"

"Rosalind, please . . ."

"Girls were always trying to take advantage of you. And would have, too, if I hadn't been around to watch out for you."

He couldn't help but smile. It was true. Only minutes older yet Rosalind had always been the big sister. Always there to protect him.

"Kate is different," he assured her. "She's good. She's sweet. You'll like her, Rosalind."

She just lit a cigarette and exhaled the smoke over her shoulder.

When Rosalind had come the last time, it had been a day much like this: cold enough to get under your skin, unnaturally cold, colder inside than it was out. He'd just married Theresa, and Russell had seen then in Rosalind's eyes exactly what she was thinking, the same thing he was certain she was thinking again now: *Why have you chosen this? This is not what Grandmother raised us to be. You could have had so much more than a two-room, paint-flaking, cockroach-ridden apartment in Hell's Kitchen. You were supposed to carry on the family name, bring a wife back to Wrightsbridge, open up the estate for the Old Town Day celebrations, play host with the mayor and the citizens while your wife entertained the ladies in the parlor. . . .*

Russell felt himself grow angry. As if *Rosalind* had followed Grandmother's dictates, with her red lace and the games she'd play with the boys up in the attic. And how *about* Bobby Shortridge? How about *him*, Rosalind? *How about Bobby Shortridge?*

"What were you doing in Europe?" he asked, choking back his anger, wanting to change the subject.

"Oh, you know me, Russell," she said, waving her cigarette in her hand. "I just got around."

He smirked. Oh, how he imagined she *had*. Rosalind had been *getting around* since she was a young girl. So what gave *her* the right to pass judgment on *him*—this tramp, this hell-raiser, this witch? He hated the look in her eyes as she surveyed his apartment, his home—for this *was* his home. His and Kate's. Not that place back in Connecticut. *This!*

"Why don't *you* go back to Wrightsbridge, Rosalind, if it's so important to you?" he asked suddenly, aggressively. "When was the last time *you* were there?"

She let out the smoke in rings over her head. "Oh, I plan on returning," she said, turning her eyes languidly to lock them on to her brother's, "if *you* will, too, Russell."

He said nothing, just crossed his arms in front of his chest.

She sighed. "I'm worried about what's become of you, Russell," she said, attempting, unsuccessfully, to sound sincere. "I don't like what I see here. And neither do you. Admit it."

"I'm married now," he said quietly.

She made a tiny, impatient sound. "What does this one do? Does she have any outside interests or is she just another happy little homemaker like the last one?"

"She's a writer," Russell said, somewhat defensively.

"A *writer!* Oh, heavens! Romance novels? Bodice-rippers? Tell me, Russell! I'm *dying* to know."

He walked away from her in disgust.

She smiled. "Oh, dear brother," she said. "My dear, dear, baby brother. How I once took such care of you. Do you remember that day, trapped in the snowstorm, down by the river? How I kept us warm by building that fire? How I gave you my coat? You would have frozen out there. Just like you're freezing here."

Of course he remembered that day. They had gotten lost in the woods behind their house, and it had started to snow. Russell tripped and fell, spraining his ankle, and they'd had to wait until the next day before the sheriff found them. Russell had thanked God for Rosalind then.

"Russell, it's not just you I'm worried about." Rosalind was changing tacts, shifting strategy. She looked at him plaintively. "It's Auntie Cee. She *needs* you."

He grunted. "We pay for a nurse to take care of her. What more could *I* do?"

Rosalind creased her brow looking at him. "Oh, Russell. And here I thought you *loved* Auntie Cee. How many times did Auntie Cee intercede with Grandmother for us? And now she's old and alone and a little daffy. She *needs* you, Russell."

He felt his back stiffen. She knew how to get him. She knew mentioning Auntie Cee would break him down.

"Why not you, Rosalind?" he railed. "Why can't *you* go back for her?"

"I told you. I will. If you do, too."

"You're lying." He was suddenly pacing the room, agitated. "As if you'd stop all your traveling around to move back into Wrightsbridge! I don't believe you, Rosalind."

She chuckled. "You know me so well, baby brother."

He grimaced. "I know the game you're playing, Rosalind. You want *me* to be there all the time, so that *I* can

take care of Auntie Cee while you're off with your men,
partying all night. That's why you want me to go back."

"It's a beautiful house, Russell! Really now! You'd
think being master of Wrightsbridge was a prison sen-
tence! What's here for you in New York? This *writer*? This
little wife you so impulsively married without talking it
over with *me*?"

He ignored her taunt. "How bad *is* Auntie Cee?"

"Quite bad. Didn't you get Mrs. Tynan's letter?"

"Yes." Auntie Cee's nurse-companion had written to
him just last week, and it had been on his mind for
days. Auntie Cee had been the only good thing about
Wrightsbridge, the kind, gentle counterpoint to Grandmother's cruel rigidity. And now she was nearing one
hundred years old, losing her mind, unable to walk,
confined to her chair in that middle room on the third
floor overlooking the garden. It was either full-time
care, Mrs. Tynan had said, or a nursing home. Auntie
Cee had said so often she never wanted to go to a
nursing home, that she wanted nothing so much as to
die in the house where she was born. Wrightsbridge.

Just then the buzzer sounded. Rosalind raised an
indifferent eyebrow toward the sound while Russell
rushed to answer it. "Yes?" he called down through the
intercom.

"Russell, it's me!" Kate's voice filled the room. "I'm
so glad you're there! I've been a dunce and forgotten
my key!"

"Just a moment, darling."

He pressed the button to let her in downstairs. He
turned to his sister. "You'll see," he promised. "You'll
love her, Rosalind. As much as I do."

Kate and Russell

"Hello, darling," he said. "My, your hands are cold."

Kate had cupped his face in her hands as she kissed him. "I'm sorry to be such a nuisance," she said.

"Not at all. I'm just glad I was here. Otherwise you'd have had to wait outside until I returned."

Kate removed her coat and hung it on the rack. She sniffed. "Russell," she asked, "have you been burning incense?"

"No, darling. Why do you ask?"

She walked into the living room. "I smell something."

He seemed a little uncomfortable. "You do? What do you smell?"

"I'm not sure. Something Eastern. Some kind of incense."

Russell sighed. "Well, yes. I suppose what you smell is my sister's perfume." He paused. "She was here."

Kate broke into a broad smile. "She was *here*? She's back from Europe?"

"Yes. She's returned."

"When did she get back? Oh, Russell! Isn't it a shame she just missed our wedding?"

He sighed. "She expressed her deep regrets about that. I wanted her to stay to meet you but she had so many things to do now that she's home. She'll be back soon, though." Russell smiled wanly. "She promised that."

"Well, where is she staying? She doesn't have a place here in New York, does she?"

Russell's face darkened. "Oh, Rosalind always has a place to stay."

Kate smiled cautiously. "A boyfriend?"

"Any number of them."

It was clear Russell didn't approve of his sister's lifestyle. But it was of no matter to Kate. She'd learned long ago not to judge other people. She'd gladly accept Rosalind for whoever she was. She was truly excited to meet her sister-in-law. Finally, some connection to Russell's life.

"Well, maybe we can have dinner with her," Kate suggested.

"She has plans this evening, I think. But soon." He sighed. "Darling, I really need to talk with you about something."

"Let me just wash up quickly," she said. "I'll be right back."

Ever since moving to New York, she'd had a compulsion to wash her hands after riding the subway. So many people touched those poles and seats. She hurried into the bathroom and switched on the light. Turning on the faucet, she looked up into the mirror.

She gasped.

The face of an old man with a beard was staring back at her.

"She doesn't want you in the house," he spoke to

her, his voice old and dry and cracking, as if it hadn't been used in years.

Kate spun around. There was no one behind her. She looked back into the mirror. The man wasn't there anymore either.

"Who are you?" she whispered. "What did you say to me?"

Her ghosts didn't often speak to her. Usually when they did, they were quite specific. They were intelligent spirits, realizing they had lost their way and were asking for directions, just as a living pedestrian might on the street. But this one hadn't waited around for a reply. She called out to him again.

"Who are you?"

But there was nothing. Silence.

What had he said?

She doesn't want you in the house.

Who didn't want her? In *what* house? This one?

Odd. Kate had never seen any ghosts in Russell's apartment before. She smiled a little. *Russell's apartment.* She had to stop calling it that. It was *hers* now, too. And if some ghost didn't want her here, well, that was too bad.

She dried her hands on the washcloth hanging beside the sink. Suddenly she thought about the little girl in the cottage out at Montauk. *She clearly hadn't wanted me in that house.* Had the old man meant her? *Well, I have no intention of going back there,* Kate thought. *If she sent you here to tell me that, assure her I'll respect her wishes.*

Yet what was it about the old man's face that had seemed so strange? Almost familiar? He *had* seemed lost. Sad and lost. Maybe his message wasn't for her. Maybe it was just gibberish. Erik said that happened sometimes.

She let out a sigh and chalked it up to another experience living with her particular "gift."

Back in the living room, Russell was sitting on the couch waiting for her. She was struck again by just how handsome he was. He was the kind of man she used to dream about as a girl. Tall and dark, with a cleft chin. He was what she imagined Cinderella's prince to look like. She smiled to herself. She still felt like a blushing bride. How lucky she was to have found him.

"What is it, Russell?" Kate asked, sitting beside him. "What did you want to talk about?"

He showed her a letter. She made a face.

"This came a couple of days ago," he explained. "Please read it."

Kate glanced down at the signature. "Who's Audrey Tynan?" she asked.

"A nurse I pay to care for my aunt."

"Aunt? Russell, you never told me about any aunt."

"Read the letter, Kate."

She did. It appeared that Miss Cecilia Wright, aged ninety-eight, had been in steady decline over the past few months and this Mrs. Tynan worried she might have to be committed to a nursing home. Mrs. Tynan could not provide round-the-clock care, and she wanted to know what Russell felt should be done. She'd apparently tried reaching him by phone but Russell hadn't returned her calls. Kate wondered why.

"I was so caught up in our wedding plans, darling," he said, as if reading her mind.

"Why did you never tell me about your aunt?"

He sighed. "I don't know. Sometimes remembering my childhood isn't pleasant."

She took his hand. "The loss of your parents? Is that it, Russell? You were very young."

He nodded. "It was never the same after they died. My grandmother was very strict. Auntie Cee—Cecilia—was so good to Rosalind and me, though. She was our saving grace."

"Oh, Russell." Kate embraced him. "I've waited so long for you to share your past with me. I'd love so much to meet Auntie Cee. I'm sure I'll love her."

He beamed at her. "Do you think we should go, then, darling? Should we go to Wrightsbridge and see her?"

"Of *course* we should." She studied him. "Why are you so reluctant to go back?"

He sighed again. "I don't know. It's just that I've made a life for myself away from there." His face darkened. "Maybe Rosalind doesn't think it's much of a life, but it's *mine*." He looked at Kate. "*Ours!*"

"Of course it is." She frowned. "What makes you say Rosalind doesn't think it's much of a life? Did she say that?"

He sniffed. "She didn't need to. But I can always tell what Rosalind is thinking. Twins always can."

"I've heard that."

"Kate, she was saying we should go back there to live."

She blinked a few times. "*Live?* Move to Connecticut permanently?"

"I told her that was absurd. That we each had our own lives here."

"Yes, darling, you have your work . . ."

He looked at her. "But perhaps . . . perhaps we could go back for a few months. Maybe through the summer. Get out of the city for a bit. It's so pretty up there in the spring. The gardens . . ."

Kate looked at him intently. "Is that what you'd like, Russell?"

He looked away. He seemed genuinely torn. "I don't know."

"Because if it is, Russell, you can work from anywhere. You could just set up your modem and if you needed to go into the city for the day you could just take the train—"

He turned and looked into her eyes. "And you could write, darling. There's plenty of space, plenty of solitude. And you could keep me from going daffy with my daffy old aunt."

She laughed. "A break from the stifling New York summer heat *would* be pleasant," she said, just as they both shivered, because it was so cold for April. They laughed. "I think we should give it a try. There's nothing keeping us here. You owe it to Auntie Cee."

Russell looked at her a little oddly. "That's just what Rosalind said."

"Well, maybe she's right." Kate smiled. "I assume she'll spend time there as well."

He nodded. "She promised."

"Good. Oh, Russell. I'm glad about this. I've been wanting so much to meet your family, to see where you grew up. When shall we leave?"

He seemed strangely drained of any emotion. "As soon as possible," he managed to say.

Kate looked at him. "Are you all right?"

Russell nodded. "I suppose I ought to call Mrs. Tynan and tell her we're coming." He stood, crossing over to the phone. He turned to Kate and gave her a weird little smile. "The master of Wrightsbridge is returning with his bride."

The Courtship of
Russell and Kate

They had met one night a little over three months ago at the video store. Russell had come to the front counter and asked if they had *Jane Eyre*. Kate had found him very handsome, but he hadn't seemed very flirtatious, just matter-of-fact. They did have the film, Kate explained after looking it up on the computer, but it was checked out. She asked if he wanted to reserve it, but he politely said no, thanked her for her trouble, and left.

The next night he came in again and inquired about the film once more, but although it had been returned that morning, someone else had checked it out not more than an hour before. Russell laughed slightly when Kate told him.

"I suppose I should've taken your advice and reserved it when I could have," he said.

"Will you do it now?" she asked.

He agreed. He gave her his name and number. "Russell Wright," he said. She liked how it sounded.

He didn't come in the third night, although Kate held the video at the counter for him. Finally, just before closing, she called.

"Mr. Wright?"

"Yes?"

He sounded distant, distracted.

"This is Kate Colson at Flash Video. We have *Jane Eyre* for you."

"Who have . . . what?"

"*Jane Eyre.* The video you reserved."

"Oh. Oh, yes. Yes, of course."

"We're open for another fifteen minutes. Do you want to come by?"

He agreed. He made it just as Kate was shutting off the neon front lights. He apologized for being so obtuse. He'd been working all night at his computer, he said, and had just gotten embroiled in figures and stocks. He was so glad she had called. He sure needed a break.

"I've been wanting to see this film again," he said. "There's just something about old gothic love stories that intrigues me."

Right there Kate had been intrigued herself. Gothic love stories were also her favorite, and although she'd read the Brontë novel, she'd never seen the film. She told Russell that.

"Never? Oh, my. It's so—so—*gothic!*" He smiled broadly as he held eye contact with her. "This may sound strange, but would you like to come watch it with me?"

"I—I don't think so," she said. "But thanks anyway."

He blushed. "Of course. I'm sorry. I shouldn't have asked."

She smiled. "No, it's very nice that you asked. I just don't know you, Mr. Wright."

He nodded. "You're right to say no. It's very unlike me to ask. I'm not sure what made me do so."

She looked at him. This man was no serial killer, no rapist, no maniac. She had always trusted her intuition. This was a good man. A man with some sorrow, some pain, but a good man nonetheless. She hadn't been on a date in a very long time, and she'd been restless recently, kidding Erik that she needed to start hanging out with more straight guys.

"On second thought, Mr. Wright," she said, "I'd *love* to watch it with you."

He looked stunned. "You *would?*"

"Sure." She hastily scribbled something onto a pad near the cash register. "But I'm leaving a note here for my coworkers telling them where I've gone. We have your address and phone in our files." She grinned. "Just so they know where to look in case I disappear into your icebox or something."

He looked horrified. "Oh, Miss Colson, I assure you I—"

She brushed away his words with a wave of her hand and a smile. "I'm sure you're quite harmless, Mr. Wright," she said. "Not to mention very attractive."

He blushed a deeper red. "As are you, Miss Colson."

"Kate," she corrected him, as she proceeded to lock up the store.

If anything untoward *were* to happen, Kate reasoned, she had her cell phone in her purse. Push one number and she got right through to Erik. Another one was the police. But she really wasn't frightened walking back to Russell's apartment. She was excited. It was something her parents would have so thoroughly disapproved of. That alone made her want to do it.

So she was taking a risk. Wasn't that why she had moved to New York?

It turned out to be a perfectly respectable evening. Russell's apartment was spartan and cold, but wasn't that the way for most straight bachelors? Kate made popcorn and actually clutched Russell's hands during the scary parts. She was quite enthralled by her handsome host, the way his eyes twinkled when he talked to her, the way he talked so passionately not only about the film but about so many things, from the stock market to Superman comic books to the way the seasons changed in New England. There was an undeniable boyish innocence to Russell that Kate found endearing.

He told her about losing his parents early, but not much of anything else about his family. He preferred to spend time attempting to explain stocks and bonds to Kate, which didn't go very well, Kate never having much of a mind for numbers. She guessed his immersion in the world of stocks and mutual funds was a way of coping with a painful past. When they said good night, Kate had already started to fall in love with him.

They saw each other every night after that. There were several dinners, many videos, and one long romantic walk across the Brooklyn Bridge, on a blue, chilly night. The East River reflected a million specks of light that danced from the city, and along its murky violet stretch, they could see, lit up in a row, all of the bridges that connected the island of Manhattan to the rest of the world. Russell was telling her about the bridge, about how it was built, how it was supported. He was so knowledgeable that Kate had to ask if he had ever been an architect, or an engineer.

"No." Russell laughed. "I guess I just know a little about a lot of things. I read a lot as a boy."

He looked so handsome standing there on the bridge, the lace of wires glowing behind him, the wind in his hair.

"I like talking with you, Kate," he said. "It's been so long since I've gotten out of the house and done things like this. I've just been so holed up, alone—"

"Why is that, Russell? Why have you kept so much to yourself?"

She suspected he was grieving someone. A broken relationship. A woman from his past. But he never confirmed it for her. From the start, they had their secrets from each other. Russell never told Kate he had been married before, and Kate never told him she could see people who were dead.

All he told her was that until he had met her, he had never felt so alive.

"Do you think it's crazy for someone to tell someone else that he loves her—even though he's only known her for a few weeks?"

"No," she said. "I don't think it's crazy."

They kissed each other in the lights of the bridge, the wind slapping at them and whistling through the cables.

A week later he asked her to marry him, and she said yes.

Erik's Caution

"Sweetie, I don't think Connecticut is a good decision." Erik folded his arms across his chest, leaning up against the bureau.

"Well, I do." Kate was packing. Russell was out at one of the brokerages he worked for, tying up some loose ends before the move. She folded a sweatshirt into her suitcase and looked over at Erik firmly. "Russell needs to go back and tend to family affairs, and I'm his wife."

"Wife or not, you don't know what you're getting into," Erik insisted. "What are you going to do in that big old house in the middle of nowhere?"

"Help him, as any wife should."

"Sweetheart, what's happened to you?" Erik threw his hands into the air. "You were so feisty, so independent. Now you act like it's 1955 and you're Donna Reed." He made a sound of impatience.

Kate sighed. "Erik, it's just for a few months. I'll have a chance to write, to finally have time to get into my head and my heart and produce a great novel—all while sitting in a New England garden in midsummer and smelling the daisies.''

"Oh, sweetie."

She smiled over at him. "Erik, I love you for caring so much. For worrying. But all I've ever really wanted was to find that special someone. We *all* want that, don't we?"

He shrugged. "Yes, I suppose so." He smiled sadly. "Maybe I *am* just jealous. I haven't found someone, and *you* have, and now you're moving away."

Kate clicked her suitcase shut. She was nearly all packed. She and Russell would leave for Connecticut tomorrow morning. Russell had rented a car. She looked forward to the drive. Connecticut was so pretty in the spring.

She placed a hand against Erik's cheek. "I'll miss you," she said. "You *will* come visit, won't you? It's a huge house. A mansion, really, the way Russell's described it to me."

Erik nodded. "Yes, I'll visit. It'll be nice to get out of the city for a couple days."

"And you'll find somebody," she told him. "I know you will. Didn't you have a date last weekend? Didn't you go up to the cottage at Montauk?"

He looked at her squarely. "Yes. I've never told you all the details."

She grinned, sitting down on her bed. "So *tell,* " she said.

"Not about the date, sweetheart." Erik sat beside her. "The guy I went with was a medium. When we got to the cottage, we held a séance."

"And what happened?" Kate leaned in closer to Erik. "Did the girl come? Did you talk to her?"

"No. She didn't come." He paused, narrowing his eyes at her. "Somebody *else* did, though."

"Who?"

"I don't know. It was an old man with a beard. I'd never seen him before."

Kate pulled back a little. "What did he do? What did he say?"

Erik sighed. "He just stood there. I asked him why he'd come when we were calling the girl. And he said—and I quote—'She doesn't want you in the house.' "

Kate gasped. It was the same thing the old man had said to her that day in the mirror. Could Erik's old man and the one she'd seen be the same?

Erik was thinking the same thing. "A short white beard, a lost look on his face?"

"Yes," she had to admit. "That sounds like him."

He reached over and took her hand. "I have a thought," he said, "but you're not going to like it. You'll think I'm saying it for my own reasons."

Kate felt impatient. Russell would be home at any minute. "Just tell me, Erik."

"The old man appeared to you in the mirror just before Russell brought up the idea of going to Connecticut. Then, when I was calling on the ghost of the little girl to tell me why she had been so upset by your being in the cottage, he appears to me to give me the same message."

She looked at him plaintively. "You think it's about me? And going to Wrightsbridge?"

He nodded. "Somebody doesn't want you in that house."

Kate felt a flicker of fear. "But who? Who's the *she?* Who doesn't want me there? The little girl? Do you think it's her?"

"I can't answer that, Kate." Erik looked at her with deep concern in his eyes. "I just know I'm worried about you going to Connecticut. Why would the same ghost appear to both of us with the same message?" He embraced her suddenly. "Oh, please, sweetheart! Take care of yourself!"

"I will, Erik," she promised.

She found it difficult to sleep that night, alert to every creak and every shadow. Even with Russell snoring beside her, she remained unnerved by what Erik had told her. She lay there expecting at any moment to see the little girl's blue face in the dark, and was terrified that she awaited her in that big old house in Connecticut. She was lulled to sleep finally by the sounds of a New York night, the sirens and the bleating of car horns. She would miss them. She hadn't realized how much they had come to soothe her, how much she had come to depend on them to ward off the fears she had known since childhood. At Wrightsbridge, there would be no buffer between her and the dead.

Wrightsbridge

Looking up at the house where he had been born took Russell's breath away. It loomed large against the bright blue sky, an oddly shaped Victorian with three stories and four gables. Maples and oaks and pines grew high around the house, keeping much of it in shade even in midsummer at high noon. Little seemed to have changed since he was a boy—little except the deaths. Once the house had been filled with people, every room filled with light and noise and movement: the radio, the television, he and Rosalind racing up and down the stairs, Grandmother's voice calling after them, Grandfather's cries at night. Now there was only Auntie Cee in the house, and she was confined to one room on the third floor.

It was called Wrightsbridge, for the simple reason that their name was Wright, and one had to cross a bridge—albeit a footbridge, but a bridge nonetheless—to access the front of the house. The bridge was built out of slate and sandstone, a charming walkway with figures of angels carved at its ends, angels whose faces had softened over the past century, noses flattened, eyes obscured, mouths pulled back as if soured. The bridge arched over a brook that wrapped itself like a lazy snake around the dwelling. In springtime, the brook often flooded, but it had never reached the house. They were, Grandmother often said, spared by God.

Or the angels.

Now Russell stood with Kate at the foot of the bridge, their rental car parked among the poplar trees that lined the perimeter of the estate. He gently caressed one of the angels' faces and listened to the soft babble of the brook below them.

"This was the angel Gabriel," he said dreamily to Kate. "My sister and I named all four of these angels. Michael the archangel is on the other side."

"Who is this one?" Kate asked, pointing to the carved figure opposite Gabriel. It was the most weathered of all the angels, a face nearly obliterated by a hundred years of rain, sun, wind, and children's hands. One wing was broken, gone.

"That," Russell said, and he smiled, "is Lucifer."

Kate was about to touch it, but she pulled her hand back.

"The fallen angel. That's why his wing is broken."

They started over the bridge, with the house standing solemnly ahead of them. Kate was fighting off a sudden regret for having agreed to this move. There was no garden. By the look of things, the shrubbery had not been tended to in years. Emerald-green ivy held the house in a fierce grip; several windows on the east side were completely covered by vines and leaves. The only flowers she could see were the bright yellow forsythia on the wild, unkempt bushes that shielded much of the front of the house.

"Maybe I can do some gardening?" she asked.

"I should think so," Russell replied. "But I should talk to Rosalind."

It struck her as odd. She was Russell's wife, after all. In the old days they would have called her the mistress of Wrightsbridge. Why should his *sister* have any say in what she did? But she supposed the house belonged to Rosalind as much as it did Russell, and so Kate accepted the fact that she needed to be consulted about any decisions they made.

Then why wasn't she here? Why had Rosalind stayed behind in New York? Still she hadn't deigned to grace Kate with her presence. Kate was starting to grow strangely uneasy about this sister, about the near-deference Russell showed her. He'd accepted her excuses for not meeting them in New York with apparent pique but with little protest. "There's nothing I can do about Rosalind," he'd told Kate. "She makes her own way." There was no word on when she'd be joining them here in Connecticut, but when she did, Russell insisted, they should just give her plenty of room. "I wouldn't like for you to cross her," he said. "She's quite independent."

They stepped off the footbridge and started up the gravel path to the front door. "Maybe Rosalind is here already," Kate suggested.

"Oh, I should think not," Russell replied. "But then again, one never knows with Rosalind."

They were on the front steps now. The porch was cracking; some floorboards needed to be replaced. "I see I shall be busy for quite some time repairing this place," Russell observed, and giving a quick, awkward rap against the pane of glass on the front door, he went inside.

Kate lingered. She turned her face to the sun and savored the warmth on her cheeks. She had an odd sensation in the pit of her stomach, something like the

feeling she used to get when she was very little and she'd
stay overnight at some friend's house. At first the idea
would seem loads of fun, and she'd be all hyped up—
but come the time when she was there, when there was
no going back home to her own bedroom and her own
stuffed animals and her own dolls lined up at the foot
of her bed, she'd feel sick. It would be too late to turn
back then, and Ann Marie's mother was turning out the
light, and Kate was trapped.

Especially when the dead showed up.

She tried to bolster her courage. So she felt a little
homesick for New York. *That's to be expected,* Kate
thought, letting the sun kiss her upturned cheeks and
the fresh spring air fill her lungs.

"I'm going to write something today, this very day,"
she vowed in a whisper to herself. "I'm going to come
out and walk along that brook and I'm going to sit on
the grass and write something today. About the sun and
the air and the forsythia."

The door in front of her creaked. Russell had apparently not closed it all the way. It swayed slowly on its
hinge, seeming unsure of whether it would open or
close. Behind its dusty panes of glass hung age-yellowed
lace curtains.

"Hello?" she called softly, peering around the door.
It was dark and dusty inside, but an overhead lamp
shone soft golden light. Kate stepped through the door,
shutting it carefully behind her. She looked about for
Russell, but saw no one.

Until she spotted the old man with the beard at the
top of the stairs.

"Auntie Cee?" Russell was calling.

He had wasted no time on the stairs, bounding up
all three flights, the way he used to as a boy. Auntie Cee

was why he was there, after all, not because of any love for this old house. At the third floor landing, he paused, realizing he'd left Kate behind. *Maybe it's best,* he thought to himself. *She'll need to learn about this house on her own.*

He heard footsteps, and turned. Rounding the corner, carrying a tray, was a tall woman with wire-framed glasses and dark hair pulled severely back in a bun.

"You must be Mr. Russell," the woman said pleasantly enough.

He smiled. "Mrs. Tynan."

"Yes." She set the tray down on a table and shook his hand. He guessed her to be close to fifty. "Welcome home."

"Thank you," he said. "How's my aunt?"

"Quite chipper today actually. *Thrilled* that you were coming."

"Let me check in with her and then we'll talk downstairs," Russell said.

"Very good. You know which room is hers?"

He laughed. "Oh, very well." He continued on down the hall.

The old man disappeared when footsteps sounded behind him on the stairs. Kate watched as a dark-haired woman carrying a tray came into view.

"Ah," she said, "you must Mrs. Wright."

"Yes." Kate smiled. "Kate Wright."

"Audrey Tynan." The nurse smiled in return, still holding the tray, leaving Kate awkwardly trying to hide her outstretched hand in greeting. "Let me put Miss Cecilia's lunch tray in the kitchen and I'll come back and take your bags."

"Oh, no, I can handle them. Do you know which room we're staying in?"

"Well, now, I would assume Mr. Russell's old room."

She twinkled, disappearing around the corner to what, Kate imagined, led to the kitchen.

Kate breathed deeply. She could smell something in the air, something she wasn't quite sure of, but *something*. Something the dust covered. Maybe wine from a wine cellar. Or maybe just the accumulated odors of a hundred years, of a hundred Thanksgivings and a hundred Christmas dinners, of babies born and old people dying. Old houses with their old, rotting wood and their old, decaying parchment wallpaper were *supposed* to smell. Still, it made her dizzy. She felt as if she had dust in her throat.

She looked back up the stairs but the old man with the beard hadn't returned. Still, he had followed her here. *Why?*

A thought struck her. Maybe he *hadn't* followed her here. Maybe this was where he'd been all along. Maybe he belonged here.

She doesn't want you in the house.

Mrs. Tynan had returned to her side. "Mr. Russell is with his aunt. Do you want me to show you to the room so you can put your things away?"

"Yes, thank you," Kate said. She lifted her suitcase and followed the spry old woman up the stairs. At the first landing, a stained-glass window of St. George slaying the dragon barely emitted the sun. Once it must have been vivid in its blues and reds and golds, but seemed now merely a puddle of muted grays and purples, the sun struggling in vain to shine through the thick veneer of dust. *It's everywhere,* Kate realized with a growing sense of claustrophobia. *Dust.*

"The house will seem so alive with you two here," Mrs. Tynan said as they turned onto the second flight of stairs, leading to the second floor. "I'll have to get used to cooking for three."

"Oh, I can handle that—"

"Tut, tut. Mr. Russell pays me quite well. I'm glad to do it."

Kate smiled. "Do you live here too?"

"No, I live in town. But it's been getting that I had to stay here overnight quite a bit since Miss Cecilia was getting worse. It'll be good to be able to go home every night to my cats now that you two are here."

"Is there anyone else in the house?" Kate asked, curious to see Mrs. Tynan's reaction.

They had reached the second floor. To their left a few lamps were lit along the hallway. To the right, a dark corridor stretched off into the east wing of the house. The windows had been shuttered on that side of the house, Kate remembered from their walk up to the porch. That's why it was so dark there.

"No, there's just Miss Cecilia and me," Mrs. Tynan answered. "Why do you ask?"

"You've never seen an old man with a beard?"

Mrs. Tynan stopped walking and looked at her. "I don't know who you mean."

Kate sensed the woman wasn't telling her the truth. Instinct again, and she trusted it. "When I came in just now," she said, "I saw a man. On the stairs. There, down on the first landing."

"Oh." Mrs. Tynan laughed, resuming her walk. "You must have seen St. George."

"St. George? Oh, you mean the window? No, no. This was a man. With a short white beard."

"If you saw anyone, Mrs. Wright," she said, as she turned and opened a door into a large, black void, "you saw a ghost."

Russell paused before he entered Auntie Cee's room. Suddenly he was twelve years old again, running to this room to cry on his old aunt's flower-print-covered bosom. "Grandmother slapped me," he'd cry, and old Auntie Cee, her face full of sympathy, would pull him to her and stroke his hair. "There, there, child," she'd say, soothing him. "She doesn't mean to be so hard. . . ."

"Auntie Cee?"

Silhouetted against the large picture window that looked out over the garden in the back of the house was a woman in a chair, slightly hunched, very frail. The silhouette shifted against the sunlight as it heard his voice. The light of the room was limited by the thick red velvet drapes, but Russell could make out the wispy features of his ninety-eight-year-old aunt, and he fell to his knees in front of her chair.

"Russell," she said in a voice like maple leaves on a dry October afternoon, "welcome back to Wrightsbridge."

Her hands, so much like Theresa's at the end, reached out and gripped his face, bringing it to her bosom.

Auntie Cee

Cecilia Elizabeth Wright was born just after the last century turned. The house was filled with photographs of her throughout her long and rather sheltered life. First there was her christening photo, on the wall beside the parlor, in which she was nothing more than a bundle of white lace, held by dour-faced matrons, with her grim father, the founder of Wrightsbridge, hovering behind. On the old grand piano, long out of tune, stood her engagement photo, showing her full of life and hope, standing beside young Samuel Hotchkiss in his army uniform. Samuel's father had been the mayor of the town from 1915 to 1919, and old Asa Wright had been tickled pink that his daughter had made such a catch. Samuel had high cheekbones and a cleft chin, and unlike in most of the photos in the house, he and Cecilia—by then known to everyone as Cee—were smiling.

Six months later Samuel's smiling face was blown

apart by a cannonball in France, and Cee lived the rest of her life as an unofficial widow.

Not that she was grim about it, not like her father, who lost his wife shortly after his children were born and whose sour portrait hanging over the mantel dominated the parlor. He'd died in 1925, a defeated, bitter man of fifty-four. But the whole town had come to his funeral, for Asa Wright had brought industry to the town, a munitions factory that rivaled Colt Firearms in Hartford during its heyday.

"Papa built guns," Auntie Cee would tell the children, shaking her head sadly. "This house was built on other people's blood."

Auntie Cee was opposed to war. In the 1960s, she railed against the war in Vietnam to anyone who'd listen. There were pictures of her from that era, too, an old woman with long gray hair in a tie-dyed dress surrounded by teenagers with flowers in their hair. Most people presumed her pacifism stemmed from Samuel Hotchkiss's grisly death in World War I. But Cee was a gentle soul from birth, who couldn't comprehend cruelty. It was a wonder, then, most folks believed, that she had managed to outlive her sister-in-law, Russell's grandmother, a woman the whole town feared.

"Let me look at you," Auntie Cee said now, her old hands moving away from Russell's face and hovering over him, as if to give him a benediction.

"It's good to be with you again," Russell said, standing up.

"Oh, my boy, you have had heartache, haven't you?" Her perceptive old face was white with talcum powder, a habit she'd never given up, and her lips were bright pink with fresh lipstick. Her eyes were as blue as the bright sky outside her window, and her hair, tied back, was shockingly white, whiter even than he remembered, almost glowing in the muted darkness of her room. She wore a flower-print dress and a cameo on her bosom, and heavy black shoes on feet that had not left this room in years. Her face was lined heavily, and her hands were little more than bones wrapped loosely in dry, spotted skin, with nails that were sharp and untrimmed.

"Heartache," she repeated. "Tell me of your heartache."

He hesitated. "Why speak of it, Auntie Cee? It's over now. Can't you see joy in my face, too?"

She studied him. She said nothing at first. "I'm glad you're here," she said at last. "But this is not a place to heal heartache."

"It's a place to start anew."

"You've brought a wife?"

"Yes," Russell said, and thinking of Kate made him feel brighter. He suddenly felt guilty for not bringing her upstairs. "I'll bring her up later to meet you."

"Good." She seemed to tire, resting her head back against her chair. "Did you know that come this fall I'll be ninety-nine years old?"

"Yes. We'll have to celebrate."

She smiled. Her false teeth clicked. "When I was a girl, celebrations in this house brought out the whole town."

"Maybe they will again." Russell sat down on a small stool in front of his aunt's chair. "Auntie Cee, have you seen Rosalind?"

She looked at him. "Not for a while."

"She'll be back, too."

Her voice had changed. "Will she?" It was a genuine question.

"Yes. She came to see me in New York. It was her idea that I return, in fact. She was concerned about you." He took her old withered hands in his. "We'll be a family again, Auntie Cee. You and I and Rosalind."

She smiled and looked at him with strange eyes. "Don't forget your wife."

"Of course not. Kate, too." He beamed. "We're all going to take such good care of you."

"No need to be concerned about me," Auntie Cee said, her eyes twinkling. "I have all the ghosts to watch over me."

"I remember those ghost stories you used to tell us as kids," Russell said.

"You would pretend not to be frightened."

"No, that was Rosalind. I'd be scared to death. She'd be the one who'd comfort me after Grandmother would put an end to the stories."

Auntie Cee smiled. "I suppose it was naughty of me to tell children ghost stories. Inger never liked me to do that."

"It was all in fun. Grandmother didn't understand fun." Russell stood up. "Do you need anything? I guess you just had your lunch."

"Oh, yes. Mrs. Tynan is very good. No, I'm fine. So long as I can sit here and watch the birds and the squirrels."

"Well, let me go downstairs and settle in and then I'll bring Kate up to meet you."

"All right, Russell. Welcome home."

He bent and kissed her on her cool forehead. She had already turned to resume her garden watching, her hands knotted together in her lap.

I have the ghosts . . .

"Cecilia," he was calling.

Oh, why must his voice still haunt me? Why has it never left this house?

"Please, Cecilia! Help me."

"Inger," she said, pleading. "It's not humane what you're doing. *Please.*"

The other woman fixed an ice-blue stare at her. "Mind your own business. *I'm* mistress of this house and I will do what I feel is necessary."

"But he's ill. . . ."

"Don't you think I know that? *Don't you know that's why I keep him there?*"

"Cecilia!" he cried, rattling the door, and all poor Cee could do was cover her ears.

The Ghosts

Kate was settled in an old, overstuffed, fraying arm-chair next to the mantel, beneath old Asa Wright's grim portrait. She was leafing through an ancient volume of poetry she'd pulled from the bookshelf (dust, again, everywhere) and wondering when it had last been opened. Among its pages she found a ticket stub: *Old Town Day, Wrightsbridge Meadow, July 4, 1947.*

"There you are."

Kate looked up. Russell had come into the room. He was looking around at the furniture, the portraits, the photograph of the young couple on the piano, and he seemed uneasy.

"Is everything okay?" Kate asked.

"Yes," Russell replied, and suddenly he resented Kate's presence in the house, sitting in his grandfather's chair. "Why are your things in my old room? Did Mrs. Tynan put them there?"

"No, I did. That's where I assumed—"

"Well, you assumed wrong," he snapped. "That's *not*

where we're sleeping. We'll sleep in another room down the hall.''

"All right, Russell. Whatever you say.''

Russell softened. He could see Kate's green eyes even in the dim light of this room, and all at once he felt warmth toward her again. "I just want a fresh start, darling,'' he said, smiling. "No bad memories.''

Kate stood and approached him. "Russell, was coming here a good idea?''

"Of course it was. Auntie Cee was delighted to see me.''

Kate gave him a small smile. "I can't wait to meet her.''

"We'll take the room on the second floor just below hers. It's actually the nicest room in the house. It's got a grand view of the garden.''

Kate's smile turned wistful. "I'm afraid there's not much garden left.''

It was true. The rosebushes had long ago grown wild and thin. Tall grass now sprouted through the azalea bushes. Some perennials continued to sprout sporadically through the dry, unturned earth, but the flowers Auntie Cee had once so carefully tended were now mostly choked by weeds and dandelions.

"Why don't you make that a project? You can restore the garden.'' Russell felt pleased at being able to offer this.

"That would be wonderful. But your sister—''

"I'll handle my sister.'' It was a promise.

"Well, then, it'll be my project.''

"Terrific.''

"So,'' Kate said, putting away the book on the shelf, "tell me about the ghosts.''

Russell looked at her oddly.

"Mrs. Tynan told me the house is haunted.'' Kate

smiled mischievously. "You never mentioned that little fact to me."

"It's utter nonsense."

"She said the whole town has long thought so, ever since she was a little girl."

"I'll speak to her about repeating such nonsense," Russell snarled.

Kate drew close to him and stared up lovingly into his eyes. "I don't mind, Russell. I'm not afraid of ghosts."

Should she tell him? Maybe Erik was right. Russell *should* know. He was her husband; they shouldn't have secrets from each other. Erik said some places were apparently more conducive than others in allowing the dead to appear and to communicate. Wrightsbridge was clearly one of those places. Kate had seen the old man with the beard as soon as she had walked through the door, and sitting here in the parlor, she'd felt the presence of many other spirits. Not necessarily hostile, just curious. She would need to share all this with Russell eventually.

But Russell insisted, "There are no ghosts in this house." He looked at her sternly, raising an eyebrow. "Are you going to tell me you saw one?"

She decided to take a chance. "Actually, I have. On the stairs. A man with a short white beard."

Russell looked away from her. "You saw St. George."

"Only if he was wearing jodhpurs."

Russell held up his hands. "Believe what you want, darling." He smiled. "Mrs. Tynan said she left some food for our dinner. Let's go look in the refrigerator."

Kate agreed. She'd save the talk about seeing ghosts for another day. "Tomorrow morning I start trying to clean out all this dust," she said.

"Oh, this house has always been dusty," Russell told

her, dropping an arm around her and leading her out
into the kitchen. "You'll get used to it."

But Kate doubted that.

They dined that first night by candlelight, eating roast
pork and applesauce. Mrs. Tynan was an excellent cook.
She'd prepared a tray for Auntie Cee and then gotten
her into bed, leaving Russell and Kate to enjoy their
first night at Wrightsbridge all to themselves. Kate
regretted not meeting the old woman yet but understood she tired easily. She was ninety-eight, after all.
There would be plenty of time tomorrow for introduc-
tions.

In the flickering candlelight over dinner, Kate marveled at how handsome Russell looked. How in love she
felt sipping a glass of wine, listening to her husband
regale her with the history of the old house. It had been
built by his great-grandfather Asa Wright in 1895, and
four generations of Wrights had lived and died in this
house. For a man who had been so reluctant to talk
about his past and his family in New York, now that he
was here Russell sounded every bit the proud scion of
a great clan. And now *she* was a part of it, too. Kate had
become a Wright.

It was an exhilarating feeling. She'd never felt part
of a family before, never considered herself to have a
place in history. Being a Wright suddenly grounded
her. The portraits that surrounded her would be the
ancestors of her children. Her name would forever be
etched into the family tree.

She wasn't even frightened anymore by the ghosts.
There had been no sign of that spiteful little girl, and
the old man hadn't seemed very threatening. Even that
day in the mirror he hadn't seemed sinister. Just lost.
She wondered who he was, if he had lived here, if he

was a Wright, too. She had scanned the photographs and portraits but hadn't recognized him. Maybe his warnings were off-base. Maybe he was just confused.

After dinner, she cleared the dishes off the table and stacked them in the sink. She'd just rinse them off now and leave them for tomorrow. She had other things to attend to. Russell had winked at her and told her he'd meet her upstairs. She smiled broadly. They would make love, this first night in the old family home. Maybe even conceive an heir.

She giggled at how grand she was sounding to herself. Oh, how she loved Russell . . .

She felt his hand on her shoulder. "Yes, darling, I'll be there in a second," she promised.

But the hand felt odd. . . . She looked over at it. She reached up and touched it. It was ice-cold.

She spun around. Behind her stood a man she had never seen, a man so horrible she was struck momentarily mute. His eyes were bulging from his face, his skin was black and blue, and his neck was twisted at an odd angle, as if he'd been hanged. He *was*, Kate realized as her horror mounted. The torn noose still dangled from around his neck.

Kate screamed. The dish in her hands slipped and shattered on the floor.

"What do you think of the garden?"

Kate gasped, turning around.

Russell was asking her a question. They were outside. The sun was at two o'clock, and very bright. It hurt her eyes. She blinked.

"What?" she asked.

"The garden. I know it's not much, but it can be rototilled, and with some new topsoil, some bulbs . . ." Russell was actually getting excited about the prospect.

"The man," she murmured, "that horrible man . . ."

Russell was paying her no mind. "Maybe it's not too late to prune some of these rosebushes. . . ."

She put a hand to her head. "Did I wash the dishes?"

"Don't worry about the dishes, darling," Russell said with a wave of his hand. "You can *write* out here. No one will bother you. What do you think?"

She looked around. It really *was* daylight. But how was that *possible?*

She had been in the kitchen. It was *dark. Night.*

And the man . . . the man with the noose . . .

"Wave up at Auntie Cee," Russell was telling her, and Kate lifted her eyes up the height of the tall crooked house. There, at the top, between two gables, was the ethereal image of a white-haired woman, obscured by the glare of the sun on the glass, but Kate could see she was waving.

Kate waved back.

"I can't wait for you to meet her," Russell said.

"Russell, what day is it?"

He looked at her strangely. "Why, it's Wednesday."

"We got here yesterday."

He looked even more strangely. "Of course we did, darling. Are you all right?"

The sun bore down on her. It suddenly seemed so bright that her eyes couldn't stand it. "I need to go inside," she said, hurrying in through the back door that led into the kitchen.

She steadied herself against the ancient gas stove, its white surface chipped here and there with black wounds. Kate scanned the floor for broken glass, but saw none. The dishes from last night were neatly stacked, drying in the drainer.

Russell had come in behind her. "What's wrong, Kate? Are you feeling ill?"

She looked at him desperately. "Did anything happen last night, Russell? After we had dinner?"

He gave her a little puzzled smile. "We made love, darling. Have you forgotten that?"

Yes, yes, she *had*. But she couldn't tell him. Something kept her from telling him. Suddenly she wanted nothing more than to get to a phone and call Erik. Nothing like this had ever happened to her before. She'd seen that horrible apparition, and then lost half a day.

"Of course I remember, Russell," she lied, putting a smile on her face. "I guess I just had a little sunstroke." She stood up tall. "I'm fine now."

"Good." He kissed her forehead. "Shall we go up now and meet Auntie Cee?"

She nodded. They walked out of the kitchen hand in hand through the parlor. Russell paused to indicate the portrait of old Asa Wright. "When I was a kid," he said, "my sister and I used to play that my great-grandfather would come down at night out of his portrait and walk the house to make sure we all were in bed."

"Is he one of the ghosts who supposedly haunts this house?" Kate asked, trying to be light.

"The townspeople say all of the Wrights come back from the grave." He made a face of annoyance. "But that's the talk of nonsense. The only Wrights left are Auntie Cee, Rosalind, and me."

She looked up at her husband with significance. "How did Asa Wright die, Russell?"

"Some say a broken heart. His wife died very young and he never got over it."

Kate looked up at his portrait. No, that wasn't the man she had seen. It had been such a quick glimpse, and he'd been horribly misshapen—but still she was certain it wasn't he.

They walked out of the parlor and began to climb

the stairs. "Speaking of Rosalind," Kate asked, "have you heard from her?"

"Not since we've gotten here."

"So you still have no idea when she will arrive?"

Russell stopped, almost imperceptibly, as if for a moment hesitant to take the next step. But he continued. "I don't know," he said. "One never knows with Rosalind."

Rosalind

She must have been eight, Russell was thinking, eight or nine, when she first caught a butterfly and stuck it in the jar with the Japanese beetles.

It was her trick. "Watch the butterfly die!" she'd say gleefully, and Russell would recoil, but watch in fascination nevertheless.

The butterfly was usually a simple, small, white one, little more than a moth, but sometimes, when she was quick, it would be a grand orange monarch. The poor creature would flutter furiously, its wings beating pathetically against the glass of the jar, a tiny echoing sound that Russell could still hear as he climbed the stairs now, more than two decades later. The Japanese beetles, slow-moving brown and yellow insects picked from the rhododendren blossoms, would crawl up and over the nervous butterfly, clawing at its tendons, ripping its wings, eating its antennae. It was quite a show, and Rosalind would end it all by dabbing a cotton ball with kerosene and popping it into the jar. "That takes care of all of them," she'd say.

In the morning, the jar would be filled with dead beetles on their backs, their tiny legs coiled, scattered among pieces of broken wing. And if you shook the jar, Russell discovered, it made a sickening thump, with all of the pieces seeming to move together. Rosalind called it a death rattle.

"Why do you kill butterflies?" he asked his sister one day.

She looked at him puzzled. "Why?" she echoed, seeming to think about it. They were standing in the garden, and the rosebushes were in full bloom. That year—the year Auntie Cee would fall and break her hip and increasingly become a recluse in her room on the third floor—the roses were more beautiful than ever, reds and whites and pinks and even a few spectacular yellows. Their scent hung heavy in the air, and the bees lumbered lazily from blossom to blossom, drunk.

"I don't kill butterflies," Rosalind said finally. "The Japanese beetles do."

"But you catch them and put them in the jar."

They were standing in the noonday sun, and Russell watched as Rosalind's face darkened. She began to cry, running into the house to be comforted by Auntie Cee. Yet she didn't stop killing butterflies after that, and Russell never raised the issue again.

The Second Night

Auntie Cee had fallen asleep in her chair, Russell explained as he came out of her room. Kate had been waiting outside the door. "You can meet her tomorrow," he said. "I'll have Mrs. Tynan go in and get her ready for bed."

How very odd, Kate thought. She was sure she'd heard them talking. Could Russell not want her to meet his aunt for a reason?

But that was silly, and Kate dismissed the thought. Auntie Cee was almost one hundred years old. If she wasn't up to meeting her just yet, Kate certainly understood.

Now, the late afternoon sun slanting through her window, casting the room with a golden glow, Kate sat on her bed, her bags still unpacked. Had she really slept here last night? Had she and Russell really made love here?

The room was large, the furniture solid oak. Beside the bed stood a tall free-standing mirror. An old-fashioned armoire rested against the far wall, directly opposite a large chest of drawers and a rolltop desk—a sign, Kate thought encouragingly, that she would write here. Maybe she'd start tonight, in fact, writing about what she'd seen and experienced so far—and *not* experienced, or at least not *remembered* experiencing. The bed was a four-poster nineteenth-century style, and while the mattress was a tad too soft, she wouldn't complain. The bedspread, smelling subtly of age, had a raised mosaic pattern and fringe around the edges. She ran her hands across it. Dust particles rose from it to dance softly in the air.

She stood and walked over to her suitcase, popping open the lid. Her nightgown was still folded inside. What had she slept in last night? Had she slept naked? She suppressed a small smile as she felt her cheeks flush.

She would call Erik in a bit. She had to find out if he'd ever heard of ghosts playing these kind of tricks with your mind. Did they have that kind of power? It was terribly disconcerting losing half a day, especially not being able to talk about it and having to cover it up. It was horrible to think she had forgotten making love to her husband. Were the spirits merely being playful? Or was there something more sinister going on?

Looking down at her sweatshirt and jeans she realized she was wearing different clothes than she'd worn yesterday, so obviously she'd opened her suitcase at some point. She let out a long sigh, and began unpacking her things, hanging them in the armoire. All at once she sneezed ferociously, unsettling a layer of dust on top of the bureau.

"That's *it*," she said, marching downstairs to find some dust cloths and spray cleaners. Underneath the sink in the kitchen she found a bottle of Windex. A roll of paper towels hung from the wall. She grabbed both.

At least she could clean out some of the dust from her room.

But once again, as she began to climb the stairs, she saw the old man ahead of her on the landing and looking at her with wide, frightened eyes. He was wearing jodhpurs again. Pants for horse-riding.

"Hello," she said urgently.

She felt as if she had stumbled upon a deer in the woods, and she had to be careful not to frighten it away. She approached him cautiously, taking small steps, keeping eye contact with him and smiling. But all at once he turned and bolted in terror up the stairs. She followed.

"Please don't run away!" she called after him. "Please talk to me!"

He stopped. His back was to her. She hurried past him on the stairs to turn around and face him.

"Please," she said. "I mean you no harm. What was it that you were trying to tell me?"

What a sad old man he was. His face seemed haunted, bereft. Kate felt nothing but compassion for him. "Please," she said, offering her hand. "Let me help you."

But suddenly his eyes moved past her to something at the top of the stairs. His expression changed to abject terror. He pulled back. "Keep her away!" he shouted. "Keep her away!"

He screamed and fell backward on the stairs. Kate gasped as she watched him tumble down to the first landing and disappear. She spun around, only to catch a glimpse of a woman's long black skirt rushing back down the hall.

Kate ran up to the second floor. The woman had headed into the darkness of the east wing. Kate could only make out a vague impression of her: tall, broadshouldered, in a long black dress. She knew it would be fruitless to pursue her. Unlike the old man, she didn't want Kate to see her.

Who was she? Was she the force who didn't want Kate in the house? Why had the old man been so terrified of her? What power did she hold?

And what connection did the man with the noose around his neck have to all of this? And the little girl? Was she here, too, some place?

The glimpse of the woman in the black dress had shaken Kate's nerves. It was the first time she had sensed evil in the house. The man with the noose had been terrifying, perhaps even threatening—but he had not been evil like the woman in the black dress. The old man had been terrified of her, even in death. "Keep her away!" he had screamed. What power did she still hold over him?

Back in her room, Kate fumbled through her purse to find her cell phone. She punched the *3* and within a few seconds she heard it start ringing in Erik's apartment. How she wished she were there with him. How she wished they were out eating burgers and fries at their favorite diner. "Please answer," she whispered. Erik might be able to figure out what was going on.

She got his machine. "Erik," she said. "Call me, okay? On my cell phone. Thanks."

She sighed. The sun was now setting, sending a spectrum of golds and reds throughout her room. There were three large windows in a bay formation that looked out over the garden, and two on either side of the curve, and she opened all of them. Fresh air filled the room— the first time, she imagined, in decades. She set about attacking the dust, wiping off every last speck she could find, longing for a vacuum cleaner. She'd ask Mrs. Tynan when she saw her again.

The room had gotten dark. How long had she been standing there? She switched on a lamp and looked over at her suitcase, intending to finish unpacking. But it was empty. She pulled out a drawer from the chest. Her underwear was all neatly folded inside.

"Dear God," she whispered. "I'm losing chunks of time."

She glanced at her watch. It was almost nine o'clock. But only a second ago the sun had just started to set.

"Dinner," she said to herself. "Russell will be downstairs having dinner."

She hurried down to the dining room. But there were no lights on in the parlor; the kitchen, too, was dark. She walked back through the parlor and ran a finger along a table, leaving a river in the dust. Somewhere a clock chimed nine o'clock.

"Have I forgotten having dinner with Russell?" she whispered to herself. "Where is he now?"

She headed back up the stairs. She felt the kind of icy terror she remembered as a girl, when seeing people who already died had left her trembling and confused. She'd come to grips with that ability, and now few things frightened her.

Except losing her mind.

Were they doing this to me? The ghosts?

Or rather, one ghost in particular?

She doesn't want you in the house.

"Russell?" Kate called, climbing the stairs. "Russell, where are you?"

The house was eerily quiet. She walked past her room, peering into others as she went by. All were dusty, darkened, and empty. Finally, at the end of the hall, she paused before a closed door. It was the room Mrs. Tynan had first indicated would be theirs. Russell's old room. Where he'd slept as a boy. She could hear something from behind the door.

It was Russell. Snoring.

She tried the knob. It wouldn't turn. Locked from the inside.

He's chosen to sleep in there by himself, she realized.

She tried to think. In those few hours she'd just lost, had they fought? Had he retreated here out of spite? She considered knocking, banging on the door, waking him up and telling him how terrified she was—but she drew her clenched fist back at the last moment, before she had made a sound.

Who is that man in there? He might be my husband, but I hardly know him. I'm here with a man I barely know in a house haunted by the malevolent dead—who are making it emphatically clear they don't want me here!

She nearly ran back to her room and closed the door, locking it against Russell as he had locked his against her. She turned the switch on a tall brass floor lamp and golden light suffused the room.

She picked up her cell phone. The screen showed she had missed one call. *Damn it!* Why hadn't she taken it with her?

She pressed the code to listen to her message. It was Erik. "Hey, sweetheart. You sounded a little frazzled. Things going okay? Call me later. I've got a hot date so won't be able to get back right away. But leave a message if you want to talk later. Love ya!"

Just hearing his voice made her feel better. *Look,* she told herself, sitting down at the desk, *you can handle ghosts. You've been dealing with them all your life. Just respect them and they'll respect you.*

But these gaps of lost time—maybe they had nothing to do with the ghosts. Maybe they were the result of nerves, anxiety. More than once, her therapists had diagnosed her with anxiety-related symptoms. Maybe the move, the marriage—

"Okay," she said aloud to herself. "I guess this means I should write."

Writing always helped clear her head and made her feel more together. She opened the large blank journal she'd brought just for this purpose. Later she'd hook up her computer, but for tonight this would suffice. Something about writing in longhand appealed to her. She opened the journal, cracking its binding slightly, and turned to the first page.

The first blank page.

"I need the right kind of pen," she said, and instantly the image of a quill came to her mind, and she laughed. She got up, searched through the drawers, and then discovered all the pens she'd brought with her neatly arranged in a small cup on top of the bureau. It was something else she didn't remember doing. She tried one, but the ink didn't flow smoothly; she tossed it in the can next to the desk. Next she tried a felt-tip, but feared it would dry up on her. Finally she settled on a plain old ballpoint, but after the first line—*What am I doing here? I am still*— the ink apparently clogged, and the pen ripped the page.

Damn, she missed her computer.

She threw the pen across the room. She briefly considered a pencil, but then slammed the journal shut and decided to go to bed. She'd call Erik in the morning after a good night's rest.

Kate sat up in bed. She could tell the sun was coming up on the other side of the house: the room had that peach-colored early morning glow. And Russell was banging at her door.

"Kate! Kate!"

She jumped up, unlocked the door, and pulled it open. She looked up into the face of her husband.

"Why did you lock me out last night?" he asked, clearly annoyed.

She steeled herself. "I could ask you the same thing."

He was still in his robe. "What are you talking about?"

"I went looking for you, and heard you snoring in your old room. The door was locked."

He looked at her as if she were mad. "You're making no sense," he told her. "I was in the library reading, waiting for you to come down as you'd promised. When I finally gave up and came upstairs, I found the door here locked. I slept in the parlor on the couch."

She turned away. What was true?

"We can talk about it over breakfast," he said. "Mrs. Tynan just arrived, and I wanted to get you up so you could meet Auntie Cee this morning. Will you be all right?"

She nodded. He looked down at her, giving her a quick kiss on her cheek before heading off down the hall.

She pulled her robe around herself and tied the belt, grabbing her cosmetics case and heading for the bathroom. As she passed the desk she paused. The journal was open. "Dear God," she muttered. There were six, seven, eight, *nine* pages in her handwriting, starting out neat, ending up sloppy and rushed. She sat down in front of it, stunned.

"When the hell did I do this?"

Mother and Dad

Russell brought some tea up to Auntie Cee, and sat with her while she ate the breakfast Mrs. Tynan had prepared. She was lost in a fog, thinking everybody was dead except for Russell, and unable to talk for more than a few sentences. He'd gone downstairs for a phone conference with her doctor, who told him not to worry. "For a woman nearing one hundred, it's a marvel that she's as sharp as she is on some days," the doctor said. "She's just weak and her bones are brittle and her memory and wits will come and go. If you're there to tend to her, and Mrs. Tynan can get her up and dressed and fed every day, she could be with us for several more years."

Russell was satisfied with the prognosis. He strolled out into the garden and sat on one of the stone benches. The sun had yet to rise over the house, so half of the garden was still in shade. The bench was cold on his bare legs; he wore khaki shorts and sneakers, and a sweatshirt he'd discovered in a drawer that must have been his when he was a teenager.

Kate was becoming a problem.

Why did he resent her presence in this house suddenly? She was his wife. She belonged with him here. But she had been acting oddly ever since they'd arrived. Last night especially.

He thought of Theresa. She'd begun acting odd, too, and that's when he discovered she'd been keeping secrets from him. He'd found the torn-off matchbook covers in her pockets, the names and numbers of strange men written upon them. He'd answer the phone only to have the caller hang up. Theresa hadn't been able to keep him from finding out her secrets.

And neither would Kate.

He sat on the cold bench and surveyed the tumble of the garden. The air was crisp, the birds lively and noisy in the trees. By eleven-thirty, he knew, this garden would be bathed entirely in sunlight, and then, hours later, the sun would set along its far edge, the poplar trees swaying in soft silhouette. A few of the poplars had died, standing out like dried-up, monstrous cornstalks, waiting to be cut down.

Well, he would *cut* them down. That was what he was here for. To set things straight.

He was master of Wrightsbridge, after all. He had come back to restore the house, to restore the place the Wrights had traditionally occupied in this small town. He stretched, watching a robin alight on the grass and peck among the blades for worms. There was still dew on the lawn. To roll in that grass now would produce grass stains on his khakis. His mother had once scolded him for getting grass stains on his pants . . .

Mother. He wondered, for a second, before quickly dismissing it, how she was. If she ever thought of him. Or Rosalind.

Mother. Molly Fitzgibbons was her name. He never told anyone he was half Irish.

"That *Roman* woman," Grandmother had called her. "She goes into that church and worships her idols. They shake perfume and she kneels in front of the priests and they touch her with their blessings . . ."

Grandmother had hated Catholics. When her son, Russell's father, had brought Molly Fitzgibbons home and introduced her as his wife, Grandmother had reared back her imposing frame and set her face into stone. And it seemed as if she never budged from that stance, remaining rigid until the day she died. Her only son, her only child, had disappointed her gravely, getting some cheap Irish bartender's daughter pregnant and bringing her into this house and daring to call her his wife.

And Grandmother had willed that disappointment to her grandson, who could not, even now, even when he thought he knew better, think of his mother as anything other than a tramp.

"Go on, take off your shoes, they're wet," Molly Fitzgibbons Wright told her son, four years old, as he came in from playing in the grass. "Look at those grass stains on your pants. Oh, Russell! Where's your sister?"

"Down by the river," he said, struggling with his shoes.

His mother was making something on the stove. "I'm making breakfast. This here is Wheatina, the kind my mother used to make me when I was a girl."

"Was she my grandmother?"

"Yes," Molly said, staring into the pot as she stirred. "She died a long time ago. You never knew her. I wish you had. I wish you knew another grandmother besides . . ."

They became aware of Grandmother in the kitchen doorway, her big frame filling most of it. Molly Fitzgibbons Wright allowed her voice to trail off, hoping she hadn't been overheard.

"What are you making them?" Grandmother's voice boomed throughout the kitchen.

His mother didn't turn around. "Wheatina."

"That is not enough for children for breakfast." Grandmother folded her imposing arms across her bosom. "They need *meat*. I'll cook some bacon."

"No, no, this is enough," his mother tried.

Grandmother snorted. "Put some of that in a bowl and bring it upstairs to him," she said in her thick, guttural Swedish accent. "He is crying for food."

Him. Russell knew she meant the old man in the attic.

Molly seemed to cringe. Russell watched her, standing over the pot, and he knew she didn't want to go up there. She didn't want to see him. Nobody did.

"Bernard feeds him," she said softly. "Bernard brings him his food."

Grandmother snorted again. "I don't know where Bernard is," Grandmother said. She was clearly angry. Bernard was her son, Russell's father, Molly's husband. He would disappear sometimes for days, returning home disheveled and hungover, and Grandmother obviously feared this was the start of yet another bender. Her lips always tightened when she got angry, tightened so much that they'd turn white. Sitting on the floor, Russell watched the color fade from her lips.

He turned his gaze to his mother. Grandmother's back was to them both, and Molly Fitzgibbons Wright was looking over at the old woman. All at once she made a face and stuck out her tongue. It startled her small son, and he never forgot it. It was a hideous face, full of hate, just the kind a bartender's daughter would make, and as much as he feared his grandmother, as much as he too over the years would want to make a face at her, Russell never forgave his mother for sticking out her tongue. *White trash,* he told himself in later years, *that's what she was: white trash.*

"Throw those boots down the stairs," Grandmother was barking at him.

"Yes, ma'am," he said, standing up to do as he was told.

His grandmother always called shoes "boots," and whenever anything seemed even the slightest bit dirty or rumpled, she would say, "Throw it down the stairs." In the basement stood an ancient washing machine, probably among the first models ever made, and a laundrywoman came in twice a week to wash their clothes. The old man in the attic soiled a lot of linens.

Russell pulled back the door to the cellar, smelling the earthen floor from below. He tossed his damp sneakers down the steps; they bumped along the wood before landing with a thud at the bottom. But before he closed the door he saw something move against the wall, a dark shape, and he looked again. It was a shadow, but there were lots of shadows in the cellar. He took a few steps down the stairs.

He saw it then, hanging to his left. He felt suddenly very light, as if his small body would just float the rest of the way. There, from an overhead beam, hung his father, swaying ever so gently—just below the spot where, moments before, his wife had stood stirring Wheatina.

And now she was screaming behind Russell, screaming and screaming. The bowl she had planned to carry to the old man upstairs because her husband hadn't done his duty was smashed all over the cellar steps, and steaming Wheatina dripped, dripped, dripped in clumps off the steps and onto the cold earthen floor below.

Grandmother rushed up behind her and shouted at her roughly to stop screaming, then hurried her bulk down the stairs to stand before her son's dangling body. Molly Fitzgibbons Wright started to scream again and Russell, suddenly terrified, bolted barefoot back out to the garden and to the arms of Auntie Cee, who stood in her bed of pansies and kept asking him again and again, "What is it, child? What is it, child? What is it, child?"

"Ah, there you are, Mr. Russell," Mrs. Tynan was saying.

He looked up at her from the bench where he was sitting. A red ant was slowly crawling up his foot, getting lost in the thick hair on his calf.

"Yes, Mrs. Tynan?"

"I'll be going along to do some shopping. I'll be back by noon."

"All right. Mrs. Tynan?"

"Yes?"

"Are you happy working here?"

She seemed a little surprised by the question. "Oh, yes, sir."

He nodded. "I suppose you would be. Auntie Cee is the only one left. The only one, out of all of them."

She smiled. "May I go now, sir?"

"Yes, of course." He wanted to ask her if Kate had come downstairs, but decided against it.

"Well, Grandmother," he said out loud once he was alone again in the garden, "I met her in a video store. Is that better than a bar? Her father was a mechanic. Is that any better than a bartender?"

As if in reply, the red ant bit him.

Grandmother

She had died seven years ago, an eternity for Russell.
It was even before he'd met Theresa. Grandmother's
lawyer, a Mr. Cartwright, had written him in New York
that she had wanted only a small memorial service and
then to be cremated. Russell had written back to Mr.
Cartwright, giving him the authority to take care of
everything. Russell did not come back to Wrightsbridge
for Grandmother's funeral, but he dutifully signed the
papers that made the estate his.

His. And Rosalind's.

She had shown up at his door two days after he had
gotten news of Grandmother's death, distraught. He
hadn't seen her in three years, not since he'd moved
to New York.

He was openly rude to her.

"I should've known you'd be back."

She brushed past him into his apartment. She was
wearing a red lace top, so tight that even breasts as small
as hers formed impressive cleavage.

"Oh, baby brother," she wailed. "Grandmother is dead!"

He sneered. "Don't tell me you're grieving her."

"Of *course* I am! She raised us! She shaped us, taught us, made us who we are—after our no-good mother abandoned us! We owe her so much, Russell!"

"She was a witch. She hit us."

Rosalind looked so angry he thought she might hit him too. "Yes, she was strict. At times, perhaps, unfair. But she was alone, too, don't forget. She suffered *too*, remember. Our cowardly father. Our insane grandfather. She raised us alone, and taught us about class, about family, about standing . . ."

And at this, Russell had laughed. "Class! Family! Standing! Oh, yes, she taught us about all that, and look how well we learned those lessons."

Rosalind's face darkened. "It is a good thing Grandmother could never see you here."

He narrowed his eyes at her. "Why? There's nothing wrong with my life."

She smiled. "Then why have you hidden here? Why have you turned your back on the family, on the estate? What now, dear brother? Shall Wrightsbridge just become a faded memory of a time long past? Will the days of the town celebrations held at the estate be over? Oh, Grandmother had so hoped you would return with a bride, take up your place as head of the family, restore the grandeur that our great-grandfather had made for Wrightsbridge. Shall you let her down?"

She had fallen into the pretentious formal speech they had used while still living at Wrightsbridge, speech intended to convince Grandmother that they were worthy heirs, that they would not turn out to be white trash like their mother. Hearing it from her now, it sickened him.

"Shut up," he said. "You sound like an actress in a bad television melodrama."

It's funny, but he never could remember how their conversation had ended, what Rosalind's response had been to his rebuff. He never knew if she went to the funeral or not, only that she left his life again for another few years, only to show up soon after he'd married Theresa, standing outside his door flaring her nostrils, refusing to come in and tempting him once more to come home to Wrightsbridge.

And now he *was* home.

Standing in Grandmother's upstairs parlor, where she would sit for hours and listen to her phonograph records—Perry Como, Frank Sinatra, Bing Crosby—and, in later years, watch her soap operas—*Guiding Light, Love of Life, Search for Tomorrow*— he could still smell her: that faint odor of soap and hair spray, sweet yet sour, sometimes overpowering. She had been a big woman, not fat, but big: tall, broad shoulders, heavy thighs, more like a man than a woman. Her voice, too, was gruff: low and deep, with a heavy Swedish accent. Her blond hair had quickly turned to gray, and she wore it up on her head, in two buns, one piled on top of the other. She cut a commanding figure, one that terrified him as a boy, even as a man. Grandmother was his father's mother and yet she was really both parents to him, and he wanted so desperately to love her for that, but he never could.

She was born Inger Johanssen just outside Stockholm in 1910. She came to this country when she was just twelve, her parents determined to rise quickly up the social ladder.

Grandmother never spoke of her life in Sweden, where her family labored as fishermen (he learned from Auntie Cee), or of their first few years in America, when they lived in a tiny fourth-floor tenement in Brooklyn.

But then her father's carpentry business had become successful, and she was sent to a posh girls' school in Connecticut. There she met one of the school's benefactors, a Mr. Edgar Wright, scion of the Wrights of Wrightsbridge, newly master of the great house since the death of his father. He was dashing, handsome, and twenty years her senior. Tongues had flapped for years that Mr. Edgar might never take a wife, but he married this tall, sturdy Swedish girl as soon as she turned eighteen and set her up as mistress of the great house. She bore him nine children, all but one—a blond, wheezing boy named Bernard—dying in childbirth or in the first few weeks of life.

Russell reached down and touched the wooden cradle that still sat at the foot of Grandmother's bed. "This is where I rocked my babies," she'd say, "some of them after they were dead."

"She's had much heartache in her life," Auntie Cee would tell him, comforting him, trying to explain what made Grandmother fly into one of her rages. "You've got to try and understand. All those babies. And then your father . . . how much can one woman bear?"

Unspoken, of course, because Auntie Cee could never bring herself to speak of it, was Grandmother's husband, Russell's grandfather, Auntie Cee's brother, the dashing and handsome Edgar Wright, who went mad one night and nearly burned the house down. It was a night of terror, of chaos, that Russell would never forget. He had been only five years old, but the memory of the curtains suddenly ablaze with crackling orange light was seared onto his memory. If he had ever doubted that it was Grandmother who ruled the house, that it was she who was the strongest person in the entire world, those doubts were erased after that night, when she single-handedly pushed her once burly husband up all three flights of stairs, his hands and arms flailing, his screams shaking the house to its foundation. And so for ten years, Grandmother kept him locked in the attic, and sometimes, Russell thought, especially on stormy summer nights, you could still hear his screams to be let out of his cell.

An Idyll

How many days had they been there now? Three? Kate thought so, but it took a moment for her to confirm it, given those two disconcerting losses of memory. Russell had been distant all yesterday, and they'd never resolved what had happened that night, whether he'd closed the door on her or whether she'd done it to him.

"They're playing games with you," Erik warned her when they finally spoke on the phone. "The ghosts."

"Nothing like this has ever happened to me before," Kate said. "I'm frightened."

"Just keep your wits about you," he advised her. "They may be just testing you, trying to get you to prove your mettle if you're going to live among them. But it sure sounds like that's a hotspot for them. If it continues, call me. We may have to . . . do something."

"A séance?"

"Something," he responded, vaguely.

For the rest of the day yesterday she'd kept mostly to her room. Russell had come by late in the afternoon to tell her that Mrs. Tynan had prepared some dinner and she'd find it in the refrigerator. He was eating with Auntie Cee. Kate had looked at him eagerly, and asked if she might join them, but Russell had turned coldly away from her and said his aunt was still not up to meeting her. Kate had felt terribly rejected, and cried herself to sleep without eating a thing.

In the morning she woke up angry. No more feeling sorry for herself. Whatever was happening between her and Russell needed to be confronted head-on. She just couldn't understand it. Only three days here, only weeks into their marriage, and she felt as distant from her husband as if he were a stranger. She felt like an intruder in this house, her presence resented by everyone, alive *and* dead. How had things changed so fast?

Had Erik been right? Had she really acted so rashly, marrying a man she barely knew and then going off with him to a house filled with ghosts?

Today she'd been writing. Not much, but some. Not as much as that first night, when she must have gotten up out of bed in a half sleep and spilled her guts onto paper. It was some of the finest writing she'd done in a long time, she realized, smiling to herself that she would need to get that tired again if she was going to be so brilliant.

She closed the journal and headed down the hall to the bathroom to shower. It was an old contraption, rigged up to hang from a hook over the ancient claw-footed tub. But the water was hot, which was all that mattered to Kate, and in a few minutes she was downstairs, ravenously eating a breakfast of scrambled eggs and bacon that Mrs. Tynan had prepared for her.

"Is there a garden center in town?" Kate asked.

"Yes. It's right on Main Street. Do you still have the rental car?"

"No," Kate said, wiping her mouth with a white cloth napkin. "We had to return it. Is it too far to walk?"

Mrs. Tynan considered. "For me, yes. For you, I'd say not."

"Great. Main Street intersects with this road, right?"

"About half a mile mile ahead, yes."

"I'm up for it."

"Up for what?" It was Russell, coming into the room wearing nothing more than a pair of khaki shorts. It was going to be hot today, and they were all glad about that, after such a cold spring. They were moving rapidly toward Memorial Day weekend, and Kate wanted to have the garden finished by then.

"I'm going into town, to buy bulbs and plants and garden tools," Kate said.

"Oh." Russell's voice betrayed nothing, no excitement, no resentment, no pleasure, no anger. But then he turned to Kate: "Would you like me to come with you? I could show you the town, where I went to school, the old fishing pond."

Kate beamed gratefully. "Oh, Russell, I'd *love* it."

Mrs. Tynan smiled at them as she left the kitchen to carry a tray up to Auntie Cee.

Russell sat down at the table next to Kate. His mat of black chest hair, in an upswept pattern, was still sprinkled with tiny beads of water from the shower. The sun caught them, making them sparkle like jewels.

"I'm sorry I was so distant yesterday, darling," he told Kate.

"Oh, Russell," she said, near tears. "I thought I'd done something to offend you."

Russell smiled. "Not at all. It's just been . . . difficult . . . for me here, adjusting to being back." His smile faded. "There are many memories here. Not all good."

"I understand."

He took her hand. "A fresh start?"

She smiled broadly. "Yes, a fresh start!"

He looked at her with such love in his eyes. "Have you been writing?"

She shrugged. "A little."

"Figure the garden will inspire you?"

"Hopefully." She raised her eyes to look at Russell's. Green met black.

Russell reached over and kissed her. It ignited a passion both had not yet felt for each other in this house. They decided the garden shop could wait an hour, and went upstairs.

"Shh," the boy was saying, but Rosalind kept giggling anyway.

They were in the attic, and the boy, probably no more than ten or eleven, was unfastening Rosalind's bra. She was thirteen. Russell stood on the steps, watching through the door that led to the attic, which they'd foolishly left ajar.

Or maybe Rosalind had left it that way deliberately, so that Russell could watch. . . .

When she had unzipped the boy's corduroy pants and began playing with his tiny penis, Russell had felt his own loins begin to stir. He touched himself. He watched without ever taking his eyes away, afraid to breathe, afraid to move.

But when the boy began putting his mouth on Rosalind's small, round breasts, she giggled too loudly, and the old man in the locked room had stirred.

"Who's there?" he cried, agitated.

The boy pulled back, just as Russell recoiled, too, but Rosalind guided the boy's head back to her breast. "Ignore him," she whispered. Then louder: "It's just my daffy grandfather."

At that the old man began rattling his door, and

Russell, sickened, turned and fled, aware that his foot-steps down the stairs would be heard by his sister and her boy, and probably by his grandfather as well.

They made love. They put on the radio so that Mrs. Tynan wouldn't hear them, and locked the door just to be safe.

"Oh, Russell, it feels so good to be with you again," Kate said, dreamily, lying back on the bed, her breasts moving in a satisfied rhythm up and down.

"Mmm," Russell agreed, resting his head on Kate's shoulder.

She stroked his hair. "Russell, are you still glad you married me?"

He didn't answer right away. Suddenly he stood, pulling his shorts back on. "Don't be silly, darling. Of course I am."

But he sounded so officious once again. "Come back, Russell," Kate pleaded. "Let's just lie here a bit longer together."

"We've got a lot to do today."

She sighed. "All right." She stood, crumpling up her dirty clothes into a ball.

"Throw those down the stairs," Russell said.

Kate looked at him strangely. "What? Throw them *where?*"

"Never mind." Russell closed his eyes, then opened them. "Well, shall we walk into town? It's a gorgeous day."

"Yes." She looked up at him, desperate not to lose sight of the love in his eyes again. "I want to see that fishing pond you told me about."

Russell smiled down at her. "You will, darling. You will."

* * *

"Lookit the little faggot," Bobby Shortridge spat at him.

Russell was catching tadpoles at the pond, hoping to bring them home and watch them turn into frogs. And Bobby Shortridge had walked up behind him, as quiet as a cat after a bird, not one twig snapping in the woods. Russell didn't like Bobby Shortridge—*hated* him, in fact. Bobby was a year older than Russell, but he had stayed back a year in school and he picked on all the other boys in his class. Russell was eight, maybe nine. Bobby wasn't nearly as good-looking a boy as Russell, but he was tough and ran fast, so all the girls had crushes on him. His face always looked dirty to Russell, but Bobby came from a good family, Grandmother said, so they should be nice to him. But Russell hated Bobby Shortridge nevertheless.

"Whatcha doing," Bobby sneered, "catchin' tad-poles?"

"Yes," Russell replied, stifling his impulse to be sarcastic. *No, I'm hanging tinsel on the Christmas tree,* he wanted to say, but he didn't, trying to ignore the intrusion, scooping his hands into the silky brown mud that ringed the pond. A slippery tadpole squeezed through his fist and escaped back into the lapping water.

"That's a faggoty thing to do," Bobby said.

"Is not," Russell snarled.

"Is too." Bobby walked over and stood behind him. Russell was stooped in the mud, barefoot, and he tried to ignore the bully, concentrating on spotting the next tadpole to come wiggling toward shore.

"Whatcha going to do with them?" Bobby was asking.

"None of your business."

Russell had sighted an unwary tadpole and reached for it. Bobby, still behind him, said, "Faggot," and suddenly shoved him, toppling Russell face first into the murky waters of the pond.

He ran off howling. "Whoooooo-eeeee!"

When Russell came up, gasping for air, his face and body covered with stinking water and clinging greenish tan mud, Rosalind was there, sitting on a rock. She'd been hiding, and had seen the whole thing.

"Don't you worry, baby brother," she said calmly. "Bobby Shortridge will get his."

By the time the sun was setting, the azalea bushes had been carved out from the overgrown forsythias, and tulips had been planted, and marigolds, and pansies. It had turned out to be a good day after all, with Kate enjoying their walk into town. She held Russell's hand as he showed her the old swimming hole where he and Rosalind used to skinny-dip as children and the old fishing pond where he used to catch tadpoles and watch them grow into frogs. Back at the house they cut back overgrown bushes and planted flowers, feeling the sun on their faces and laughing all the while. By the time darkness settled in, they were tired but happy, and the garden was well on its way to recapturing its former glory.

"Wave up at Auntie Cee," Russell said, and they did, proudly, standing in front of their garden.

In the Attic

"Russell?" Kate called quietly.

She'd expected to meet him here in the parlor after breakfast, but the room was empty. It was a dark room, one of the darkest in the house, shielded from the light outside not only by the thick draperies but by the ivy growing over the windows. Kate ran her fingers along the spines of the volumes in the bookcases. Ancient tomes of poetry and New England history. They smelled musty and damp.

Russell had seemed distracted at breakfast, and it made her anxious that he was distancing himself yet again. She couldn't fathom these mood swings. Yesterday working in the garden, they'd been so happy, and last night, making love and holding each other all through the night, she had allowed herself to believe they'd never be unhappy again.

But at breakfast he'd barely made eye contact with her, and only when she asked if she might finally meet Auntie Cee did he look at her.

"All right," he'd said, but there had been no joy in his voice.

Now, looking for him in the parlor, Kate had a sinking feeling in her gut.

She turned, hearing footsteps. "Russell?" she called out hopefully.

It was Mrs. Tynan. "I'm sorry, Mrs. Wright," the nurse said. "But Mr. Russell told me to tell you he'd been called back to New York unexpectedly. Urgent business."

"*New York?*" Kate was dumbfounded. "But we just had breakfast. I went upstairs to shower and change and he was going to take me up to meet Auntie Cee."

Mrs. Tynan made a sympathetic face. "I'm sorry, Mrs. Wright. But he left in a cab about ten minutes ago."

Kate didn't know what to say. "It must have been *very* urgent," she stammered at last, awkwardly. She felt suddenly embarrassed in front of Mrs. Tynan. "Oh, well. I guess I'll get to meet her when he gets back then." She hesitated. "Did he say . . . when . . . ?"

"I'm sorry, he didn't."

Kate tried to smile. "I'm sure he'll call me later."

"Of course, Mrs. Wright." Mrs. Tynan looked at her with pity. Kate turned away.

She didn't know what to think. What could have happened to make him leave so early? And why did she feel so unnerved being in this house without him?

She spent the morning in the garden, planting more bulbs and trimming some of the hedges. She filled the dry, slightly cracking birdbaths with water. A blue jay sang garishly in a red maple tree behind her. Out here in the garden, she felt safe, especially as the sun climbed higher in the sky and another warm spring day revealed itself. But she knew she was only avoiding what scared her, and until she faced her fears, she'd never be happy in this house.

"I'm going to explore Wrightsbridge, from top to bottom," she said all of a sudden, setting her can of water down.

Ever since they'd arrived, Kate had confined herself to just four places in this big old house: the bedroom, the dining room, the downstairs parlor, and the kitchen. She'd never been told *not* to explore, but she felt the edict anyway. As much from Russell as from the ghosts.

She hadn't seen any of the dead in over twenty-four hours now, nor had those disconcerting blackouts returned. Maybe Erik was right. Maybe they *had* just been testing her. Going inside now and exploring the place would only deepen their respect, she surmised. *We'll learn to live together,* she thought to herself.

She walked in through the kitchen, where the refrigerator kicked into its usual monotonous groan. She passed through the dining room into the parlor, where she paused briefly to look up at the portrait of Asa Wright over the mantel. She smiled sardonically.

"There's a new master of Wrightsbridge," she announced, "and he's brought home a bride. You all will just have to learn to make room."

Then she headed up the stairs.

In and out of the rooms on the second floor she went, even in the dark, closed-off east wing. Nothing remarkable, just cobweb-shrouded beds and bureaus. She saw nothing, no one, heard not a sound except the clock chiming downstairs.

It was the third floor where she paused. She had not yet ascended this flight of stairs, leading up to Auntie Cee's room—and who knew what else. But she took a deep breath and began to climb, feeling a little giddy, like a kid, doing something she knew her parents wouldn't allow if they were home. Here, on this landing, was another old stained-glass window, with an even heavier coat of grime. It was hard to make out what this one depicted, but it looked perhaps to be St. Sebastian, because of the figure tied to a pillar.

The third floor looked almost exactly like the corridor below, but here there was no rug covering the wooden floorboards. Below, on Kate's floor, there was a long oriental runner, but here, the old floorboards exposed just how unevenly the house had settled. There were also what appeared to be gas lamp fixtures along the wall, lamps unused in decades.

All the doors on the floor were closed, except the one immediately to her left, which she presumed to be Auntie Cee's room. From within, she could hear whispered conversation, obviously Mrs. Tynan feeding the old woman her lunch.

Kate surveyed the rest of the corridor. To the side of the stairwell was a smaller staircase, built into the wall, clearly leading to the attic. She decided to take it, figuring she'd be less intrusive there. Besides, attics often held a house's most important secrets. She knew instinctively that if she were to learn about Wrightsbridge, she needed to start in the attic.

It was just the way she might have imagined it. Funny how there was always a dressmaker's dummy in old attics. An old brass birdcage rusted off to one side, and dozens of old trunks were piled on top of each other. Boxes of papers, bundles of old newspapers—a real firetrap, Kate said to herself. On some surfaces, the dust was nearly an inch thick, and as she started to cough, she almost regretted coming up here.

From every beam cobwebs hung in long, loose lace that managed to catch the slivers of sun spearing their way through the slots in the boarded-up windows. A four-poster bed frame stood at one end of the attic, but no mattress sat upon its network of coiled, dusty springs. There were two portraits hanging crookedly from nails on the far wall, and as Kate drew closer she discerned they were, in fact, very old photographs, of an unsmiling man and a broad-faced woman, maybe in their thirties. The writing in the corner, the photographer's stamp, was in some language she couldn't read.

"Swedish," she surmised, whispering.

Then she spotted the room. It seemed to have been specially constructed, for it made a perfect square in the northwest corner of the house. It stood at the opposite end of the attic with its open door facing her, revealing the blackness within. A servant's room, Kate surmised. Between the room and herself hung a dozen layers of cobweb, like laundry on a line, but even still she could detect movement inside the room. She walked slowly toward it, peering through the door.

That's when she saw him. The old man with the beard, inside the room.

But he didn't look lost anymore. He looked very much at home, and no longer did his face reflect fear or sadness. For the first time Kate was frightened looking at him, and well she should be—for suddenly he grinned and pulled from behind his back a flaming torch, and came running toward her.

"No!" she screamed, and all at once the sound of flapping, angry, leathery wings arose from the dust of the attic, and a storm of bats, maybe as many as fifteen or twenty, swooped down from the rafters and then up again, into the dark beyond the beams.

The old man was gone.

Kate had instinctively covered her hair, but as quickly as they had appeared the bats were gone, hiding their nearly blind, beady little eyes from the rays of the sun that spilled increasingly into the attic as the sun rose higher in the noonday sky.

"Dear God," Kate said. Her heart was racing in her chest. She wasn't sure what had frightened her more, the sudden malevolence of the old man or the startling appearance of the bats. Still, she couldn't resist going ahead, looking into that room. She parted the cobwebs in front of her as if they were draperies, silk curtains leading to the sultan's inner chamber. When she stood in front of the room, trying to make out its darkened interior, she found it difficult to breathe, her throat clogged up again with dust.

She pushed into the darkness of the room, guided by a faint glow at the far end, a shuttered window, which she tugged at, releasing the latch. It finally opened, allowing unfettered sunlight to fall into the room. For the first time in how many decades? she wondered.

There was nothing remarkable about the room; no ghost sat on the broken chair in the corner or on the rusted Murphy bed that was attached to the west wall. That was it for the room's contents: a cot and a chair, and lots of dust. Yes, this must have been built for a servant, and a lowly one at that.

She was about to leave when she noticed the carvings on the wall next to the window. Crude scratchings, as if made with a blunt tool, or another piece of wood. She touched them, feeling even here the layer of dust. The largest of them read: *EW, EW, EW, EW.*

And below that: *I am Edgar Wright.*

"Edgar Wright," she read, the name meaning nothing. Which generation of Wrights had he belonged to? What had he been doing in this attic room?

And might he be the old man with the beard?

Then suddenly, farther down, closer to the floor, she noticed other carvings. She bent down to read them. They copied the carvings above, with a slight variation: *RW, RW, RW, RW.*

She strained her eyes in the dim light to read what was carved below: *I am Rosalind Wright.*

* * *

Auntie Cee could hear something, like someone walking above her.

Someone in the attic.

"Bats," she said, staring into the garden.

No, not bats, that's too loud for bats. Pity it's just the mind that's going, she thought, not the hearing. Why did she still have to hear them up there?

Dear God, there it was again. Sounds from the attic. Soon they'd be calling for her. She covered her ears.

"Cecilia!"

"Auntie Cee!"

Dear God, she thought, holding her old, veiny hands to the sides of her head. *Will it never go away?*

Kate and Auntie Cee

As she stepped off the stairs into the corridor on the third floor, she heard her cry.

"Mrs. Tynan?"

Kate looked around. Where was Mrs. Tynan? Auntie Cee was clearly upset, distressed, calling from her room. What if something was wrong? She stopped, peering into the old woman's room.

"Oh, please stop, *please!*" she heard Auntie Cee cry from inside her room.

Kate stood outside her door, not knowing what to do. She was afraid Russell would be angry if she met Auntie Cee without him there. Inside the room the light was muted, and it smelled of talcum powder, and air freshener, and something else, something very old, the way old ladies' houses often smelled, as if old flesh itself had its own unique aroma.

"Miss Wright?" she called gently into the room. "Do you need something?"

"Eh?" Auntie Cee's voice seemed startled. "Who's there?"

"It's Kate, ma'am," she said politely. "Russell's wife. We haven't met yet."

"Oh, yes, yes," she said. "Do come in."

Kate stepped inside. Past the half-closed door she saw her, sitting in her chair, the large picture window overlooking the garden in front of her. Her profile was elegantly silhouetted in the glare of the window; she served as a kind of human eclipse, and around the contours of her face danced orange fire.

"I heard you calling," Kate said shyly. "I thought maybe you needed something."

"No, no, I just thought it was Mrs. Tynan."

"No, ma'am," Kate said, trying to smile. "It was just me."

"And where is Russell?" Her brow creased. "He's not in the house, is he?"

Kate could tell that the old woman was able to sense things like that. You didn't live for nearly a century without getting in touch with the rhythms of life.

"No," Kate told her. "He's gone into New York. On business."

Auntie Cee smiled. "He's been so busy since he came back."

"There's a lot to do in fixing up this place."

The old woman nodded. "He told me he was going to have carpenters here, and roofers, and plumbers."

"Yes, ma'am, he is."

Auntie Cee looked out the picture window down at the garden. "The two of you are making it your home, aren't you?"

Kate hesitated. "Yes, ma'am."

They were both appraising each other. She seemed pleased by her, Kate thought, and she liked her. Her old blue eyes shone with intelligence, and understanding.

This was hardly the dithering, confused creature she'd come to expect.

"Please, sit down," Auntie Cee said, patting the stool behind her.

"Thank you," Kate replied, taking her seat.

"Now tell me about yourself."

Kate smiled. "What would you like to know?"

"Where are you from?"

"California, originally. . . ."

"Are your parents still alive?"

Kate sighed. "Yes, they are."

"And do they still live in California?"

"Yes."

Auntie Cee narrowed her eyes, studying Kate. "You're not in contact with them, are you?"

"Not very often," Kate admitted.

"They don't even know you're married, do they?"

"No, ma'am," Kate said, marveling at this old woman's insight.

"Do you love Russell?"

The sudden question took Kate by surprise. "Of course, ma'am," Kate finally managed to say. "He's my husband."

"Husbands and wives don't always love each other." Auntie Cee smiled. "But it would be nice to know this house had love in it again."

Kate smiled. "You've lived here all your life," she said.

"Yes," said Auntie Cee. "Almost one hundred years."

"That's amazing."

Auntie Cee looked at her. "Why do you think so?"

"Well, you've lived a long time. Think of all you've seen."

The old woman shrugged. "Oh, I haven't seen all that much. It wasn't often that I left this estate. Since breaking my hip and then my stroke, almost thirty years ago, I haven't left this house, except a few times to the hospital. And now, for six years, I haven't left this room. I'm determined not to leave here until I die. I suppose they think it eccentric of me. Poor Mrs. Tynan has to climb three flights of stairs several times a day. But it's my last whim, you understand. Everybody comes to me. My doctor. My minister." She smiled warmly. "And now, my nephew and his pretty wife."

Kate smiled back at her. "Your niece will be coming home soon, too."

Auntie Cee looked at her intently. "Did Russell tell you that?"

"Yes," Kate replied. "He said Rosalind would be arriving soon."

Auntie Cee seemed to consider this. "Get me a glass of water, will you? There's a pitcher over on that table."

She did. The old woman drank. Kate watched her throat accept the liquid, a tangle of veins shifting in her neck. She finished and set the glass on the small table to her left.

"Russell said you were a writer," she said at last. "Do you write stories?"

"Well, I'm trying to."

Auntie Cee laced her bony old fingers together. "I used to read the stories in the *Saturday Evening Post.* And the *Atlantic.* I miss those periodicals. I don't watch the television anymore."

That's right, Kate noticed. There was no TV in her room. The only clue that this room existed in the present was the modern telephone on the table at the old woman's left elbow. Otherwise it could've been 1920, with its ornately framed photographs of people long dead, its rich red velvet draperies, the fireplace with its antique andiron, the grand canopied four-poster bed in the corner. There was a radio next to the bed, but it too looked as if it was made long ago.

"I used to love moving pictures, went a couple times a week down to the picture show in town," Auntie Cee was saying, "but I haven't seen one now in over thirty years."

"I love old movies," Kate said, suddenly getting an idea. "Tell me some of your favorites and I'll get a VCR up here and we'll watch them together."

Auntie Cee smiled, false teeth clicking. "Remember, now, dear, I'm almost a hundred years old. When I was a girl, movies were shown in nickelodeons, and they lasted no more than five or ten minutes each."

"Mary Pickford?" Kate asked, raising her eyebrows and cocking a smile.

The old woman grinned, seemingly in disbelief that Kate would know the name. "Have you ever seen a Mary Pickford picture?"

"Sure. In New York, I worked for a video store. We had a whole section on silent films."

"They still show the old silents?"

"Sure. Mary Pickford, and Charlie Chaplin, Douglas Fairbanks, Lillian Gish . . ."

Auntie Cee was positively rapturous. "Oh, my Lord— to think, to be able to see again—" Her eyes seemed to move off toward a far distant place, where Kate couldn't follow. "Of course, by the time I was engaged to be married, they showed pictures in grand movie houses, palaces really . . . That's what they called the theater here in town, the Palace, and Samuel and I would go to see Gloria Swanson. She was my favorite, yes, Gloria Swanson, Samuel and I. She was just a girl then, not a very big star, not like she became, just a girl, like me, and Samuel was just a boy . . ."

She trailed off. She slowly moved her eyes to take in Kate again. "Did you know Samuel?" she asked suddenly.

Kate was startled. "No. No, I didn't."

"Did you go over there? In the war? To France?"

"No, ma'am."

"I wanted to. I wanted to be a nurse." She looked out the window. "But my father wouldn't let me, and Samuel died, you know . . ."

"I'm sorry, ma'am."

She was quiet for nearly a minute, then looked over at Kate with eyes she didn't recognize. "Who are you again? Why have you come to see me?"

"Kate, ma'am. I'm Kate, Russell's wife."

"Russell," she said weakly. And then she covered her ears with her hands and began rocking back and forth in her chair, crying, "Oh, dear, dear, dear, dear, dear, dear."

"Miss Wright—" Kate said, reaching out to her.

"What is wrong with her?"

It was Mrs. Tynan, suddenly behind Kate.

"I'm sorry, I was just—"

Mrs. Tynan fell to her knees beside the old woman, attempting to take her into her arms.

Kate backed out of the room. She could still hear the old woman wailing inside, and Mrs. Tynan's attempts to calm her. But she could hear something else now, too.

The old man crying to be let out of the room in the attic.

Theresa

Russell sat in the town square, on one of the iron benches that edged the green, the statue of LaFayette on his horse behind him. It was a Saturday, he realized: funny how the days of the week no longer mattered to him since he'd returned to Connecticut. He'd lied, of course, to Mrs. Tynan and through her, to Kate—lied about going into New York when he was just coming here, to town. But he'd had no choice. He wanted to be alone. He needed to think.

He watched the children pass him on the sidewalk, children with their mothers, come "downtown" for a day's shopping, free from the confines of school for a couple of glorious days. Russell remembered what school was like in late May: a rush of everything, of heightened anticipation for summer, a truce between teachers and troublesome students, an accelerating energy that rose with the warm temperatures. And Saturdays were simply coming attractions for summer.

Oh, how he'd loved Saturdays as a kid. He'd often

come into town like these kids, except of course he came alone, without a mother to hold his hand. He and Rosalind would come and they'd buy comic books: *Superman, Adventure Comics, Wonder Woman.* Bobby Shortridge had once come upon him sitting there on this very same bench, reading *Wonder Woman.* "What a fag you are, Russell Wright," he'd said. "What a fag."

Russell hated Bobby Shortridge. He hated the memories being in that house had brought back to him. He hadn't thought of Bobby Shortridge in years, and now suddenly there he was, behind every tree, around every corner. He hadn't thought of his father, either, and now he saw him every time he closed his eyes, hanging from that beam in the cellar. This morning Russell had awakened consumed with the desire to get out, to clear his head, with no one—not even Kate—around to confuse him. Yesterday had been such a good day, and he'd felt so together with Kate—but today he simply couldn't bear it, not there, not in that house.

"It's a good thing Grandmother never knew your wife," Rosalind had said, meaning Theresa, of course, but she might as well have meant Kate. "Grandmother would never have approved. She'd never have approved of how you lived your life after you left Wrightsbridge. It's a good thing she can't see you now."

Oh, but she can, dear sister, she can, Russell thought. *And even though her ashes are still sitting in some attorney's office, still unclaimed, she's expressing her disapproval to me every day, every single day.*

He had, of course, been raised to make up for the shortcomings of his father, that coward who'd hanged himself in the basement. Grandmother determined that Russell Wright was to be the true heir to Asa Wright and the glory of Wrightsbridge—a glory debased not by one but by *two* generations of Wright men. Both Edgar and his son Bernard had proven to be failures, disappointments, bums. It was left to Russell to carry on the name, to keep the family prosperous, to restore the fortune, to revive the glory.

He remembered the last Old Town Day celebration held at the estate, right before Grandfather went mad. Russell was very young, but he remembered all the people, and the mayor standing on their front porch, graciously thanking the Wrights for their generosity. People were crammed onto the lawn over the bridge, and there were jugglers and face-painters, magicians and clowns. Tents had been set up in the meadow on the other side of the brook, with cakewalks and raffles and even a pony ride, out near the barbed-wire fence that divided the meadow in two. Once, when Asa Wright had kept a farm, the barbed wire had kept the cows from wandering. By the time Russell was a boy it was just a rusting relic of the past. The fair committee had decorated it with pink and blue crepe paper, and tied smiley-faced helium balloons to its old wire.

Oh, such parties were those Old Town Day celebrations! The street in front of the house was closed, and a Ferris wheel erected. Russell rode to the top with Rosalind, and the operator, knowing who they were, stopped while they were at the top, giving them a glorious view of the treetops and the meadow and the softly winding brook. The entire fair was subsidized by Wright money, and the town was grateful for that. At the end of the day, Grandfather and Grandmother stood at the bridge, shaking everyone's hand as they left, and Russell had watched them, thinking them very important people indeed.

What had changed all that? When had it happened? Soon after that last fair, his grandfather had gone mad. Two years later, his father had hanged himself, and the factory, long floundering, was finally closed. There were enough investments to keep the family going, but their fortune dwindled. Russell could live off his trust fund for the rest of his life if he wanted, but he wasn't rich, and the thought of doing nothing, nothing but taking care of Auntie Cee and fixing shower heads and floorboards, oppressed him, especially this morning, sitting in the town square.

How different it had all been, when he'd left, when he'd finally worked up the courage to leave and move to New York. Never had he imagined coming back. He was free. *Free!* He had finally escaped. Grandmother hadn't even known he'd left for good. He never said good-bye. He'd gone to New York, he said, for a weekend, to explore career opportunities. After college, he'd hung around Wrightsbridge for a while, but Rosalind was gone, and he was bored. Four years of relative freedom had taught him he didn't want to live under his grandmother's thumb, not ever again. A degree in business management from the Wharton School at Penn allowed him to set himself up in business, and after a few years he was pretty much on his own, playing the role of an eccentric Wall Street investor with panache. How happy he'd been in those first years in New York, finally free of Wrightsbridge and its memories.

Then he'd met Theresa.

"You've got to face the truth, Russell," Rosalind had said, sitting on his couch, smoking a cigarette, just as she had often done when they were teenagers, sneaking a smoke in the far meadow, out by the barbed-wire fence.

He sat next to her with his face in his hands.

"*Your wife has been cheating on you!*" Rosalind snarled. "Making a fool of you!"

He'd started to cry.

"Don't tell me you actually *loved* her?" Rosalind

asked, her face all pulled back as if she'd been sucking a lemon. "Russell, she is common *trash*. Beneath you."

"No, Theresa is not—"

Rosalind exhaled smoke. "Oh, please, Russell. You could never take her back to Wrightsbridge. What would Grandmother have ever thought?"

"What am I going to do?" he asked his sister, looking up at her through the tears in his eyes.

She had smiled. "Don't you worry, baby brother. I'm here now. I'll take care of things."

Rosalind always did. She always took care of things when they got too much for Russell. Within weeks, Theresa was dead. She died on the couch, her lips drawn back from her teeth so far that she already looked like a skeleton.

Russell was crying, sitting on the bench in the town square. It was the first time he'd cried since that day with Rosalind. He hadn't shed a tear at Theresa's funeral, or even on the day she died. But he was crying now, and suddenly he missed his wife more than anything in the world, and Kate seemed such a sorry substitute.

He looked up the road that led, half a mile down, to Wrightsbridge. "I'm sorry, Theresa," Russell whispered. "I'm sorry."

Kate and Russell, Part Two

His screams hadn't stopped. Kate sat in her room, huddled in a chair, and from the attic she could still hear him, if faintly: his cries to be let out, the rattling of the door, the banging on the wall.

Why had Edgar Wright been locked up there? What had he done? Who put him there?

"Stop!" she called out, placing her hands over her ears. But still she heard him.

Let me out! Let me out! Someone, please, let me out of here!

She thrust herself from her chair and grabbed her cell phone. She would try calling Erik again. She'd already left two messages.

"Kate?"

"Oh, Erik! Thank God you answered!"

"Sweetie, I was just going to call you. I just got your messages."

"They're wild here, Erik. I feel like I'm going mad. I can't tune them out today."

"Hold on, Kate. Start from the beginning. What happened?"

She told him about the attic. The room. The old man.

"Okay," Erik was saying, considering the situation. "That's obviously his focal point. Where his spirit is stuck. If you can help him move on—"

"He's *not* stuck there," Kate said. "Remember I saw him in New York. You saw him out at the cottage in Montauk."

"I don't mean literally stuck, Kate," Erik told her. "I mean that's the place that holds him here, that won't let him move on. Something about that place is significant to him, and from the sounds of it, not in a good way."

"He was locked in there by someone. For a long time, I think. Because of the carving on the walls."

"What about the other name? Rosalind? That's the sister, right?"

Kate sighed. "Yes. I'm not sure why she was in there. Maybe it was a prank."

"Or maybe she was locked in there, too."

Kate ran a hand through her long red hair. "She's supposed to be here soon. Maybe she'll be more forthcoming about all this than Russell is."

"Sweetie," Erik said, and his voice had taken on a serious tone she recognized. "I think it's time you talked to him. Tell him about what you see. Otherwise you're going to go crazy. You *need* to tell him, get his support."

Kate agreed, walking over to the window and looking down into the garden. "I guess you're right. Maybe if I understood what happened in this house I could better deal with my fear." She shivered. "I've never been this frightened by my visions since I was a little girl."

* * *

She turned and pressed a pansy to her nose. It startled her.

"Erik?"

She looked at her hand. She was holding a flower, not her cell phone. When had she hung up with Erik? When had she left her room and come down here, to the garden?

Oh, dear God, it's happened again.

She turned and looked up at the window—her window—where she'd just been standing. She saw someone there, talking on a cell phone: *myself,* she thought with wonder. *I'm seeing myself.*

"Mrs. Wright?"

It was Mrs. Tynan. Kate turned, and now she wasn't in the garden, *or* in her room, but down by the brook. She was sitting against a tree, and her journal was open in her lap. She was here, writing, just as she'd hoped to do before the day was done.

She looked down at the page. She'd written two full pages. She was eager to read them, but there was Mrs. Tynan, scuffing through the grass behind her.

"Yes?" she asked impatiently.

"Mr. Russell is back. He's looking for you."

"Tell him I'm out here," Kate told her.

"Oh—" Mrs. Tynan stopped. "Very well," she said, turning to leave.

"Oh, Mrs. Tynan?" Kate shouted, over her shoulder.

"Yes?"

"What time is it?"

"Nearly half past four."

Four? She felt her armpits dampen. It was not even two o'clock when she'd been on the phone talking with Erik.

She turned to her journal. She had written nonsense.

There's no getting away from it, not really, not really. In the end, that's what it is: the end. Why pretend anything else? You are trapped. They have won. In the end, that's all it is: the end.

"Dear Lord," she said to herself.

And after that: *I am Kate Wright.*

Followed by a page and a half of: *KW, KW, KW, KW, KW, KW . . .*

She slammed the volume shut.

"Have you been writing?"

Russell had come up behind her.

"If you can call it that." Kate had torn out the pages; they were now several yards downstream.

Here, at the brook, daisies had sprouted in abundance, and the clover had pretty much obliterated the grass. Kate was breathing easier now, and her heart had stopped racing.

"I'm sorry about today," Russell said awkwardly.

"You had business." Kate wouldn't look up at him.

Russell sat down next to her in the clover. "No, I didn't. I just freaked out."

Kate now turned to face him. "You, too, huh?"

"Bad day?"

She shrugged, and then laughed, bitterly. "I don't know. I can't remember. What did *you* freak out about?"

"Oh"—and Russell gestured futilely—"everything. Nothing. Being back here. You."

"Me?"

Russell nodded.

"Oh, Russell, are you having second thoughts about our marriage?"

He put his arms around her. "Not second thoughts. Just worrying that I'm not being fair to you."

She looked up at him. "Maybe I'm not being fair to you, either."

He looked puzzled. "What do you mean?"

"I mean, I need to talk to you. Things are happening to me . . . things maybe I should have expected . . . things I should have told you about long ago."

He stiffened. She could feel it. "Kate, please don't keep secrets from me."

"I don't want to. Not anymore."

Russell looked around, the river babbling clean and clear over the rocks, the daisies swaying in the cool, late afternoon air. "You know," he said, letting Kate go, seeming to drift away with his thoughts, "over in the woods there is where I almost froze to death one winter, when Rosalind and I were skipping school and got lost. I fell and sprained my ankle, and couldn't walk, and Rosalind had to give me her coat. She was always taking care of me."

"Why did Rosalind have to take care of you?" Kate pressed. "Why did the two of you have to depend so much on each other?"

He looked at her blankly. "I've told you. Our parents were dead."

"But you had your grandparents . . ."

He shivered. "Grandmother was cruel. She hit us. She punished us for the slightest indiscretion . . ."

Kate moved in close to him. "*How* did she punish you?"

He looked at her.

"Did she ever lock you in a room?"

"*Stop!*" Russell stood suddenly, his hands over his ears. "I don't want to talk about the bad things! I came out here to be happy with you! Why do you bring up the bad things?"

Kate had gotten to her feet as well, and was trying to

embrace her husband. He pushed her away. "I'm sorry, Russell. I'm sorry, really I am."

He seemed to calm down, staring at the brook rushing by. He allowed her to take his hand.

"I just want to understand," Kate said softly.

Russell just sighed, a long, sad sound, and then brought Kate's hand to his lips for a kiss.

"Speaking of Rosalind," Kate ventured, "any idea when she'll be arriving?"

"No," Russell said, sharply. Then he smiled, reaching down to pat Kate's hand. "Darling, I don't want anything to get in the way of us being happy together."

"Neither do I, Russell."

They stood there quiet for a long time. Russell slipped his arm around her. Kate, suddenly exhausted, rested her head on Russell's shoulder. She would wait a while longer before telling him about her visions. But she knew she couldn't wait too long.

They made love right there on the grass, beside the babbling brook. The sky was a canvas of color as the sun set behind the trees, splattering reds and golds and deep, deep purples. They didn't even care if Mrs. Tynan was watching through a window.

"You know," Kate said, rolling onto her back, "I met your aunt today."

"You did?" Russell leaned up on one elbow to look down at her.

"Yes." She glanced up into the darkening sky. "I admit it—I was exploring the house. I heard her call, so I introduced myself."

"That's great." Russell gave her a small smile. "What did she—what did you two talk about?"

"Little things. Silent movies. Her health. Then she started rambling . . . she thought I was someone else."

"That happens." He looked at her deliberately. "Sometimes Auntie Cee gets confused. Says people are dead when they're really alive."

"And vice versa," Kate said.

"Yes. Vice versa."

Kate sighed, closing her eyes against the night sky. "Your attic really does have bats," she added.

There was a pause. "You went into the attic?"

"Yes." She hesitated, not wanting to set him off again. "Russell, who was Edgar Wright?"

"Why do you ask?"

"Because I saw his name, carved in the wall, in a little room up there. And your sister's name, too, underneath it."

Russell closed his eyes. For a moment, he didn't say anything, and Kate thought maybe she'd gone too far. But then he spoke, and his voice bore no sign of emotion.

"Edgar Wright was my grandfather," he said. "That's where my grandmother locked him when he went mad. And after he died, that's where Rosalind was punished. Left in there for days, with no food, no water, nowhere to go to the bathroom." He stood up, buttoning his pants. "Do you understand now what a monstrous place this is?"

Kate tried to respond, but found she couldn't. Instead, she took Russell's hand and together they walked back to the house.

The old man's screams were silent.

Rosalind Arrives

It was Memorial Day weekend that Rosalind finally arrived.

The garden had been restored. Auntie Cee had clapped her hands from her window, and they both had taken bows before her. Afterward, they all had dinner—even Mrs. Tynan—in Auntie Cee's room, watching the sunset. The tulips and the pansies were beautiful, they all agreed, but it was the roses for which they waited most eagerly to bloom.

"Well, we'll have to give them a few years," Russell acknowledged, "since the bushes have been untended for so long."

"I think," Auntie Cee said, raising a bony finger, "that Kate is a magician."

They all laughed.

"They will be beautiful *this* year," the old woman pronounced.

It had been an uneventful couple of weeks. Kate had neither heard nor seen anything else; she also had not gone venturing very far. Most thankfully, she'd had no more of the mysterious blackouts, and told Erik when she spoke to him on the phone that she thought maybe her visit to the attic had been the final step in convincing the ghosts to accept her.

"Any sign of the little girl?" he asked.

"No, none at all." Kate laughed into the phone. "I think she's *your* ghost, Erik, not mine."

So she'd delayed, yet again, telling Russell anything about what she could see. They were so happy once more. Why risk spoiling it?

"Let's have a Memorial Day picnic," Russell had suggested. "Nothing too big. But something to let people know Wrightsbridge is back."

"And *different*." Kate smiled.

"Oh, *quite*," Russell agreed.

And so old Mr. Shortridge and his son Bobby were invited, and Mrs. Tyrwhit from the house down the street, and the Lacey sisters, Beatrice and Barbara, and Mayor Miller, whose late father had been the last mayor to preside over an Old Town Day at Wrightsbridge, back in 1969.

"Make sure they all wave up at me," cried Auntie Cee, gleefully.

"Of course," Russell assured her, kissing her forehead. Kate did likewise.

That night, Russell came into the parlor, where Kate was writing in her journal. He'd heard from Rosalind, he announced.

"Finally," Kate said.

"I told her about the picnic," he said. "She promised she'd be here."

It was a glorious day. Kate awoke early. She went to the large window overlooking the garden and threw open the sash. She breathed deeply of the fresh cool morning air. The weather had simply been spectacular ever since they'd arrived. Not one rainy day in all that time.

Russell was already awake, no doubt already preparing the yard for the picnic. Over the past few days all sorts of workers had swarmed all over the estate, replacing rotted floorboards, rehanging shutters, painting trim, putting in new drainpipes. The house was emerging as an aging dowager might after a careful face-lift. Kate had even managed to wipe away much of the dust from the parlor and dining room, and once more St. George shone in brilliant blue and green stained glass. Surely their visitors would marvel at the restored grandeur of Wrightsbridge.

Kate looked forward to meeting the people of the town. She was especially anxious to finally meet her sister-in-law. *Rosalind.* She'd finally stand face-to-face with the famous, mysterious Rosalind.

She did herself up in bright spring colors, a green sundress to complement her red hair, which she tied back with a yellow bow. Downstairs, she found Mrs. Tynan helping Russell prepare casseroles and salads. Kate quickly pitched in, chopping vegetables and slicing eggs.

"This will be such fun," she gushed.

In the yard they set up lawn chairs and scraped down the old grill. The sky was startlingly clear and blue.

"Are you excited, Russell?" she asked. "Opening up Wrightsbridge again?"

He smiled. But she could tell he was tense. It was only natural, she supposed, seeing all these people after all this time.

The first to arrive was Mrs. Tyrwhit, an old lady about eighty who still dyed her hair bright orange. She wore a hat with a plastic blue jay perched among yellow silk flowers. She'd baked four pies.

"One cherry, one apple, one peach, and one lemon meringue," she chirped, coming up the steps, lugging the heavy, four-pie wicker basket. Kate took it from her. "Course, none of the fruit's in season, so I hadda get 'em from cans." She kissed Russell, enthused about how handsome he'd gotten. Then she looked over at Kate. "Who's this one?"

"I'm Kate Wright," she said, offering her free hand to help Mrs. Tyrwhit up the stairs.

"None of the fruit's in season," the old woman said again, almost apologizing. Kate assured her that they'd be delicious all the same.

The next to arrive were the Lacey sisters, Beatrice and Barbara, in their late sixties and who considered Mrs. Tyrwhit much older than they ("I could never call her anything other than Mrs. Tyrwhit," Beatrice confessed to Kate). Barbara had been positively *ecstatic* about returning to Wrightsbridge. "Why, I couldn't *sleep* last night," she gushed to Russell. "You have done *such* wonders in restoring the place."

"Well, there's still a lot of work to do," he said.

"But the garden—" She gestured to the flowers and neatly trimmed bushes. "Miss Cee must be delighted. Oh, *yoo hoo!*" she called, turning arthritically to look up at Auntie Cee, who waved down from her open windows.

From the parlor, Russell noticed Mr. Shortridge getting out of his car on the other side of the bridge. In the shade of the poplars, he couldn't yet make out if Bobby was with him, but in a moment two figures walked into the sunlight and began crossing the bridge.

So he'd brought Bobby after all. Russell went outside to wait on the front porch and greet them.

"I'd heard you'd come back, Russell," Mr. Shortridge

called from the bridge. Bobby was behind him. "Welcome home."

"Thank you, Mr. Shortridge," Russell called back. His eyes moved to the younger man behind him. "Hello, Bobby."

There was a wave. Bobby looked hunched, and Mr. Shortridge paused at the end of the footbridge to wait for his son, extending his hand. "Come on, Bobby."

As they walked up the path, Russell kept his eyes on the father. How old he'd gotten, this bear of a man, how thin, how fragile. Clem Shortridge had been the basketball coach at the junior high school, and he hadn't much liked Russell then, because Russell wasn't an athlete. Russell preferred to read books in the library rather than try out for the basketball team. Russell wasn't the popular, rough-and-tumble, all-American boy his own son was—or at least, had been, before the accident.

But then again, Grandmother had made quite a substantial gift of money to Coach Shortridge after the accident, and ever since then, the Shortridges and the Wrights had been very close. Very close indeed.

"Can't wait to see whatcha done with the house," Mr. Shortridge said, winded from his walk, continuing past Russell through the front door.

Bobby was a few minutes behind him.

"H'wo, Wuthew," he said, and Russell extended his hand to him.

"Hello, Bobby."

They shook. Bobby smiled. Or at least, the muscles behind what was left of his face shifted, in what passed for a smile. Bobby's features—his eyes, his nose, his cheeks, his lips—were obliterated into one torn and twisted mask. They had never grown back, as Rosalind had promised they would.

She had turned Bobby Shortridge into a freak.

* * *

Picture a day as cold and gray as Memorial Day was warm and sunny. Picture Russell at fourteen, with his shiny blue parka with the big fur-lined hood. And Rosalind, in wool hat, big red mittens, a green wool coat, and a scarf with every color of the rainbow. And picture Bobby Shortridge, itching to get into Rosalind's too-tight blue jeans, arriving on the scene, in heavy sweater and denim jacket.

"Hey," he said, his way of greeting.

"Bobby," Rosalind cooed. "Want to go snowmobiling?"

Russell glared at her. "Rosalind," he reprimanded—but she just looked at him, all eyes beneath the wool hat she had pulled down over her forehead.

They had just decided to haul out the snowmobiles themselves, and they only owned two. Russell resented Bobby's intrusion. Oh, how he *hated* Bobby Shortridge, and Rosalind knew that. Bobby had stopped beating Russell up after the seventh grade, but still he taunted him with calls of "faggot, faggot" in school. Russell was a brain where Bobby was a jock, and so had classes far more advanced than Bobby. But still Bobby would see him in the hallway, taunting him and asking him about Rosalind.

"I hear your sister puts out," he'd say. "Why don't you have her give me a call?"

"She wouldn't sniff at garbage like you," Russell spat back, bracing himself for a fight.

But Bobby had simply started chanting: "Faggot, faggot, faggot, faggot," louder and louder, till it echoed down the hall, bouncing off the tin lockers, causing girls in ponytails carrying their books against their sprouting breasts to titter, giggle, and look wildly at Russell.

"They're up in the barn," Rosalind said of the snowmobiles, and Russell gave a deep sigh, accepting the inevitable. Rosalind had decided to let Bobby have his way with her, damned tramp that she was. There was nothing Russell could do about it. He just trudged along after the two of them, crunching through the deep snow. Oh, wasn't this just like her? Rosalind was so unreliable. If she got it into her head to flirt with a boy, she'd just forget about Russell, leave him behind.

But *Bobby Shortridge?* How could she go off with *him?* Rosalind knew Russell hated him more than anyone in the world.

They'd just had a wicked storm. A classic New England nor'easter. Nearly four feet of snow, even higher at the drifts. Beyond the frozen brook that ringed Wrights-bridge was a large meadow, once used as farmland when Asa Wright had raised horses and cows. Now the barn was used only for storage, and in a few years, it would burn mysteriously to the ground one night. Some in town would whisper it was the ghost of Edgar Wright, come back to finish what he'd tried to do the night he'd taken a torch to the parlor curtains. But on this day, this day of brightness and reflecting white snow, the barn still stood, and Rosalind pulled open the heavy door all by herself. Inside, next to the rusting, rotting tractor, were two new snowmobiles, Christmas gifts from Auntie Cee. Rosalind had wanted one, *begged* for one; Russell was more ambivalent. "I'll pay for them if you go down and pick them out," Auntie Cee had promised.

Grandmother had given her consent. "If it will keep you outside, and give me some peace, go ahead," she told them, turning her attention back to *Search for Tomorrow.*

Russell had come to enjoy his gift, riding over the crisp hills of snow, his face stinging from the cold wind, but feeling more alive than he could ever remember before. He bought a pair of sun-and-snow-glare glasses, and he thought he looked really cool in them. Rosalind had laughed: "You look like a dork." But he paid her no mind.

Auntie Cee gave them only one admonishment: "Be careful of the barbed-wire fence."

The first time he strapped himself onto the snowmobile, Russell had been terrified—scared to death that he'd be zipping along and suddenly find himself ensnared in the fence, covered as it was by drifts of snow. But Rosalind had mocked his fear: "You're afraid of *life,* baby brother. Follow me. I know where it is. I'll keep you away from it."

And she had. When she reached a spot marked by an old, dead tree sticking ungainly from the snow, she lifted her hand, signaling the end of their run. "It's over there, right beyond the dead tree," she'd yelled to Russell over the roar of the snowmobile motor. "Turn around!"

They did, making smooth arcs in the snow, and in the days to come, when he'd be riding by himself, he always made the same curve—getting a fast, straight start from the barn and then cutting the handlebar swiftly to the right, safely missing the sharp teeth that hid under the snow.

Now Rosalind was standing far too close to Bobby Shortridge for Russell not to get the message. "We'll go first," she said, "then I'll come back and let you ride with Bobby." Bobby grinned from over her shoulder, probably copping a feel of her butt.

"I'm not even sure I *want* to ride today," Russell said, considering going back inside to sit with Auntie Cee.

" 'Fraid I might beat ya?" Bobby laughed, swinging his leg over Russell's snowmobile and grasping the handlebars.

They gunned out of the barn, into the snow, Rosalind first and Bobby following. Russell watched them for a few seconds, then turned his head, deciding to trudge back to the house. He walked a few feet in that direction when he stopped in his tracks. It was probably the sound of the motors that made him look back, the steady, unchanging sound.

They should be turning back by now, he thought.

He looked across the white meadow. Bobby and Rosalind were both zooming straight ahead, the dead tree on their right. To an observer, it would look as if nothing impeded their way, that they could continue for almost another mile, so smooth and unfettered the snow appeared. But Russell knew differently. He knew that dead claw sticking out of the snow was the sign to turn back.

"Oh my God," he whispered to himself.

They just kept going straight ahead, and he heard, over the motors, Bobby's "Whoooooeeece!" Then came Rosalind's laugh, a laugh like shattering glass. Finally, at the last possible second, she suddenly veered to the right in almost a ninety-degree turn, while Bobby barreled on, straight ahead, into the fence beneath the snow.

Russell had started running. Bobby's screams, his endless screaming, filled his ears, even muffled as they were by the snow. The snowmobile, on its side, shot a geyser of soft, fluffy white snow into the air. Suddenly the white was mixed with a horrible red, and as Russell approached, he could see blood splattered everywhere, like paint shaken from a brush onto a canvas. The snow around them began to turn pink.

The ambulance came, and so had the police, who asked both Rosalind and Russell many questions. But it was an accident, everyone agreed: two kids out for a lark. "I tried to call out to him, to warn him," Rosalind said, so calm, so smooth, "but he didn't hear me over the motor."

Bobby's face had been ripped off. Between the barbed-wire fence that took hold of his chin and his lips and the blades of the snowmobile that crashed down on top of him, his entire face was ripped off, and he broke his back and both legs, too, in several places. He lost his right eye too, and the left would sit at an odd angle the rest of his life. His mind, too: his mind would never be right again after that day.

He never taunted Russell again.

"His face will grow back," Rosalind casually informed Russell and their grandmother after the policemen had left. "Don't eyes and noses grow back?"

Grandmother had just glared at her.

On the morning of the second day after the accident, Grandmother had awakened Rosalind by pulling at her arm, saying nothing as the girl screamed, waking the house. Rosalind fought like a tiger, but Grandmother was bigger, stronger, and just as she had overpowered Grandfather, she dragged Rosalind up the stairs to the third floor, and then to the attic, where she put her in Grandfather's cell. There she left her, for two whole days, without food, without water, without any place to go to the bathroom.

Her cries were worse than Grandfather's had ever been. Russell had to stick cotton in his ears at night to drown them out.

Now, on the porch, ten minutes after Bobby Shortridge had shuffled past him, his face not having grown back, Russell watched the bridge. There was a woman starting over it, a tall, dark woman, dressed in black jeans and a red lace top. He watched her silently move across the bridge, her hand on the rail, her hair moving sensuously down her back. Slim, shapely, she was a woman he would have found desirable had it been permissible, and even though she wore dark sunglasses, he knew her eyes would be just like his, big and dark and deep-set and beguiling.

Gracefully she continued up the walk, getting larger and larger as she approached. Finally she was at the foot of the front steps, and she removed her glasses.

"Rosalind," he said.

"Well, baby brother," she said, breaking into a wide smile. "I'm home."

Memorial Day

Out in back, the guests were laughing.

"Yes, yes," Barbara Lacey was saying, "I remember one year when Edgar Wright got up on the picnic table with a drink in his hand and a basket on his head and sang some little ditty he picked up on one of his travels."

"Edgar Wright picked up a lot of little ditties on his travels," her sister stage whispered, followed by a look of mock shame, as if she were a naughty girl to say such a thing.

Barbara pretended to ignore her. "It was some song about the Irish, some drunken sailor kind of thing. It shocked everyone, but of course we were all delighted, really. Edgar could be such a cutup when he'd had a few pips."

Kate was standing over the grill, her back to the sisters. Russell had asked her to take over hamburger duty while he went back into the house to help get Rosalind settled. Kate kept glancing up at the house, expecting to see brother and sister coming down the garden path, anxious to finally meet this woman who loomed so large in her husband's life.

She tried to keep up the small talk with the guests as she ran the grill. "I wish I'd known Mr. and Mrs. Wright," she was telling the Laceys. "I see their portraits on the walls and feel as if I know them."

The old mayor, vodka in hand, looked over Kate's shoulder at the grill and then turned back to the Lacey sisters. "I think Edgar had more pips than he should have had, mosta the time." He laughed. It was a horrible kind of sound, a raspy, throaty chortle.

Kate tried to smile. She was peeling the hamburgers from their ready-made wax-paper coating and arranging them over the coals. She kept glancing back at the house, anxious for Russell to get back out here and help her. The burgers began sizzling and popping over the open flame, the smoky smell of burning flesh wafting out across the yard.

"Smells mighty good," Mayor Miller said, lifting his vodka and tonic to Kate.

"I hope they don't burn," Kate fretted.

"Oh, I think you're doing a fine job," the mayor said, rasping that horrible laugh again.

Kate felt his hand on her butt. She spun around to glare at him.

"I'm sorry, my dear," he said, smiling nastily. "Just lost my footing there for a moment."

She kept glaring at him, outraged. His tongue, pink and plump with blue veins, licked his thin, dry lips.

Kate shivered and turned back to the grill.

Barbara Lacey walked over to her, apparently oblivious of the mayor's indiscretion. "I can remember Edgar grilling duck on this grill, duck he'd shot himself," she said. She smiled at Kate, her cheeks dimpling. "He was a wonderful man. How I used to love to watch him riding his horse out through the meadow. I have such

lovely memories of Edgar, and of course, the children."
She sighed wistfully.

"It was the *wife* who caused all the trouble," observed
Mrs. Tyrwhit, who so far had been mostly quiet, sitting in
a red-and-blue plastic lawn chair, sipping a screwdriver
she'd made herself. Her comment seemed to put the
other guests on edge. Kate noticed Mr. Shortridge close
his eyes; Beatrice Lacey actually looked around the yard,
as if to see if anyone had heard.

"Oh, now, now, Mrs. Tyrwhit," Barbara Lacey muttered uncomfortably. "We really shouldn't be . . ." But
she didn't finish her statement.

Old Mayor Miller made a face, shifting his weight
from foot to foot. "I think we should remember Edgar
as he was, here at Wrightsbridge for the Old Town Day
celebrations, having had one pip too many, singing his
silly songs."

"Here, here," Barbara Lacey said, holding aloft her
rum and Coke.

"Well, at least Inger had the sense not to expose all
of us to things we shouldn't have to see," Mrs. Tyrwhit
said, more to herself than to anyone else. "Some things
shouldn't be brought out into the daylight, you know."

Kate followed the old woman's gaze. Her black eyes
were focused over the rim of the glass on the pitiful
form of Bobby Shortridge, sitting in a lawn chair behind
his father. What was left of his face was looking down
at the grass.

Kate shivered. She turned, flipping the hamburgers,
hearing the flames seer away at the soft, pink, dripping
undersides of the meat. The grease agitated the flames,
causing them to leap more boldly. She drew back from
the sudden heat, feeling her cheeks suddenly on fire,
and threw her eyes across the lawn, scanning the ragtag
group of old-timers around her. Every now and again
they'd struggle out of their lawn chairs and move slowly,

painfully, through the grass to replenish their drinks at the bar. Only Bobby Shortridge, that pathetic, misshapen creature, stayed in his seat, idly picking blades of grass and splitting them, carefully, down the middle.

Kate wished Russell would come back. What was taking them so long? They'd probably gone upstairs to see Auntie Cee.

"So how long have you been married?" old Mayor Miller was asking her.

"A little over four months," Kate replied, not looking at him, finding him more repulsive than Bobby Shortridge.

"Four months! Newlyweds!" The mayor grinned from ear to ear. "Still in that stage where you can't get enough, huh?"

She looked at him again with utter contempt.

"Me, I've been married for fifty-three years," he said, grinning, seeming oblivious of her pique.

"What a lucky woman," Kate said dryly.

"No! Four *different* women!" He laughed in that phlegmatic way of his, roaring back on his heels.

Kate did not like this man. Or any of them here. They were mean old gossips, she felt suddenly, and the only reason they were here was to satisfy their prurient curiosity. How she wished Russell would come back outside. She turned back to the grill. The hamburgers were burning; the flame was too high and she'd left the meat on too long. She tried desperately to rescue the tiny round slabs of burnt flesh, fumbling with a spatula, losing a few to the hungry flames.

She looked up in despair. And Bobby Shortridge was staring at her, with the one pulpy eye he had left in his face.

* * *

They were sitting in Grandmother's upstairs parlor, which Russell had avoided since his return to Wrightsbridge. All the furniture was still there: the nineteenth-century chaise longue, the vintage 1960 television set, the Victrola that still housed the old woman's records, stacked neatly, covered with dust, as if Bing and Perry and Old Blue Eyes himself were merely waiting for Grandmother to return and set them spinning again.

Russell took in a deep breath.

"I don't want you to do anything," he said, staring at Rosalind.

"*Do* anything?" his sister asked, leaning back on Grandmother's chaise longue, kicking off her black pumps, and sighing. "Whatever do you *mean?*"

"Things have been going well. I don't want you to interfere."

"*Interfere?* Why, baby brother, you know the only reason I'm here is that you need me. I'm always there when you need me. Admit it. This house has been doing strange things to you. You've felt out of sorts, not yourself, isn't that right?"

It would be futile to lie to her; it always was. How could he pretend what she said was untrue? "Yes," he said, looking away from her. "It *has* been hard being here."

"Especially with *her.*"

Russell stood up and peered down at the picnic from between the drawn curtains. Kate was standing over the barbecue, nearly obliterated by the gray smoke that billowed out from the coals. She was having difficulty, Russell realized.

He looked back at his sister. "Oh, Rosalind, why did you have to come back?"

"You *wanted* me to. Remember?"

"You're not here to take care of Auntie Cee. You're here to make trouble between me and Kate."

She narrowed her eyes into tiny slits, just as she used to do when they were teenagers and he wouldn't listen to her or take her advice. Those eyes were meant to remind him that she only had his best interests in mind, and that he would be a fool not to listen to her.

"Russell," Rosalind said, patiently patronizing him, "I'm *worried* about you. Your *mind*. You're not right in your mind, are you? What if something were to *happen* to you? Who would take care of you? What would we do? Lock you up in the attic?"

He glared at her. "You're obscene, Rosalind."

She sighed, swinging her legs around to place her stockinged feet against the floor. "So aren't you going out there to help that poor little wife of yours? It must be hard for her, don't you think? A little video store clerk like her with people whose families built this town. People with some standing, some history. She could be making a fool of herself down there, and a fool of *you*, too, Russell."

He looked at her with such hatred. "Oh, as if *you* ever worried about what people thought."

She laughed, clapping her hands. "Oh, there you go again, Russell. I'm not nearly as bad as you make me out to be."

He drew up close to her, his face in hers. "Why should I care what people think?" he asked. "I don't want to live like Grandmother did, never admitting that Grandfather was sick in the head, crazy as a loon. 'It's his arthritis,' she'd say to the people. 'That's why he can't come down and see you.' That was a crock. He was crazy, and she kept him locked in the attic, but she made it seem as if he was lounging in his room, being catered to by the servants, receiving us grandkids as a king would receive his subjects. But she'd fired all the servants and kept him locked up there because she didn't want anyone to know he was crazy."

Rosalind shook her head. "Grandmother would be so disappointed in you," she said softly.

"Why do you act as if you're *defending* her?" Russell shouted, exasperated. "After what she did to you?"

There was a knock at the door, a sharp successive series of raps that jolted both of them.

"Shh," Rosalind said. "I don't want anyone to know I'm here yet."

He looked at her. "Why not?"

She seethed. "Just do as I say."

Russell sighed, turning around and opening the door a crack.

It was Mrs. Tynan, who peered inside, her eyes moving past Russell's face and over his shoulder. "Are you . . . *with* someone, Mr. Russell? I thought I heard—"

"No, no," he said. "I guess you . . . caught me talking to myself." He looked around warily; Rosalind had gone into hiding. He eased the door open a bit more, allowing Mrs. Tynan in a few steps.

"Well, it's just that Mrs. Wright was wondering where you were. She's having some trouble with the barbecue. I timed the casseroles to be done when the hamburgers were, but now it seems she's . . . well, a number of them are too well done for some of the guests' tastes."

"I'll be right down," Russell said. His face looked dark, even darker than usual, even darker than the dim light of the room should have allowed for. "Tell Mrs. Wright to stay away from the grill, that I'll handle it when I get down there."

"Yes, Mr. Russell," Mrs. Tynan said, heading downstairs to relay the message.

He shut the door and turned his face back into the empty room. "Where'd you go?" he whispered.

Rosalind emerged from the behind the draperies. "Go down to your party," she purred. "Tell everyone I'll join them in a minute."

"Well, hurry up," he said. "I might need you."

And well he might. Kate was proving to be of little help.

Rosalind was smiling. "Won't Bobby Shortridge be surprised to see me again?" She parted the curtains to spy on the people below. As Russell closed the door, he saw the old clever smile creep across his sister's face, the smile he remembered oh so well. He could not tell what emotion he was feeling, seeing that smile return: Fear? Wonder? Gratitude?

"If it's too crisp," Kate was apologizing, "I'll make you another." Mrs. Tyrwhit took a bite into her hamburger and made a face. Black grease ran down her painted lips and powdered chin.

"No, thank you," she said. "I'll wait for the tuna casserole."

Kate walked over into the garden to look up the side of the house. She saw a hand at the curtains in one of the rooms. Someone had been watching them.

She turned and discovered the mayor close behind her. He was clearly already drunk; his eyes were bloodshot and his speech slurred. "You're a very beautiful woman," he said to her, spitting as he tried to talk. Kate tried to move past him but he blocked her way. The others were intent on their plates, and the rosebushes partially obscured them from view.

"Do you know what my second wife used to call me?" Mayor Miller slobbered. "Donkey Kong. Can you guess why?"

He impulsively reached for Kate's hand and pressed it against his crotch. She struggled free and slapped him across the face. She turned quickly and rushed off toward the women.

But something was happening. It was as if suddenly

there was no more sound, only a dull, distant thudding in her ears. In the far distance, across the meadow, she spotted a figure, walking toward her.

Russell came outside, and the world skidded into slow motion. He was half running, apologetic, saying something about his sister, Kate thought. But he moved like a videotape on slow advance, or an old-fashioned Super-8 home movie, jerking along, frame by frame. Kate turned her head, just as slowly, away from Russell, panning the picnic scene, the old folks appearing to her like dried sculptures from a wax museum. She let her sight come to rest on the garden gate, coiled with wispy strands of reddish ivy. The figure had gotten closer. She gasped.

It was Erik.

"Get out of there, Kate, get the hell out," Erik was saying, but his voice didn't come from his lips, although they were moving. They came from inside Kate's head. She turned and saw Russell, slapping down fresh meat onto the grill, glancing once over at Kate, a glance that was chilling in its silent nothingness.

She turned again, and Erik was gone.

"His sister's home," Kate said softly to herself.

"Eh? What's that?" Mrs. Tyrwhit asked.

She looked down at the old woman without emotion. "He said his sister's home," Kate repeated.

"His *sister?*" The old woman grunted. "His *sister?*"

Bobby Shortridge was staring at her again. Except now it wasn't the deformed Bobby Shortridge sitting in that chair playing with the blades of grass. It was the man with the noose around his neck, and he was crooking a finger at Kate, beckoning her to him.

"No," she murmured.

"Kate!" It was Erik at the gate again. *"Get out of there!"*

His voice seemed to echo, as if he were in a long tunnel, not out here in the bright sunny outdoors. But the sun no longer felt warm, and the day seemed not nearly so bright.

The hanged man had struggled to his feet and was now staggering toward her.

"*Who are you?*" she shouted. "What do you want from me?"

A snaky tongue darted from the dead man's mouth.

"This house won't let you have secrets," the man spoke at last. "Can you guess mine? Can you guess?"

She screamed as his cold blue hands closed around her neck.

The last thing she remembered seeing was the old women rising from their chairs to loom over her as she collapsed onto the ground. They were all laughing at her with hideously distorted features. And among them was Russell, who was speaking to her, although no sound came from his lips.

"Are you deaf as well as dumb?" Russell was saying, and he realized it came out harsher than he would've liked people to hear.

Kate could hear her breath laboring in her ears. She was looking up at Russell. She was lying on her back in the grass. Old Mayor Miller stood over her as well, the ice of his vodka and tonic tinkling in his glass.

Soon others appeared in her vision, hovering above her. The Lacey sisters, looking down in wonderment, and Mr. Shortridge and Bobby. His one eye seemed to bore down at her.

Kate tried to sit up but didn't have the strength.

"Why won't you answer me, Kate?" Russell demanded. "What's happened to you?"

"Go easy on her, old boy," Mayor Miller was saying. "She had a fainting spell."

Barbara Lacey looked at her sister. "But who was she shouting at?"

"Does she suffer from delusions?" Beatrice asked Russell.

Her husband glared at her. "Not that she's ever told me."

Kate remained fixed on Bobby Shortridge's pulsing eye.

"You'd better take her inside," Barbara Lacey told Russell. "Maybe call a doctor."

Russell scooped her up into her arms. "She'll be fine," he said, and the most terrifying thing she'd seen all day was the look he gave her. "She'll be just *fine.*"

Nightfall, and the Rain Came

Kate was propped up in bed with several pillows. "Do you need anything else, Mrs. Wright?" Mrs. Tynan was asking her.

"No, thank you," she said softly.

"Well, if you're still feeling weak in the morning, Mr. Russell said he would call a doctor."

"I'll be fine," Kate assured her.

Mrs. Tynan smiled at her. "Have a good night's rest now. I'm going home and I'll see you in the morning."

Kate nodded. Mrs. Tynan closed the door behind her. Kate took a long, deep breath and let it out as slowly as she could.

Why was she so weak? She could barely lift her hand. Somewhere in her purse on the other side of the room was her cell phone. She wanted to get to it and call Erik. Somehow he'd been trying to communicate with her. Telling her to get out.

She heard old Edgar Wright then, screaming to be released from his cell in the attic. She could hear the horrible rattling of the door, the pounding on the walls. She was too weak to cover her ears. She just closed her eyes.

When she opened them, Russell was in front of her.

"How are you now?" he asked. His voice was stark in its lack of concern or compassion.

"Russell, I'm sorry," she said. "Please don't be angry with me."

"You made a fool of me this afternoon. What must the town think? You know they're already spreading the story from one end to the other."

"Russell, I see things . . ."

He glared at her. "I heard Mrs. Tyrwhit call you 'white trash.' That's what she said. *White trash.*"

Kate began to cry. "Russell, I'm sorry."

He folded his arms across his chest. "What do you mean, you see things?"

"I should have told you before. I wanted to, but—"

"You've kept secrets from me," he said evenly, but the whiteness of his lips betrayed his anger. "You've kept secrets."

"I see things, Russell," she said, urgently. "Please understand. I have seen these visions ever since I was a child. I see people who have died. It's a gift, really, but sometimes it can be frightening. I've been frightened ever since coming to this house. I've seen your grandfather, Russell, the one who was locked in the attic. And others, too—a hanged man, Russell, I've seen a hanged man."

He slapped her hard across the face. She gasped.

"Shut up!" Russell shouted. "You are no better than Theresa! Telling me lies! Rosalind was right! Rosalind told me you were trash! She was right!"

Kate managed to place her hand against her cheek. It stung from where Russell had hit her. She watched as he turned in a terrible fury and ran from the room.

Dear God, she thought to herself. *He's crazy. He's gone crazy.*

The cell phone . . .

Dear God, I have to get my cell phone.

But it was no use. Whatever force that had attacked her in the garden today had left her too weak to move. She would need to conserve her strength and recover.

She allowed herself to think. Her cheek still stung. *Her husband had hit her.*

But that wasn't the husband she had fallen in love with on that long romantic walk over the Brooklyn Bridge. Oh, how long ago now that seemed. Russell was a different person, a changed man. What had this house done to him?

And Theresa? Who was Theresa? And why would Russell's sister say she, Kate, was trash? *Why does Rosalind hate me? We've never even met!*

The old man in the attic pleaded to be set free.

"Cecilia! Help me!"

"Please make him stop," Kate muttered, hands over her ears, a pathetic little prayer.

Just then, from across the room, Kate heard her cell phone ring, a muffled sound from deep down within her purse. "Erik," she whispered, and began to cry.

It rang eight times, like a furious little honeybee trapped in the folds of her purse. Kate's tears ran down her cheeks and dripped off of her chin as she listened to it ring. Then the phone went silent.

At that moment Kate heard the tappity-tap of rain on the windows, and then a long rolling drumroll of thunder. The rain came hard and fast, beating against the house, and kept up all night.

Lilacs

In the morning, it was the smell of lilacs that woke her, lilacs everywhere, dewy lilacs, newly blossomed, urged on by the rain.

Kate found that she could stand, and the first thing she did was pull her cell phone from her purse. The battery had run down; she couldn't even check to see if Erik had left any messages. She carried it to the recharging cradle she kept plugged in on the desk, and slipped the phone inside. A half hour was all it needed. Then she'd call Erik.

She walked shakily down the stairs, holding firmly to the banister, feeling a rush of intoxication from the scent of the lilacs. In the parlor, the damp, lavender flowers filled the room, big, tall, bushy bouquets on the tables and on the mantel, threatening to obliterate Asa Wright's portrait.

"Aren't they lovely?" Russell asked, emerging unheard from the kitchen.

Kate, startled, looked over at him.

He doesn't remember. She knew this instinctively. *He doesn't remember hitting me or any of the unpleasantness of last night.*

Her suspicions crystallized instantly.

My mind isn't the only one the ghosts are playing tricks with.

"Rosalind picked them first thing this morning, over in the meadow," Russell was telling her, pressing his face into the flowers. "There's literally a *forest* of lilac bushes over there. She's always loved them. Isn't it *fantastic?*"

Russell seemed overjoyed by his sister's work, and Kate, carefully monitoring the situation, was pleased to see the darkness had lifted from Russell's eyes. If lilacs made him happy, Kate was happy for the lilacs. But she would remain cautious. Very cautious.

"They *are* beautiful," Kate acknowledged. "Their scent is so . . . strong. It actually woke me up."

"I want to *fill* the house with lilacs!" Russell proclaimed, throwing his arms out in an exhuberant gesture.

"Where *is* Rosalind?" Kate asked, looking beyond Russell into the dining room.

She wanted to add, *Where is the bitch who called me trash?* But she held her tongue. All in good time . . .

"She's out walking along the brook," Russell told her. "She was up at the crack of dawn, picking these to surprise us."

Kate ran her fingers through her tousled hair. She needed to test her husband, see if he really was free of the ghosts' influence. "Russell," she asked carefully, "how do you think the picnic went yesterday?"

"Wonderfully!" His eyes danced, and Kate saw nothing there but joy. "Oh, darling, I called Mayor Miller this morning and told him I wanted to host Old Town Day again here on the estate! Just like old times!"

He seemed so ecstatic by the idea. He seemed to have completely forgotten about the scene she caused—as well as hitting her. Kate tried to smile, but felt a growing knot of terror in her stomach. How long could each of them go on having these blackouts? She glanced at the old grandfather clock. In fifteen minutes, she'd call Erik.

"I'm looking forward to finally meeting Rosalind," Kate ventured, still watching Russell's eyes.

He smiled warmly. "As she is looking forward to meeting you," he assured her.

They had moved into the kitchen, where Kate poured herself a cup of coffee. "Is Mrs. Tynan up with Auntie Cee?" she asked.

"That she is," Russell replied, looking out the window. The sun was hidden behind clouds. "It's supposed to rain again today. What's on your agenda, darling?"

"Nothing." She looked at Russell deliberately. "I'd like to spend time with Rosalind."

"Of course." Russell smiled. "She should be back inside shortly. Why don't you wait for her? We'll have coffee and biscuits."

Kate suddenly realized she looked a fright. Her long red hair was tangled and matted down from a restless night. She'd never washed her mascara off from yesterday. She couldn't meet Rosalind looking like this. "Well, I'd like to shower first . . ."

"Go ahead then, darling. We'll be waiting for you here." Russell freshened his coffee and walked out the back door to settle himself at the patio table. Kate smiled a little awkwardly and then walked back out into the parlor. She paused to inhale the aroma of the lilacs one more time, and then made her way back upstairs.

She checked her cell phone. Erik had indeed tried calling her, leaving three messages, each increasing in urgency. "I've *got* to talk with you, Kate," the first one said. The second repeated the first, adding Erik's concern that she was all right. The final message had said that if he didn't hear back from her that night, he was getting on a train and coming to her. Kate called him back, got his voice mail, and told him yes, yes, to come as quickly as he could. Maybe he was already on his way here. By the time she stepped into the shower, she knew everything would be all right.

The Meadow

Russell was watching a bumblebee hover between the lusty lilacs and the fading forsythias, as if unable to decide which it would suckle. The clouds had thickened, and moisture hung heavy in the air. Far off to his right, deep into the meadow, waist-deep in the grass, moving in and out among the clusters of lilac bushes, was Rosalind. Occasionally she would pause and wave over at him. Occasionally he would wave back.

The old dead tree was still there, a giant mitt protruding savagely from the yellow-green grass. He wondered if Rosalind remembered it.

He watched her for some time. With a simple flick of his eyelids, he'd switch his gaze from her back to the bee gathering its nectar. Sometimes Rosalind, like the bee, would disappear into the bushes, only to emerge at a point he could not have guessed, always in motion. He marveled at her energy. He felt tired suddenly, despite the fact that he'd had a full night's sleep, a solid rest in his old bed, his *real* bed, the bed he'd slept in as a child. Once, in the deepest part of the night, when everything was dark and quiet, he woke up and missed Kate, but that was just once. By the time the morning came, he was glad he was alone, and he had hurried downstairs to find Rosalind.

He had lost her now. His eyes searched the meadow, but her form had disappeared. She had gone too far, wandered too long. He stood up from his bench and peered harder, trying to discern the movement again, but nothing broke the soft wave of grass that stretched to the far blue sky. Except the barbed-wire fence, now stretched crookedly across the meadow, rusted and ragged. That, and the old dead tree.

The bee, sated, had departed too.

Kate was there now, behind him.

"Where's Rosalind?" she asked.

Russell turned to look at her. Her red hair, the color of the grass in the meadow with the sun falling upon it, was still wet from her shower. She had pulled it back in a bow, and she looked beautiful to Russell, but he pushed the thought away.

"She's gone," Russell said simply, returning his gaze into the meadow.

"Gone? Where'd she go?"

"Who knows with Rosalind?" He sat back down with a long sigh. "She's out collecting nectar, out smelling the lilacs."

"When will she be back?"

Russell shrugged. "I don't know. My sister has always been a free spirit. She comes and goes as she pleases."

Kate looked at him sharply. "Russell, you need to tell me the truth. Rosalind didn't stay here last night, did she?"

Russell was silent.

Kate leaned down close to him, and her words were defiant, confrontational. "I just talked with Mrs. Tynan.

There was no extra room prepared. No bed rumpled. No towels used." She narrowed her eyes at him. "If she was here, where did she sleep?"

Russell's face clouded over. "Probably in town. She probably went into town and slept with one of her old flames." He suddenly threw his coffee cup and it shattered against the stone pathway. "Maybe with a dozen different guys!"

Kate sat down beside him. "Did the two of you argue?" she asked, trying to sound gentler. "Is that why she left?"

"I don't want to talk about Rosalind anymore."

Kate sighed. "Fine. Then it's time we talked about other things, Russell." She tried to find his gaze but he kept it from her. "About last night, Russell."

Russell's voice, when it came, was far away. "You have to understand about Rosalind," he said, ignoring her. "She's always been there for me. No, we don't always see eye to eye. There's a part of me that hates her. Hates her for what she's done. What she does to me." He looked across the table to his wife. "But she's *strong*, Kate. Stronger than I could ever hope to be. We're twins, she and I. She's the dark half, maybe. That's what Grandmother used to call her. But she's the strong one, too, the one who could take care of herself, the one who always, in the end, would land on her feet. Not like me. She always wanted to protect me. Make sure nothing bad came my way. Nothing, no *one*, was good enough for me. She wasn't the type of sister who showed you a lot of love, or affection, or even attention. But she was always there, watching out for me. Just like she still is."

They were quiet. Then Russell added: "No one's ever cared about me like that."

Kate stood and walked around behind him. She wrapped her arms around his neck, resting her face on Russell's shoulder.

"*I* care about you like that, Russell," she said.

She knew she shouldn't so quickly forget his actions of the day before. After all, he had slapped her. He had been cruel and callous. But that hadn't been Russell. She had to believe that. That had been someone—*something*—else.

He seemed near tears. "Here at Wrightsbridge," he was saying, "if you were strong, you had to be *hard*, too. And *dark*. And *bad*."

"Russell, let *me* be strong for you," Kate said quietly. "And we don't have to be hard or dark or bad. We can fight off those things if we do it together."

He said nothing.

She pressed her lips close to his ear. "Do you remember that night, on the Brooklyn Bridge?"

He sighed, and a tear came unexpectedly from the corner of his eye. "How could I ever forget it?" he whispered.

"Russell, we can still go back there. Maybe we ought to leave Wrightsbridge—"

He stiffened suddenly, furiously wiping the tear away with the back of his hand. "Leave Wrightsbridge?"

His voice had changed. Kate stood up, placed her hand over her heart. "We were happy in New York—"

He spun on her. "And what would you have me do with Auntie Cee? Put her in a nursing home? After she single-handedly saved me from Grandmother's wrath? I might have been put in that room, too, but Auntie Cee wouldn't let her! Not after what she had done to Grandfather and Rosalind!"

"I'm sorry, Russell, I didn't mean—"

Kate tried to touch him again, but Russell stood and pulled away, taking several long strides toward the meadow, toward the last spot he'd seen his sister.

"Russell! Please don't run away from me!" Kate

shouted after him. "We have so much we need to talk about! The things that are happening in this house!"

"Please," he said, and his voice sounded strangled, "let me be alone for a while."

He didn't turn to see Kate break down in tears and run back inside. He kept walking out into the tall grass, watching it sway gracefully in the morning breeze. He searched for a shape, a form, anything, the slightest indication of his sister. A shock of black hair, a flash of red lace. But nothing. Nothing disturbed the soft pattern of the grass, not as far as the eye could see, and he could see all the way to the end, to where the meadow met the sky.

Waiting for Erik

Kate couldn't stay in the house. She arranged to borrow Mrs. Tynan's car and drove into town, calling Erik repeatedly on her cell phone to see if maybe he'd be arriving at the train station. She would meet him and fall into his arms and ask him what she should do.

But it just rang and rang. Why wasn't he picking up? Why didn't she at least get his voice mail? Terror began to seize her irrationally. Had something happened to stop him?

Overhead the sky still threatened rain. She wandered into the old post office, inhaling the marble-chilled air and gazing up at the frescoes of Washington and Lincoln. She had no business to do. She just felt lost, and the idea of returning to Wrightsbridge unnerved her. She wished at that moment she never had to go back.

"Aren't you Russell Wright's wife?"

The voice came from behind her. She turned and saw no one for a second, then realized the woman standing there was very short, rising only as far as her chest.

She dropped her vision. The woman was plump, gray haired, and dark eyed, with full, red cheeks. She appeared to be about sixty, and her eyes were bloodshot, as red as her cheeks. She wore a red kerchief around her head, and she completed the color scheme with bright red lipstick. A cigarette burned between her fingers.

"Yes," Kate said hesitantly, "yes, I am."

"Excuse me," a postal clerk interjected from the counter, "but there's no smoking in this building."

"Jeeziz," the woman muttered, dropping the cigarette to the marble floor and stubbing it out with her toe. "And I just lit up. Whole damn thing wasted."

Kate could smell whiskey in the air as the woman talked.

"So what do you think of the place?" she was asking. "Of Wrightsbridge."

Kate wanted to get away from her but didn't want to be rude. "It's—it's quite historic," she said.

The woman raised penciled eyebrows. "How many ghosts have you seen?"

Kate didn't answer.

The woman smiled scornfully. "Have you seen the old man? Or the old bitch, his wife?"

"Excuse me," Kate said, turning to leave.

"Wait," the woman said, grabbing Kate's arm. "If I were you, I'd make my stay there brief. Take Russell and go back to New York."

She wanted to tell her to mind her own business, fearful that such talk would get back to Russell. But she couldn't help asking, "Why?"

"Because people die there," the woman said plainly.

Kate and Auntie Cee, Part Two

The only thing she could do was go back to Wrights-bridge and wait for Erik. Russell was nowhere to be seen. She sat in the garden, preferring to be there than in the house. She allowed herself to marvel at the cycle of life. Just as the crocuses and forsythia had given way to the daffodils and the lilacs, now the roses were nearly ready for their glorious burst into brilliance.

Auntie Cee was right, she thought to herself, caressing the vines that she and Russell had so painstakingly cleared and trimmed from the tangle of weeds. The roses *would* be beautiful this year.

She heard a rapping at the windows above her. Leaning back, she saw Auntie Cee, three stories up, gesturing to her. It appeared as if she was motioning for Kate to come upstairs.

She pointed at herself and then up at her. The old woman nodded emphatically. Kate smiled and headed inside.

She'd never been summoned like this before. She'd

always gone up to see her with Russell, except for that first time she'd stumbled upon her, after her exploration of the attic. What if something was wrong? Mrs. Tynan had taken the car to the market when Kate got back, and Russell was nowhere to be found.

People die there.

But Auntie Cee was fine, just excited about the roses. "They're getting ready to bloom!" she exclaimed.

"Yes," Kate said, feeling a swell of pride. "I think you were right. They *will* be beautiful. *This* year."

Auntie Cee beamed. She brushed at some wisps of white hair that had fallen onto her face. She smelled of her usual talcum powder, and when she smiled Kate noticed the old woman's wrinkles were outlined in white. "I remember when I first planted those roses," she was saying dreamily. "It was right before I got engaged."

She rested back in her chair. She looked even smaller, more fragile, than Kate remembered. In her hand she held an ancient yellowed lace handkerchief. On it were embroidered the initials *C-W-H.* Cecilia Wright Hotchkiss. A premature wedding gift, Kate surmised.

"Tell me," Auntie Cee said, looking seriously at Kate all of a sudden. "How is Russell?"

"He's fine." But Kate knew the old woman had lived far too long for her to be able to get away with anything less than the full truth. "I think it's still hard for him, being here, sometimes."

Auntie Cee sighed. Yes, Kate was certain the old woman suspected something was wrong, but how much should she admit to her? How much would she understand?

"If only his mother hadn't left," Auntie Cee was saying, looking out the picture window down at the garden.

Kate blinked. "What? I thought his parents both died in a car accident."

Auntie Cee seemed not to hear her. "That's the hardest thing of all, losing one's mother. It made losing all the others even more unbearable, if that's possible."

"Where did she go?" Kate asked. "Russell's mother?"

The old woman sighed, looking over at her with eyes weary of too much life and too much heartache. "Back to her father. He had to take her in, because Inger wouldn't let her stay here with any degree of peace. Not after Bernard's death. In some ways Molly had more courage than I did. I should have joined her the night she packed her things and left."

Kate reached over and took the old woman's hand. "But then Russell and Rosalind would have been all alone here, and their grandmother was so cruel—"

"But what good did I do?" Auntie Cee cried, and the guilt on her face almost caused Kate to look away, embarrassed by its rawness. "*What good did I do?*"

Kate didn't want to upset her, not like last time. She stroked her hand, conscious of the brittleness of her bones. "You comforted them. Russell loves you a great deal for that."

"Molly looked back at me when she left," Auntie Cee said, staring straight ahead, and Kate knew she was seeing her own ghosts. "She just looked at me, for a long, long time, before she walked out that door. Inger was standing in the doorway to the kitchen, telling the children to look, to watch their mother walking out on them, to always remember that she abandoned them. Rosalind was by the fireplace, refusing to look around. She was playing with her doll, making out like she didn't care. But Russell—he stood there crying, that poor little child, crying and holding out his little arms to his mother. And she just looked at me, not at him, and I knew she was saying, 'They're yours now. Take care of them.' "

"Is she dead?" Kate asked.

"No, no," Auntie Cee said, turning to look into her eyes. Their faces were very close now, with Kate sitting on the stool next to her chair. She saw the moistness in her old eyes, the guilt and regret she had lived with all these years. "No, she's still right here, still in town. I see her name in the phone book, still listed. I check for it every time a new phone book arrives in the spring, to see if she's moved or if she's died. I don't know why I do that. But I do."

"She's *here*? In town? Russell's mother? And *was*, all those years?"

"Yes."

"And Russell never saw her?"

"No. Not once. Maybe by accident, I don't know. But he never said so. He said he hated her."

Kate thought for a moment. "But she was *driven* out. By the grandmother. Maybe if she and Russell were to meet now—"

"It's been too long, dear. Too much of life has passed by."

An idea was forming in Kate's mind. "He resents her for not being there. I understand better now. I can understand the pain, the feeling of rejection." Suddenly she was seized with compassion for her husband. "She could have tried to gain custody. That must be what he always thought. But now . . . I think it might do wonders for Russell to reconcile with her, especially with Rosalind back home."

"Rosalind?" Auntie Cee asked. "Back home? Did he tell you that?"

Kate looked at her strangely. "She didn't come up to see you?"

The old woman returned an equally strange look. "When was she here?"

"Yesterday."

"No, she was not here."

"Yes, yes, I saw her—I saw her, through the window, I thought—"

"No, dear. Rosalind was not here."

Had she dreamed that, too? No, no, that much had been real. She was sure of it. "She was here last night," Kate told her, "though she didn't sleep here. She came back this morning. She picked lilacs. Russell spent time with her. She didn't come up and see you?"

The old woman was silent. She had resumed staring out of her window, looking down at the garden.

"Look, Samuel," she said at last. "I think one of the roses has started to bloom."

Kate took a deep breath. She waited a few seconds, then stood and gently kissed the old woman's cool forehead. "I'll see you later, Auntie Cee," she told her. "You rest now."

The poor old thing had forgotten. Surely Rosalind would have come upstairs to see her beloved aunt. How quickly Auntie Cee's mind came and went.

But she had been right about one thing: Kate flipped open the phone book to the Wrights. There, at 44B Morning Glory Circle, was an *M F Wright*. Molly Fitzgibbons Wright.

She was unable to rid herself of the image of Russell as a toddler, crying after his mother as she walked out the door. Just then the skies opened and the rain came crashing down again.

The Snowstorm

They were skipping school, and talking about their mother. "Do you think she'll ever come back for us?" Russell asked his sister.

"She's *trash*," Rosalind shot back at him, dismissing the idea.

Grandmother would be furious if she ever caught them skipping school. But they *had* to—especially after what Rosalind had done yesterday to poor Amy Duggerman. She hadn't even known what hit her.

They would learn later that they needn't have bothered skipping school today. They would simply have been sent right back home. The snow had been falling since four o'clock that morning, and the wind was whipping feverishly through the trees. Already the old yellow school buses were screeching their way back through the snow-drifted streets just an hour after delivering the children to school.

"What if Amy Duggerman finds out it was you?" Russell aked his sister, who was about a yard ahead of him, trudging through the snow on the riverbank.

"She won't, if you don't tell," she called back, not turning around to look at him.

But why would he tell? Russell knew she had done it for him. Just as she was always doing things for him. He'd had a crush on Amy Duggerman, until she'd joined in with Bobby Shortridge taunting him in the corridors. So late yesterday afternoon, when no one was around, Rosalind spied Amy leaning into her locker, and made a mad dash for her. She'd shoved the poor unfortunate girl into the foot-and-a-half-wide space, and crushed the door of the locker in on her.

Her wails had sounded so muffled, with not even enough room for her little fists to beat upon the metal door.

"Listen to her," Rosalind had told Russell. He had, fascinated.

"She could've died in there," Russell scolded his sister now.

"Aw, they heard her. They let her out."

"She was all bloody," Russell said.

It was at that moment that he slipped on the riverbank, sliding down the slippery slope, twisting his ankle. It hurt badly, and he howled. Rosalind rushed to his side. He couldn't stand on it, couldn't abide the slightest pressure on it. His sister tried to lift him and carry him out of the woods, but, strong as she was, couldn't hold him for more than a few seconds. He kept falling back into the snow.

The temperature dropped. They huddled in the same spot for several hours, hoping the swelling on Russell's ankle would go down enough for him to be able to limp back to Wrightsbridge. But it didn't. The sun began to sink lower in the sky and the wind grew even more fierce. Rosalind tried to think of something to do.

Grandmother would begin to suspect something. Maybe she should walk back to Wrightsbridge herself and explain that Russell had fallen. . . .

"You'll never find me again!" he cried. "We've never been in this part of the woods before!"

"Russell, I'll just follow the river!"

But he wouldn't be persuaded. "Please, Rosalind! Don't leave me! I'm going to die here!"

He bawled his eyes out. Rosalind told him to stop acting like a baby, but after all, he was only nine years old. He started to call for his mother.

"Mommy! Mommy!"

Rosalind grew furious, clenching and unclenching her fists. "Stop it, Russell! Stop it!"

"I want my mother," he cried.

"Your mother is trash," Rosalind scolded.

He looked at her fiercely. "Don't you ever want her, Rosalind? Don't you ever want her to come back?"

It wasn't often that he saw anything that passed for vulnerability in his sister's eyes. But he saw it then. Her own eyes filled up, but unlike her weak little brother, she choked back the tears. He had begun to shiver, his coat and pants having gotten wet from falling in the snow, so Rosalind removed her own coat and put it around him. They sat that way until someone found them, a man with a farm nearby, who took them back to Wrightsbridge.

Grandmother thanked the man for bringing them home, and made a pretense of looking at Russell's ankle. But as soon as the man had left, she beat both children for their truancy and their lies.

Meeting Inger

Finally, the next day, an answer at Erik's.

"Erik? Oh, Erik, I've been frantic! Is that you?"

She'd given up on his cell phone and called his apartment.

"No," the voice at the other end of the phone said. "This is Martin."

"*Martin?*"

"I'm a friend of Erik's. I'm staying here until he gets back."

"Well, this is Kate Wright. I'm a friend of his, too. I think he's coming to visit me."

"I know he was going to Connecticut, that's all," Martin told her.

"Yes. That's where I am. When did he leave?"

"Two nights ago."

"Well, he hasn't shown." All of a sudden Kate felt panicked. Why hadn't he called her?

She told Martin that if he heard from Erik, he should tell him to call her right away. She hung up the phone and put her hand to her face. Should she call the police? No, it was far too early to report him missing. *Oh, dear God, don't let anything have happened to Erik!*

In the garden, a rosebud had indeed begun to bloom. Kate sat looking at it, trying to calm her thoughts. How lovely was its potential, such deep, bold, crimson petals emerging slowly from their modest green shroud.

She glanced up at the house. A hand at the window. The same window as before.

Kate gasped a little. It was Rosalind. She couldn't see her clearly, but she could definitely make out her long dark hair, just as Russell had described it. She was wearing something red. She must have gotten back last night from wherever she'd gone off to.

"Well, you're not getting away from me this time, lady," Kate said to herself, hurrying into the house and up the stairs.

She had seen Russell at breakfast; why hadn't he told her that Rosalind was back? Maybe he didn't know either.

It was the grandmother's room she'd spotted her in. The one at the end of the hall with the old Victrola. The door was closed. Kate rapped against it briskly. "Rosalind?" she called. "Rosalind? Is that you in there?"

She heard scurrying from within. "I can hear you," she said. "I saw you from outside. I don't know why you're avoiding me. I need to talk with you. *Please.*"

The sound from inside had stopped. She was reluctant to just walk in on her, but she had no choice. The things that were happening to her had reached a crisis point. And they weren't just happening to her; they were happening to Russell, too. She believed Rosalind would understand what she had to tell her. She believed Rosalind knew about these things. She believed Rosalind could help—but only if she wanted to.

And she wanted to find out why her sister-in-law hated her. Or had that been unreal too?

Kate turned the doorknob and found it unlocked. She walked into the room.

She could see no one. Around the old Victrola she walked, passing the dust-covered television set and the slightly frayed chaise longue. She passed by the armoire, its door partly open. Suddenly there came the rustle of fabric, but by the time she had turned to look in the direction of the sound, something had hit her on the head, and she fell, elbow first, against the floor. The pain surged fast and excrutiatingly through her before she passed out.

"Wake up!"

Someone was telling her to wake up, but she couldn't seem to focus. She tried opening her eyes but they kept shutting.

"*White trash!*"

Kate gasped.

"I don't want you in this house. Have I made that clear to you, little girl?"

Kate forced her eyes open. She looked around.

There was no one in the room.

The pain hit her then full force. She tried to move her right arm but found it impossible. It was broken. Her head thumped too, where she'd been hit.

How long had she been lying there unconscious? It was night. There was no sound at all in the house. The only light came from the moon at the window. There was a light rain tapping at the glass.

With great effort Kate managed to get to her feet and stumbled over to the door, her useless right arm swinging at her side. With her left hand she tried the knob. It was locked.

She banged against it. "Help! Let me out! Russell!"

"He can't hear you," the voice came from behind her.

Kate turned around.

It was she.

The grandmother.

Inger Wright was sitting in her chair beside the Victrola, a big bear of a woman, with heavy features and enormous hands clutching the armrests. Right away she realized she hadn't wanted to be seen, that she'd hoped her mind games would be enough to force Kate to leave. But Kate had defied her, and indeed had forced her hand. The dead woman was angry about that.

"I don't want you in this house," she said in her deep, guttural accent. "Why did you come here?"

Kate braced herself. She would not tremble before this evil woman the way everyone had in life. "Is that what you said to Russell's mother?" she challenged the ghost. "Is that how you drove poor Molly Wright out of this house?"

The dead woman growled in her throat, like a mad dog.

"Do you have any idea what you did to him? To Russell? Your own *grandson!*" Kate shouted at her. "You were inhuman! He's still carrying around the emotional scars from what you did to him!"

The grandmother bared her teeth. They were long and sharp and dripping, like a rabid dog's.

"You can't hurt me! I won't let you!"

A bright light blinded Kate's eyes.

And suddenly the grandmother was gone. Kate turned, only to face something even more terrifying.

It was the little girl. The little dead girl she'd seen on her wedding night. She was walking slowly across the room toward Kate, carrying that legless Raggedy Ann doll. A mischievous little smile played with her lips. A smile that held back a secret. Kate knew somehow that this little girl was far more powerful than the old woman had been. The little girl kept approaching. Kate screamed.

Erik Arrives

"Hello, I'm here to see Kate," he told the woman who opened the door, his voice breathless.

"Please," Mrs. Tynan said. "Come inside."

Erik stepped into the house. He looked around. How dusty the place was. How cold. Right away he sensed the spirits here. Incredibly strong, and *riled*. There was indeed a lot of unrest in this house.

"If you'd like to wait in the parlor," Mrs. Tynan was saying, "I'll see if I can find her."

Erik thanked her, taking a seat on the old couch. He listened as her footsteps faded away up the stairs. He lifted his eyes to the portrait of Asa Wright. He shivered.

He was glad he'd stopped on the way here to meet with his old professor at Yale. It meant he'd first had to go to New Haven, making his trip a day longer than necessary. He'd tried to call Kate to explain, but her voice mail didn't appear to be working. He suspected something was deliberately interfering with it. But the side trip had been worth it. Professor Stokes had more experience in the occult than anyone else he knew, and unlike Erik, he hadn't spent his career making friends with ghosts. "Some are indeed malevolent forces, in league with evil," he explained. Stokes had a way of communicating with the dead that made Erik feel like an amateur. Together they'd held a séance—a séance that revealed just how much danger Kate was really in.

He hoped the delay hadn't been too disadvantageous. Still he'd been unable to reach her on her cell phone. He prayed to God that Kate was okay.

"Erik!"

He jumped to his feet. But it was Russell who was coming down the stairs, greeting him. He shook Erik's hand warmly.

"How are you, Erik?" Russell's voice was booming. "What a surprise!"

Erik wasted no time with small talk. "Russell, is Kate all right?"

Russell looked surprised. "Why, of course she is, my man. In fact, she's on her way to see you right now—in New York!"

Damn, Erik thought. But *good.* At least she was out of the house.

"When did she leave?" Erik asked.

"This morning," Russell told him cheerily. "Oh, what a mix-up, huh? I thought going into the city would be good for her. Didn't she call you?"

Erik sighed. "Our cell phones haven't been very reliable."

"Well, I imagine she'll stay at our old place. I'm sure you'll catch up with her." Russell smiled. "If you head back right now, that is."

Erik looked at him intently. He was suspicious of Russell's manner, his apparent warmth. But how much of that was merely Erik's own dislike for the man? "She called me two nights ago," Erik said, "asking me to please come up. She sounded frantic. Is she all right? Did something happen? Is that why she left?''

Russell's face shifted a little. He no longer looked quite so friendly or warm. "She called you, huh?" He looked up at the portrait of Asa Wright and his face clouded over. "I suppose *you* knew about the things she claims to see. Why did she keep it a secret from me, Erik?"

"She should have told you, Russell. But don't hold it against her." He sighed. "Did you fight? Is that why she left?"

Russell wouldn't look at him, just kept his eyes glued to the portarit. "She's kept a lot of things from me apparently," he said. His voice now sounded hard and distant. "Did you know she spent time in an institution, Erik?"

Erik hesitated. "Did she . . . tell you that?"

Russell turned finally to look at him. He smiled cruelly. "Oh, no. I had to find that out on my own." He crossed his arms over his chest. "I called her parents. I was concerned about her, you see. How strangely she'd been acting." He looked off into space, at something Erik couldn't see. "They told me about the mental hospital. And the years with psychiatrists. I didn't realize I married a crazy woman who has delusions about seeing ghosts."

"They're not delusions," Erik said hotly. "That's why she didn't tell you. She knew that's what you'd think."

Russell looked at him strangely. "You'd better go, then, Erik. If you believe in them, I don't think you'd enjoy meeting my family's ghosts."

"Russell, whether you believe these things or not, you had no right to pry into Kate's past! You had no right to contact her parents. Is that why she left here? I don't blame her for being angry! She had reasons for not wanting to be in contact with her parents! You should have let her tell you about all of that in her own time."

Russell glared at him. "Better to find out my wife is crazy sooner rather than later."

"Kate is not crazy!"

Russell laughed. "This from a man who makes his living writing about how to talk to ghosts!"

Erik drew up close to him. "I never liked you," he seethed into Russell's face. "Not from the start. If anything has happened to Kate, I hold you responsible."

Russell's eyes looked insane. Erik pulled back, suppressing another shiver. He turned and stormed out of the house.

Leaning against the mantel, Russell put his head back and laughed. A wild, devious, roller-coaster kind of laugh. Erik could hear him all the way down to the bridge.

The Roses

The roses bloomed a week later—big, beautiful, magnificent.

"Russell!" Auntie Cee called, looking down at the garden. The morning was still dewy, the garden still in blue shadows, but the roses, almost before her eyes, were unfolding their petals and greeting the day. "Russell! The roses!"

He stepped into her room and grinned broadly. "They're beautiful," he said.

"Kate must take the credit," Auntie Cee told him. "Is she feeling better? Will she be able to get out and see them?"

He smiled enigmatically. "I hope so, Auntie Cee. I hope so."

The day was extraordinarily hot, the beginning of the season's first heat wave. Summer was officially here. Schools had let out and the children had been set free. Even here on the third floor in Auntie Cee's room, Russell could hear the children in the woods, sounds he had not heard in a long, long while. Shouts from the kids jumping from the rope that dangled like a long, impotent snake over the muddy pond. Hoots from the boys and screams from the girls as they tossed slimy frogs at one another. From the street there came the jangle and screech of passing teenagers' cars, a blast of music suddenly shattering the solitude of the old house, especially with all its windows open.

For a moment Russell thought wistfully of summers as a boy, of lazy days reading his comic books, eating Cheez-Its from the box. He might, on a day like today, drag himself down to the brook, especially if Grandmother was harping at him about being a sissy hidden away in his room. He'd retreat to the brook, where he'd sit on the bank dangling his feet into the cool babbling water, watching the sky for cloud formations. Those were peaceful times, good times.

But other summer memories intruded: hot, hot days like this, the stench from Grandfather's room invading the house, the taunts from the open windows reaching his ears: "Crazy man! Crazy man! Crazy man!" And Russell peering out from his window down to the front porch, watching Grandmother emerge from the door brandishing a broom in the air, hollering in Swedish after a pack of his schoolmates, chasing them down the walk and over the bridge, past St. Michael the archangel and Lucifer, too. The fleeing boys would change their chant to "Wicked old witch! Wicked old witch!"

And then Russell smiled, remembering Rosalind. He wondered idly where she'd gone off to, and for a second the old anger swelled again in his chest. *Off with some guy,* he was sure, some guy like the ones he'd find her with in the barn, or up in the attic, or down in the basement—in the *basement*, of all places, under the very same spot where her father had once swayed from the beam. Usually the boys she seduced were much younger than she was, boys from town, boys from the trailer park, or sometimes even, from the home . . .

"But he's *retarded*, Rosalind!" Russell had shouted at her.

"So? He liked it."

"You're going to hell," he'd told her, backing away.

"Yes, maybe I am. To hell and back again." And she had laughed.

Russell turned away from the window. He kissed his aunt and went back downstairs to look for Rosalind.

It was a fortuitous move, perhaps, because he did not see the children sneaking across the meadow, just as they had years ago, when he was a boy.

They didn't go unnoticed, however, by Auntie Cee. A flash of color in the noonday sun, a whirl of motion from below. She strained to see, but the glare was in her eyes. When she sensed what was happening, she began banging on the floor with her foot, calling, "Mrs. Tynan! Mrs. Tynan!" She reached for the bell on the table at her side, but she knocked it over, sending it clanging to the floor.

Russell had gone to his room, his head in his closet, pushing aside a pile of old, rubbery-smelling shoes, searching for the cardboard box that contained his old comic books. The dust down at the bottom of his closet was thick and rich. He sneezed several times, and between his third and fourth sneeze, he thought he heard something: something from the back of the house.

From the garden.

"Crazy man! Crazy man!"

His heart began to thump in his ears.

* * *

Kate was in bed. How long had she been here? Her arm was set in a cast and held up against her chest by a sling. How had she broken it? She tried to remember, but she couldn't.

She vaguely remembered the doctor, and Russell hovering behind him, seeming so solicitous of her welfare. *Russell loves me,* she thought wearily, groggily. *Russell loves me. . . .*

Why couldn't she think? What had she forgotten? Wasn't she supposed to call someone on the phone? Why did she feel so weak?

She looked over at the breakfast Mrs. Tynan had brought her. She hadn't touched it. Somehow she thought eating it would only make her sleepy again, and she'd been sleeping so much lately. . . .

And then she heard the high, evil-sweet laugh of a child.

"Crazy man! Crazy man!"

She struggled to her feet. She almost fell to the floor putting her weight on her legs. How long had it been since she'd walked? How many days? With her left hand she braced herself against the bed and pulled herself to the post, where she leaned, out of breath. She stumbled over to the window and looked down below, pressing her hand to the windowpane.

She saw a band of marauding children invading her garden. From this angle, from above, they were partially obscured by the storm of petals that raged around them.

They were destroying the rosebushes.

"Get out! Get out! Get out!" Russell was screaming, flying from the back door, lunging at the children, their vicious cries of merriment stopped short, their beastly little legs beginning to turn and run.

He grabbed one boy as the others ran off, rounding the corner of the house, heading for the bridge. Russell wrestled the boy to the ground, pushing him down on the blanket of red and pink rose petals. The boy looked up at him with big black eyes, the eyes of a demon.

"What the fuck did you do this for?" Russell screamed into his face.

He was only vaguely aware of the frantic rapping at the window upstairs, or of Mrs. Tynan shrieking from behind him. He had the boy pressed to the ground by his shoulders, and his knee was on his chest.

"I could snap your neck very easily," Russell spat.

The boy began to cry. "Please let me go!"

"It would happen so fast. You'd barely feel it. I'd just break that scrawny little neck of yours and you'd be dead."

"Mr. Russell! Please!" Mrs. Tynan was hysterical with fear.

Russell stared down into the eyes of the terrified child. He realized he couldn't be more than twelve years old.

"Mr. Russell, please let him go. Don't hurt him!"

He hesitated several seconds, then stood, staring down at the boy.

"Get out of here," he said to the child, wearily. "And don't come back."

The boy stumbled as he got to his feet, disturbing the rose petals, sending a few to float ignobly through the air like wounded snowflakes. Then he ran, in the direction his companions had gone.

The rosebushes were gone. Every single flower had been ripped from its vine, crumbled in the dirty, sweaty hands of the boys. The vines had been torn from the trellis, and in some cases, the very plants themselves had been uprooted. Rose petals were everywhere, a pretty carpet, but already browning. Russell looked at his hands and the front of his white shirt: specked with blood. Then he realized the boy's little hands, fighting him, had been bloody, cut by thorns.

"How could they *do* such a thing?" Mrs. Tynan was crying. She got down on her aged knees, trying to save the ragged remains, pressing sundered roots back into the soil, lifting broken vines to replace on the trellis.

"This is the legacy of Wrightsbridge," Russell said without emotion. "How could I ever have thought we could restore beauty to this place?"

He looked up the side of the house. He could see Auntie Cee crying. He could see Kate, in the window directly below her, staring in disbelief.

"Oh, Mr. Russell," Mrs. Tynan was saying, her voice breaking, "that was the little Parsons boy. He delivers my newspaper at home. He's always been such a good child. I can't understand what possessed him."

"Oh, I can, Mrs. Tynan," Russell said suddenly, moving away from the roses and walking past her into the house. "I can."

Kate's Question

"Why didn't you tell me you'd been institutionalized?"

Kate sat in the chair, overcome. The roses, destroyed. And now Russell was telling her he'd spoken with her parents. *Her parents.* Gone behind her back and called her parents.

"Russell, please, I'm so weak—I can't think . . ."

"Of course you can't. You've had another breakdown. Your father described it very well to me."

Russell looked at her with hostile, accusing eyes. He seemed like someone she didn't know. A stranger. No— not a stranger. Like the doctors who had treated her, disbelieved her—who had patronized her and pumped her full of medications. Like her father even: cold and distant and disapproving.

"It was just like the breakdowns you had as a girl," he was saying. "Thinking you saw things. Thinking people were after you. People who were dead."

"Please, Russell, please—"

"And no doubt you had other episodes like this after you came to New York, refusing to have anything to do with your parents." He leaned in close to her, like an angry schoolmaster. "You *lied* to me, Kate."

"No, I never lied—"

He sniffed. "Not telling me about your—your *condition*—is just as bad as lying outright. You *deceived* me. You made me think the woman I was marrying was strong. *Good.*"

"Russell, please. I want to talk to you about this. About everything. But I feel so weak . . ."

He turned away from her. "I don't appreciate being lied to by my wife."

"The things I see are *real,*" Kate insisted, summoning all of her strength. "And there are forces here that don't want us in this house. Russell, they've affected you, too. You've changed! Can't you see that?"

He looked at her. "What you see is illusion."

"*No!*" She tried to stand, but managed only to stumble over to the bedpost, where she braced herself. "They are *real!* Who hanged himself in this house, Russell? *Who is the hanged man?*"

Russell's eyes grew wide.

"Yes! You know who I'm talking about, don't you, Russell? How would I know about the hanged man if what I saw wasn't real? Tell me, Russell! *Who is he?*"

Russell's face twisted in rage as he rushed out of the room, slamming the door behind him. Kate heard the key in the lock. She began to cry.

Why was she so weak? She needed to get her wits back, her strength. She had to try calling Erik again. Had he tried to reach her? He had said he was coming . . . but he never came. . . .

She stumbled over to the other side of her bed. She found her purse turned upside down. Her wallet was empty; the little cash she'd had was gone. Her cosmetics were scattered all over the floor. But the worst thing was that her cell phone was gone.

"Dear God," she whispered. "He's keeping me a prisoner here. Letting them do whatever they want to my mind. . . ."

She had to keep her wits. She had to think. She had to find a way out. But she could barely walk.

She looked over at the tray of food Mrs. Tynan had prepared, still untouched beside her bed. She'd eat something, try to find her strength again. She knew now that she had to get out of this house.

The Return of Rosalind

Russell knew his sister was coming home even before she presented herself. It had always been that way between them.

He heard her laugh, off somewhere in the meadow, a short burst of merriment, laughter like purple flowers, like grape Popsicles on a summer day. And he strained his eyes to see, trying to find a disturbance among the waving yellow grass. Finally he spotted her, as she made her way along the clusters of lilac bushes, pausing to stop and sniff, pressing her face at times into them as one might a washbasin, sometimes disappearing entirely into the bushes, but always drawing ever closer.

When she finally stepped into the garden, it might have been minutes, or hours, later. She regarded the tattered rosebushes with a disinterested eye.

"Were they beautiful?" she asked.

"Rosalind, where did you go? If you'd been here, none of it would have happened."

"The roses," she repeated, impatient. "Were they beautiful?"

He tore his eyes from her and forced himself to look upon the remains. "Yes," he said, "they were beautiful."

She sighed. The sun caught a shock of blue in her black hair, and tiny beads of sweat had risen on her bronzed skin, just above the low-cut neckline of her tight red lace blouse. Something foreign stirred within her brother. She removed her blazer, and folded it over her arm.

"Let's go swimming," she said suddenly, her black eyes dancing.

"Rosalind, please. Things have gotten bad here again."

She laughed. "Oh, baby, baby brother ..." She walked over to him, bent, and kissed him on the forehead. He could smell her cologne, the tangy Indian scent she'd worn since she was twelve.

"Rosalind, I don't want to be angry with you," he said tiredly.

"Then don't be."

"Where did you go?"

She sighed. "Does it matter, Russell? I'm here now."

"Kate lied to me," he said, sounding like a boy tattling on a friend. "Just like Theresa."

"Didn't I tell you?" Rosalind asked, smiling, the corners of her mouth twitching.

"Oh, Rosalind. I don't know what to do."

"Of course you do. Aren't you already doing it?"

He ran his hands through his hair. "Rosalind, you aren't planning ... anything bad for Kate, are you?"

She threw her head back and laughed. "Oh, baby brother—whatever do you mean?"

"Don't, Rosalind, please, no more bad things," Russell said, and his voice suddenly sounded desperate, a little boy again, the little boy who had turned his ankle in the snow, who lay face first in the muddy pond.

"It's not Kate I'm angry with right now," she said plainly.

Russell was caught short. "Who are you angry with then?"

She had walked over to the dried limbs of the rosebushes. "Were there any pink ones? The kind Grandmother used to put on her dressing room table?"

"Yes," her brother said. "There were pink roses."

"What a shame," she mused.

"Will you stay now, for a while?" Russell asked, aware of the plea in his voice.

"I think so."

"Will you see Auntie Cee?"

She arched an eyebrow at him. "Do you think that's wise?"

"She would love to see you. Why haven't you gone up to see her yet?"

She looked at him with her big black eyes and took his hands in hers. "Will you have Old Town Day here on the Fourth of July?"

"Yes, I'd like to. What do you think?"

She smiled. "Oh, but we *must*, Russell. We must bring back the glory days."

He took his hands away from hers, and looked away. "Oh, Rosalind . . ."

"Let's go swimming," she said again. This time he didn't say anything. He just got up and followed her, through the meadow and into the woods, down to the old swimming hole, as brown and muddy as ever, and together they took off their clothes, like children no more than ten, and swam for hours among the tadpoles and the dragonflies.

* * *

"Rosalind's back," Russell said, greeting Kate as he brought her dinner in on a tray.

Kate blinked. Had she fallen asleep again? How many days now? How many days had she been in this bed?

She'd been trying to get her strength back. When was that? When did she last consider getting out of this house? Why did she fall asleep again when she'd been trying so hard not to?

"Did you hear me?" Russell asked, settling the tray on the table beside her bed.

"Yes," Kate said. "You said Rosalind's back."

He nodded. "Perhaps she'll come up and see you tonight."

Kate looked at him. She tried to form the words, but couldn't. She just looked at him.

"I told her how we met," Russell said, smiling fondly and sitting down on the edge of her bed. "That silly video mix-up. And watching *Jane Eyre*. And how we walked out on the bridge . . ." He turned to Kate. "Do you remember?"

She found the strength to touch his hand. "Yes," she said, desperate to believe that he was really here, in his right mind, the husband she had married, the man she had fallen in love with. "Yes, I remember, Russell."

He smiled. "And I remember how you told me you'd never been to the top of the Statue of Liberty, and so we went . . ."

Kate shook her head. "No, no, Russell, we didn't," she said. "We wanted to, but we never made it. . . ."

He looked at her with eyes she didn't recognize. "Oh, but we did. Don't you remember going out on the ferry with all those tourists? How warm it was, with the sun on our faces?"

"No, no, Russell, we didn't do that," Kate told him.

"Have you lost your memory, Theresa? Of course we went to the Statue of Liberty."

Kate felt her mouth go dry. "What—what did you call me?"

"Oh, Rosalind can't *wait* to meet you," he said, standing up. He looked at her and then at her dinner. "Eat well, now. So you're strong for Rosalind."

He smiled and left the room, locking the door once again behind him.

Who was Theresa? It was the second time he'd used that name, Kate thought. Oh, if only she could remember. If only she didn't keep falling asleep . . .

She *did* need to eat. She needed to get her strength back. She reached over toward the tray . . .

But someone stopped her. She felt a hand on hers, and a voice entreating her: "No."

Kate gasped. There was a woman standing at the side of her bed, blocking her access to the food. Whether she was an apparition or flesh and blood Kate couldn't tell immediately; she just knew somehow that the woman didn't belong in this house. She wasn't one of them.

"Don't eat the food," the woman told her in a voice like smoke and wind chimes.

The woman was drawn and haggard, but pretty nonetheless, and she wore modern clothes, a wool sweater and jeans. Her blond hair was disheveled and she wore no makeup, and her lips were cracking a little. She shook her head ferociously. "Don't eat the food," she repeated.

"Who are you?" Kate asked.

The woman just stood there, looking down at her, with some of the saddest eyes Kate had ever seen.

Suddenly it hit her. The *food.* That's what was wrong with her. Russell was drugging her. Maybe even poisoning her. That's why she continued to sleep so much, feel so weak and tired.

But who was this woman? *And why does she want to help me?*

As soon as Kate understood the message she'd come to deliver, the woman disappeared. *She doesn't belong here,* Kate thought again. *She came here. Deliberately. To help me.*

The question of who the spirit was faded with the growing realization that her husband was poisoning her. The man she married. The man she loved.

"It can't be," Kate said out loud. It was Mrs. Tynan who prepared the food after all. But for the past few days it had always been Russell bringing it to her.

No, I won't eat well, Russell, she thought, looking up at the door. *I won't eat at all.*

If she had to face Rosalind, she wanted to do it with her all of her strength and all of her wits.

Rosalind Has a Plan

But Rosalind never made it to Kate's room that night. Something else occupied her mind.

She was stretched out like a glamour queen on Grandmother's chaise longue, her legs crossed and shoes kicked off. "I keep thinking about the roses," she told Russell. "I can't seem to get my mind off them."

Russell glared at her. "You promised you'd meet Kate tonight."

"All in good time, baby brother." She arched an eyebrow. "Don't tell me you haven't thought about the roses?"

He admitted that he had.

"Of course you have." Rosalind swung her legs down to the floor, getting ready to stand. "In fact, it's really all you've been able to think about. Don't you think we ought to take one thing at a time?"

He looked at her. "What are you planning?"

"What makes you think I'm planning anything?"

He scowled. "Because you always have *some* plan, Rosalind."

She laughed, standing, brushing the lint and dust off her jeans. "Tell me," she said, "does Bobby Shortridge still live in the same house?"

"Rosalind." Russell stood to face her. "What are you going to do?"

She just smiled. "Do you think he'd be glad to see me?"

Russell's eyes widened in fear. "Rosalind! Please tell me what you are planning."

She laughed again, the sound of breaking glass. "Russell, just answer my questions. He always did have a crush on me, didn't he?"

Her brother glared at her. "Yes, Rosalind. He did."

"And he's gone a little simple, hasn't he? Since the accident?"

Russell folded his arms across his chest. "He's never been the same."

Rosalind's eyes twinkled. "But still smart enough to do a little job for me, no?"

"Rosalind! *What are you planning?*"

She kissed him softly on the lips. "You'll see, baby brother. You'll see."

The Boys' Club

It was Jimmy Parsons, she learned, who plotted the most dangerous missions. Like the raid two weeks ago on Wrightsbridge. Sitting in a circle in the dampness of their clubhouse crypt, they'd all concurred that the raid on Wrightsbridge to destroy the rosebushes had been a true success. And in broad daylight, too.

For three days now she had been following them. She'd discovered their rites, their rituals, their secret meetings in a crumbling brownstone crypt in the old section of Pine Grove Cemetery. In the moist darkness under the tall blue-green pines, the boys made their plans among the dead. And she stood outside, in the purple shadows, hearing them all.

It was Wrightsbridge she heard them talk about, again and again. It was a natural target: boys loved invading haunted houses as much as they loved harrassing crazy men, sissy boys, and wicked old witches. It showed they were tough. Boys. *Men.*

"My father told me strange things have always happened up there," one boy was saying, a horrible bright red case of acne lighting up his face.

"They're all fucking weirdos," Jimmy Parsons spat.

A fat kid pointed a finger at Jimmy. "You gotta get the faggot back who pinned you down."

"Oh, I will," Jimmy promised. "I *will*."

She eavesdropped as they planned a second raid on Wrightsbridge. They wanted to steal something this time—an artifact of some kind, something to prove they'd been inside the house. They never mentioned anything specific; they were only clear as to the time. Somehow they knew that Kate was bedridden, and that of course the old woman on the third floor was helpless. That left just Mrs. Tynan, who Jimmy reported went to the market on Wednesday afternoons, and the faggot owner, who usually took a walk in the middle part of the day. They'd been casing the joint, like the crafty little boy adventurers they were. Oh, they were so smart. They thought they'd accounted for everyone.

But they hadn't considered Rosalind.

So she went back to the house to await their little broadside, which came at precisely the day and hour they'd planned. Wasn't that precious? Such crafty little soldiers. So brave. So flushed with testosterone now that school was out and their budding little male aggression had nothing to do.

She watched them now, two little warriors in baggy blue jeans, T-shirts, and baseball caps turned backward on their heads. Apparently these were the bravest of the barve, all of the others wimping out. Of course it was Jimmy Parsons to lead the way. He was crouched down in the bushes on the other side of the bridge with the other boy, and although she couldn't see their faces clearly, she could imagine them very well—especially Jimmy's, intent on revenge.

She laughed to herself, thinking how arrogant youth

was, how secure they felt in their war games. The little general thought no one could see them, hidden among the fir trees that lined the estate. But she watched eagerly as they crept over the bridge, hunched down, moving more like giant crabs than little boys.

Little boys like the ones who had tormented Russell all those years ago.

And hadn't she taken care of them, too?

Oh, they were right that Mrs. Tynan had gone shopping, and yes, that had indeed been Russell walking off into the woods. But Wrightsbridge held more than just two helpless women.

How she laughed when she saw the boys stop short just as they approached the front porch. The one with Jimmy—a chubby little brat wearing an Eminem T-shirt—stopped and began to show second thoughts, but Jimmy slapped him upside the head and called him a faggot. *Ah, Jimmy,* she thought. *How brave and strong you are.*

"The front door's open," she heard one of them whisper. Strange how sound carried in this house, echoing off the old wood, not muffled in the least by all the dust.

In the parlor, they were unaware of her presence on the stairs.

"It's creepy in here, fuckin' creepy," the fat boy said. Such a mouth for a twelve-year-old.

"Wanta take that portrait up there?" he was asking.

"It's too high," Jimmy said, looking around the room.

"How about a vase? We can rip all those lilacs apart and throw them around the room. They're all brown anyway. Why didn't they throw them out?"

"Shut up, Sean," Jimmy snapped. "The old lady will hear you upstairs."

"She can't do nothing. She's a hunnert years old. Let's write 'faggot' on the walls."

"Shut your face," Jimmy growled, and she could hear the other boy dodge out of the way of a fist, or the back of a hand. "I'm expedition leader."

"We have to get something that proves we were actually in Wrightsbridge," Sean said, his voice getting high and whiney.

"Let's go upstairs," Jimmy said.

She narrowed her eyes, listening intently for Sean's reply. But he said nothing. She smiled. They were afraid of the stairs.

And not without reason.

"The wife is up there," Sean finally said. "I heard my mother saying so. She said she was sick and in bed."

"So then she'll do nothin'," Jimmy said. "Come on. We talked about all this."

"But that's where the ghosts are," the scared boy said, his bravado completely gone now. "That's what everyone says."

"It's *daytime*, Sean," Jimmy snarled. "Don't be such a fuckin' wuss."

She had moved off the stairs now, standing in an alcove in the hallway past the parlor, still eavesdropping.

"But it's still so dark in here. What if we can't see up there?" Sean cried.

"Come *on*." Jimmy started up the stairs, his friend reluctantly following him. They stopped on the first landing to gaze up at the stained glass of St. George and the dragon.

"It's like a church," Sean said.

There was a sound; it could have been Kate trying to get out of bed, or Auntie Cee, having a nightmare, or a squall of bats from the attic. It was short, muffled, high-pitched.

"What was that?" Sean asked, his eyes wide.

"Nothing," Jimmy said. "Just the wind. Or something."

She moved to the bottom of the stairs, looking up at the boys on the landing. The sun had become oscured by dark gray clouds, and she knew she would appear suitably frightening, shrouded in shadows when they looked down at her.

"Hello, boys," she said.

They both froze, their small frames silhouetted against the purple-and-red glass of St. George and the dragon.

She smiled up at them. "Are you looking for some-one?"

Her voice was silky and calm, and she saw in their frightened eyes that they felt something was not right with her, that something didn't fit. But they had been caught: she was in control here, not they, and they would not give her any trouble, despite whatever they might think about her.

She stood at the bottom of the stairs, a long black cape draped around her shoulders that came to the floor, her black jeans and red lace blouse barely showing from beneath.

"Yes," Jimmy finally said in reply, trying to sound fearless. "We're looking for Mr. Wright."

"Mr. Wright isn't here," she said pleasantly.

"Okay, we'll come back," Jimmy said, not taking his eyes off her, starting to move forward, to walk back down the stairs toward her.

Her voice was sweet. "You weren't here to *steal* any-thing, were you?"

"No," Sean said fiercely. "Really, we were just here to—and—we came up here—looking—" He gestured wildly with his hands, whipping his head back and forth, looking between her and Jimmy.

She smiled at his pathetic little attempt to lie. "Why don't you boys come with me? I have something to show you," she said, smiling, taking the first step up the stairs toward them.

Jimmy stopped moving but remained calm. "We can't. We got to go now."

"Oh, no," she said, smiling broadly and taking another step, "I wouldn't hear of it. My little party has just begun."

"She's a ghost!" Sean cried suddenly, and in a burst of energy ran down the steps, brushing past her and pulling open the front door. She didn't turn around but she could see in her mind's eye his fat little figure getting smaller and smaller as he fled, cartoonlike, into the distance.

She kept her eyes on Jimmy, who stayed where he was, staring back at her.

She smiled. "Now it's just the two of us," she said sweetly, taking her third step up the stairs.

And finally Jimmy ran. Not down, not past her, but *up.*

Ah, that's where you weren't very smart, my little commando. The boy turned and ran up the next flight of stairs to the second floor, and then up again toward the third. She continued to ascend the steps, one at a time, slowly but deliberately, hearing his little feet galloping above her.

"That's it, Jimmy," she called softly after him. "Run, run, run."

In her room, Auntie Cee, dozing in her chair by the window, was awakened by a sound, the sound of a child, and then footsteps on the stairs.

"Leave him alone, Inger," she muttered to herself, and, as she had so many times before, closed her eyes and found Samuel waiting for her there.

* * *

In the attic, Jimmy was cornered. It had all worked out so perfectly.

She came downstairs after finishing her task, and tiptoed delicately to Auntie Cee's room. Yes, the dear old lady was sleeping. She gingerly closed the door, and then returned to stand with her ear against the door to the attic.

When at last she heard little Jimmy scream, finally acknowledging his terror, finally acknowledging that he was no man at all, she opened the door. Stepping inside, she ascended the first few steps.

"Did you take care of him?" she asked.

"Yeth," Bobby Shortridge answered, coming down the attic steps, the torn flesh on his face shifting, an expression that passed for a smile.

Kate and Theresa

The humidity had risen along with the heat. Kate sat in her room, listening to the sounds of footsteps on the stairs, the scream from the attic. Whose ghosts now?

She'd eaten nearly nothing in three days. The food Russell would give her was scraped off the plate and hidden inside her empty suitcases in the closet. Even the water he brought was poured into the potted plants. Her only hydration came from the faucet in the bathroom, from which she drank as much as she could during her twice-daily visit, Russell standing outside the door waiting for her. Except for a slightly stale pack of peanut-butter crackers, discovered among the debris of her purse, she'd had no nourishment. Yet despite her light-headedness, she felt better, more alert, than she had in days. It *had* to be the food. The ghost was right.

Russell had been poisoning her.

To fool him, she'd continued to act weak and drugged in his presence. She couldn't keep up the pretense long. *I have to get out*, she told herself. But the drop from the window was too high, and Russell always locked the door behind him. She considered making a break for it and running the next time he took her to the bathroom, but she worried she still wouldn't have the strength to be faster than he was. Maybe if she could call to Mrs. Tynan downstairs, she could convince her to listen to her tale of being imprisoned and drugged.

But that would do no good. Kate could hear Russell saying, "She's delusional. Pay her no mind." And Mrs. Tynan would agree. Of course she would. Russell had probably already told her what he'd found out from Kate's parents—that she'd spent time in a mental institution, that she was prone to emotional breakdowns.

No, it was not a good plan: she had to think of something else.

"You're feeling stronger. You can think clearly now."

Kate looked up. At the foot of the bed stood the woman who had helped her. Her arms were wrapped around herself as she stood looking at Kate.

"Yes," she replied softly. "I can think now." She paused. "Thank you for helping me."

The woman nodded. Kate had the feeling she would disappear now that her work was done, that she might not see her again.

"Who are you?" Kate asked. "Please tell me."

The woman just looked at her. A ray of sunlight seemed to penetrate her, as if she would fade away into the light.

"It was the food," the ghost told her.

"Yes, I know. I'm stronger now that I've stopped eating it."

"He was poisoning you."

Kate felt the tears well in her eyes. "But he's my husband. I thought he loved me."

The ghost's eyes too were shining with tears. "I thought so, too. . . ."

Who was this woman who felt so much compassion for Kate? "Please tell me who you are," Kate cried. "How did you know what Russell was doing?"

The pain on the dead woman's face was clear. "He thought I lied to him. He thought I was cheating on him."

"You? How do you know Russell?"

More sunlight filled the room and the woman was nearly obliterated.

"Please!" Kate shouted. "Don't go! Please tell me who are."

"My name," the woman said, just before the sunlight obscured her, "is Theresa."

The Last Boy

Russell set the electric fan on the floor facing up at Auntie Cee. They were in the midst of a heat wave, and the old house of course had no air-conditioning. Although nothing could match the horridly humid summers in New York, Russell had to admit this was close. There was no breeze, just oppressive, damp heat, and everything was so maddeningly still. This was a bad omen, he thought: if late June was this hot, he loathed to imagine July and August.

"Is that a little better?" he asked his aunt.

"Much, dear. Thank you."

Sweat dappled her old forehead, leaving little streaks in the talcum powder. The old metal fan squeaked as it began slowly rotating on the floor.

"Do you need any more ice water?"

She smiled over at him. "Thank you, Russell. I'm fine."

"Mrs. Tynan has gone out, so if you need anything, ring the bell on your table. I'll just be in my room."

Her hand reached out to stop him from leaving. "Russell?"

"Yes, Auntie Cee?"

She looked up at him. "I heard noises yesterday, coming from the attic."

He stiffened. "You always think you hear ghosts, Auntie Cee."

She looked off through the window. "Yes. But these were different. . . ."

"What do you mean different?"

A look of terror filled her eyes. "I think they're restless."

"Who?"

"All of them."

He sat down on the stool beside her. "There's no reason to be frightened."

"Oh, but there *is*, Russell. I've lived in this house all my life. I've learned to accept the ghosts that come with an old house. But in the twenty years since the deaths up there, I've never heard them so restless."

Russell said nothing. It was the first time Auntie Cee had spoken directly to him of the deaths. He couldn't bear it. He looked away from her.

"Russell." Auntie Cee's voice was suddenly direct and commanding. "Has she returned?"

He looked back at her slowly. "Who?"

"Rosalind."

He put his face in his hands. "She was here for a while, but she's left again."

"Are you sure she's gone?"

He nodded into his hands.

"And what did she do while she was here? Did she go up to the attic?"

Russell got to his feet abruptly. *Rosalind. The attic.* Oh, how she had *loved* to defile the attic when she was a girl. She'd lure boys up there, unbuttoning her blouse on the very cot where Grandfather had died, in the very cell where he'd rotted away, mad. She'd taken such perverse pleasure in that. Fornicating with those boys, usually younger than she was, sometimes simple, the way Bobby Shortridge was now . . .

He remembered the boy's eyes as if it were yesterday: big and brown, wide-eyed with terror. Russell had watched him backing away from her, terrified by the suddenness of Rosalind's advance. Russell hadn't been able to tear his gaze away from the boy's eyes. He was like an animal, cornered. When the lightning abruptly lit up the darkness, the boy's face had looked much like that of a deer.

He was the last boy Rosalind would ever bring to the attic. Grandmother had discovered them, which Russell secretly thought Rosalind had really wanted all along, each time she snuck another child up the stairs. Rosalind had been smoking and the attic reeked of tobacco and Rosalind's heavy Indian perfume. Maybe Grandmother had smelled something. Maybe she'd just sensed it. For suddenly she was there, looming large over Rosalind and the boy.

"You filthy creature!" Grandmother had croaked in her horrible accent, punctuated by terrible claps of thunder. "How *dare* you defile my house? *How dare you?*"

Russell had backed close against the wall. The power was out, and he managed to hide in the shadows. He did not want to risk Grandmother's rage if she discovered that he had been there watching Rosalind's little tryst. The terrified boy was now backing up across the attic floor, and Grandmother loomed after him with her big hand clenched in a fist. All at once he turned and ran, his footsteps falling in rapid rhythm down the stairs. And then Grandmother turned her full wrath upon Rosalind.

"You filthy spawn!" She held out her big hands as if to choke her. "You are the devil's child!"

Russell tried to disappear into the shadows. But he made a noise, a sound, something—for Grandmother's wide bright eyes suddenly turned on him, her terrible face lit up by lightning.

"*You!* It was a a twin demon seed that made you both!"

She grabbed Russell by the hair and pulled him toward her. He was crying, but Rosalind, as ever, stood stoic and unbroken facing their grandmother.

"No blood of mine," the old woman snarled. "No blood of mine!" She picked up a chair, intending to crash it down upon them. She was enraged, insane.

"No!" Rosalind cried. "You witch!" She knocked the chair out of their grandmother's hands and turned to cover Russell with her body.

Grandmother's face went white with rage—but she had been defeated, for now. She promised revenge against the little black-eyed girl, and stormed off down the stairs. Auntie Cee was crying, calling up to them, begging Inger not to hurt the children.

"She'll never hurt us again," Rosalind vowed, stroking Russell's hair.

But of course she did, for it was only a few months later that Rosalind took Bobby Shortridge for a ride in the snow, and that Grandmother at last overpowered her, despite her kicking and screaming, to lock her in the cell.

The cell she had used for her unholy trysts.

The cell where Grandfather had died.

The cell where . . .

"You see?" Auntie Cee was crying. "There it is again."

Russell listened.

"Please! Let me out!" The door of the cell rattled against its frame just as it had all those years ago.

Was it Grandfather? Begging to be released?

"Please! Please! Somebody let me out of here!"

Edgar Wright

"That is the beast from which you came," Grand-mother spat at them that first night, as the house sat in terror and shock, listening to the old man rattle the door of his cage in the attic above.

There was a lightning storm that night, too. Father was still alive, and Mother had not yet left the house. They sat in the parlor, dumbstruck, listening to the crazy man upstairs, the curtains charred and smoldering. Russell, terrified, had climbed into his mother's lap for sanctuary. They were a family back then, of sorts, but the secrets had a way of eating them all alive.

How had it started? It was late summer, Russell remembered. In the meadow the stalls from Old Town Day had still not been broken down. A few tattered streamers still flapped from fence posts. The moon had turned yellow. The pumpkins were ripening in the garden.

How fierce, how strong, how horrible Grandmother had seemed that night. She had never been kind to them, not for as long as Russell could remember. Once he had asked his mother why Grandmother hated them all so much. Was it that night, the night Grandfather was locked away, that he had asked the question? Yes, Russell believed it was. He'd asked it as his mother held him in the rocking chair by the fireplace, while the old man screamed from upstairs.

And how had she answered?

"It's not you she hates," Mother had said. "It's me."

But Mother was wrong: she hated all of them, and that included her own husband and son, Russell's father, who even that night was drunk and surly. He had said something: that's what started it all. Russell was never sure exactly what he had said, but whatever it was, it made Mother upset and Grandmother angry. And Grandmother's rage had sent Grandfather into his madness, for he tried to burn the house down with all of them in it, and as a result he was locked in the old caretaker's room in the attic. And left there to die.

Russell remembered the smoke. He and Rosalind were coming down the stairs, and started to cough, watching the blue-black smoke billow from the parlor. Inside, their grandfather was on the floor, rocking on his knees, sobbing for forgiveness. Grandmother was trying to pound out the flames that lapped up the curtains, and she called to the children to help her. They each took pillows and began slapping them against the flames, until the fire was out.

By then Mother and Father had appeared to stand mutely in the doorway, watching without saying a word as Grandmother pulled her husband to his feet, and forced him up the stairs. Rosalind had remained in place, not moving from the parlor, her little face set in stone. But Russell had followed them, up all three flights of stairs, both of his grandparents breathing fast and heavily. When they turned and continued up into the attic, he found he had had enough and bolted—down the hall and into Auntie Cee's room. There she sat, on her bed, her face contorted, her hands to her ears. He sprang at her, like a cat, and her arms encircled him.

"Sing me a song, Auntie Cee," he cried. He buried his face in her bosom. She tried, as best she could, but Russell could barely hear her words. Grandfather's cries had already begun.

The Room

"Kate! Kate! For God's sake, you've got to help me!"

It was before dawn. Kate glanced over at the lights of the digital clock glowing in the darkness. It was four-fifteen. And Russell was at her bedside, frantic.

"What's wrong?" Kate asked, not wanting to appear too alert, too strong.

"Please, you've got to get up," Russell was saying, his face a mass of lines and contortions. Kate had never seen him look so terrified. "You've got to come with me! It's Rosalind!"

Was it a trick? Kate couldn't be sure, but the door was open, and Russell didn't appear to be in any state to stop her if she tried to make a run for it. She swung her legs out of bed and with her good left hand reached for her robe.

"Can you walk, darling?" Russell asked, suddenly sounding like his old self. "Can I help you?" He helped her steady herself on her feet, solicitous of the cast on her arm.

She looked at him. He was crying.

"Darling," he said, taking her hand in his and looking her in the eyes, "Rosalind's been drugging you. Oh, Kate, I'm so sorry. I've just found out. Oh, darling, are you all right?"

She nodded slowly. Could it be true? Had Rosalind been doing this to her? And Russell unaware?

"Please come with me," he was urging. "I've just learned that she's done something even worse. Oh, darling, I'm so sorry. Please! You've got to help me!"

Maybe she was being foolish, but she believed him. She believed anyway that he was sincere in his sorrow. Could it be that he'd broken free of whatever force held him in its grasp? Had Rosalind, too, been under a spell?

"What has she done, Russell?" she asked him, trying to make sense of it all. "What has Rosalind done?"

The air was still as sticky and hot as it had been during the day. Kate's bare feet stuck to the hardwood floor. Russell was already in the doorway. "Please, darling," he was urging. "Please come with me!"

"What's wrong, Russell?" Kate asked, following him into the hallway. A slender spear of moonlight sliced through the dusty darkness.

Was it a trick? she wondered again. Was he trying to lure her into something even worse? But he was moving off down the hallway, leaving the stairway within easy reach. She could run. She felt certain of that. She could evade him and run down the stairs and out into the night.

But she didn't. She looked at the desperation on her husband's face. She just couldn't run. Not now. Not yet.

"Please tell me what is wrong, Russell," she demanded, staying in place by the stairs.

He ran a hand through his hair. "She's done something," he told her, "something horrible."

"Drugging me was horrible enough," Kate said.

"Yes, yes, it was. I am so sorry, Kate. If I had known what she was putting into your food I would have stopped her. I never would have brought it to you. You believe me, don't you?"

Kate hesitated. "Yes, Russell," she said finally, looking deep into his eyes. "I believe you would have stopped her had you known."

"Oh, God," he said, covering his face with his hands. "It's happening again—she's come back, and it's happening again. . . ."

"*What's* happening again?"

Russell looked her square in the face. "What she used to do when we were young. She'd play these games . . . horrible games . . . to teach lessons." He shivered. "To get revenge." He swallowed hard. "She locked that boy—that boy who wrecked the rose garden—in the attic."

"*What?*"

"He's there now, Kate. We've got to get him out! It's been so . . . *hot!*"

Kate couldn't process the information right away. The sounds she'd heard . . . not ghosts? But a living child? A horrible thought hit her. "How long has he been in there?" she asked.

Russell was trembling. "Since yesterday morning, I think. Oh, Kate, it gets so hot up there. . . ."

Kate looked at him. "You're afraid to go up there, aren't you? That's why you want me to go with you."

He looked ashamed. "You've been up there. I haven't. Not since I've been back."

How much like a child he seemed. Despite everything, her heart broke for him. With her good left arm she embraced him partially, bringing him close to her. His whole body was convulsing.

"How do you know the boy's up there?" she asked.

"Rosalind told me! She just admitted everything! Kate, *please!* We've got to go! We've got to get up there!"

She nodded, feeling suddenly as if she might faint. "Yes, yes, we've got to go," she said. Together they headed up the stairs.

But on the third floor, just before heading up the steps to the attic, Russell pulled back. "I can't go up there!" he shouted. "You go, Kate. Please!"

"No, Russell. I won't go up there without you."

"Kate, please!"

"How do I know you won't lock me up there? That this isn't a trick?"

He looked terribly hurt. "You don't trust me."

"I want to trust you, Russell, but you've just kept me prisoner for several days while your sister slowly poisoned me! I'm not going up into that attic alone, Russell!"

He began to cry. Tears of shame as well as grief and panic. "All right, Kate, all right."

She looked at him sharply. "Tell me something, Russell. Where is Rosalind now?"

"I . . . I don't know. I told her to get out. She's gone. I told her never to return!"

Kate nodded. That's the answer she wanted to hear.

"I'm only going up into that attic if you go first, Russell," she insisted.

He looked as if he might cry again, but he obeyed. He pulled open the door and started up the narrow flight of stairs to the attic, shaking so hard Kate thought he wouldn't make it. But they did. They emerged into the attic, where it remained as Kate remembered. Slivers of moonlight cast a pale glow through the dust and cobwebs.

Suddenly a furious shriek and movement overhead. The bats. Russell shouted and covered his hair. Kate cringed as dozens of red eyes swooped down past them, the flapping of wings riling the dust. The bats settled back into the rafters, but Kate was certain they remained aware and watching.

"I can't bear this place," Russell was crying.

"Try the door," Kate urged him.

Unlike last time, the door to the cell was closed. And when Russell tried to open it, he found it locked.

"Rosalind gave me a key," he said, fumbling in his pocket.

"Hurry, Russell!"

His hands shook so badly that Kate feared he'd drop the key, but he managed to insert it into the lock. "It won't turn," he said. "It won't turn!"

He suddenly began banging upon the door. "Jimmy! Jimmy!" But there was no sound from inside.

"What's wrong with the key?" Kate asked frantically.

"I don't know," Russell said. "This was the key Rosalind gave me."

Kate shivered. "She didn't really want you to let him out."

"Damn her!" Russell banged on the door. "Jimmy! Can you hear me?"

"You'll have to break it down," Kate told him. "I'm too weak to help you."

Russell paused. He turned to Kate, having apparently just thought of something. "I know why Rosalind didn't give me the right key," he said.

"Why?" Kate asked, instantly on guard.

"She knew the boy, if let out, would tell his parents, and the police." He looked at Kate strangely. "And *I'd* be the one to get in trouble, not she."

"Why you?"

"Because she's not around. There's no evidence she was here. I'd take the rap for her."

Kate moved closer to him. "No, Russell. That won't

happen. Now break down the door. That boy may still be alive!''

Russell smiled calmly and his eyes misted with tears. ''Once again, Rosalind was trying to take care of me. Even in the midst of all of this, even as I ordered her out of the house, she had the foresight to take care of me. As she always does.''

''What are you *talking* about, Russell?''

''We need to call the police first,'' Russell said simply. He was no longer shaking, no longer desperate or panic-stricken. ''Let them handle this. Let them find the boy. We call them, they come, they let him out.''

Kate looked at him bewildered. ''What good would that do?''

Russell's eyes darkened. ''Remember, Kate, that little punk has vandalized this house before. He came back here, got trapped in the attic. We heard something in the night, we thought it was a prowler up here, and we called the police. . . .''

Kate was listening, shaking her head. ''I don't know. . . .''

''Do want me to go to jail?'' he asked sharply.

How quickly he had changed. From terrified child to master planner. Could she trust him? After all this, could she ever trust him again?

''It's this house,'' he said suddenly, as if reading her thoughts. He gripped her by the shoulders to look down into her eyes. ''It's done things to me, Kate. And it's affected Rosalind, too. She would never have done such horrible things to you or to Jimmy had it not been for this house. You're right, Kate. There *are* forces here. Forces here that would harm us and drive us apart.''

''You believe me?'' she asked, her hopes rising. ''You believe what I've seen?''

''Yes, darling, I do. Forgive me for doubting you.''

She felt as if she'd cry. "Then go quickly, Russell! Call the police! There may still be time to save the boy!"

They both hurried back downstairs to the kitchen, where Russell nervously dialed the emergency police number. "Yes, this is Russell Wright, out at Wrights-bridge. I think . . . a prowler might have gotten into our house. . . . Yes, we think he's in the attic now. . . ."

The doorbell rang much too quickly. They'd barely hung up the phone.

Russell opened the front door. Two police officers stood there, their features obscured by the glare of the rising sun behind them. Between them stood a short red-haired woman, her face knotted in shadows.

"Mr. Wright?"

"Yes?"

"I'm Officer Piatrowski," said the taller of the two cops. "We'd like to ask you a few questions."

"Aren't you responding to my call?"

"No, sir. This is Mrs. Parsons. She thinks her son might be in this house."

"Her . . . son?"

"Yes," the woman spat. "Sean O'Brien admitted just a few hours ago, after we were going out of our minds with worry, that he last saw him here, in this house."

"In this house?" Russell asked, surprised at his own calmness.

Behind them, across the bridge, another cruiser, and then another, pulled up. Four cops were out of the cars instantly, walking quickly over the bridge toward the house.

"I'm sorry, Mr. Wright, but I'd like to ask if we can look around," Officer Piatrowski said.

"Certainly. Come in." Russell stepped aside to allow them to enter. "And I'd check the attic first. I just called the police myself. My wife and I were just awakened by some sounds from up there. I thought maybe it was a prowler—''

Mrs. Parsons shot him a hateful glance.

Four new police officers, three men and a woman, now entered the house, briefly conferring with the first two, and then, followed by Kate and Russell, the whole army started up the stairs.

The heat of the attic hit them like a physical shove. The sun's arrival had immediately jacked up the temperature another five degrees. Kate's eyes caught a glint of sunlight reflecting off the old photographs hanging on the far wall. Grandmother's Swedish relatives. Or maybe, Kate thought now, it was Grandmother herself, as a young woman, and she was watching this entire charade.

"Please," Mrs. Parsons whispered, "please find him."

The officers swung their flashlights through the gray shadows. There was no sign of any disturbance, let alone a little boy. One beam fell upon the door to the little corner room. "What's in there?" asked Piatrowski.

"It was a servant's room," Russell said, "decades ago." Kate could hear the edge in his voice. She wondered if the others could.

Two officers approached. One turned the doorknob. "It's locked," he said.

"I'm sorry I don't have a key," Russell said. "As you know, I've just moved back here. I can't imagine where the key might be."

"You've got to break it down!" Mrs. Parsons shrilled. "Jimmy could be in there!"

"Of course, you have my permission to do so, if you think the boy might be in there," Russell said. "And we did hear noises from up here, didn't we, darling?"

He looked over at Kate, who remained silent.

Two officers immediately positioned themselves opposite the door and with quick, well-aimed kicks, broke the old door from its hinges. Flashlights converged in a single ray to illuminate the interior. There, in the far corner, huddled against the wall, below the crazy carvings left by a crazy man and his crazy granddaughter, was the very small figure of a boy.

"Jimmy!" his mother screamed, rushing in to him.

Kate peered in, her heart in her throat.

Piatrowski followed, and for a few seconds they hunched over him, and the attic was deathly quiet. Kate realized the room stank of urine. The boy had pissed his pants, and then some. Finally Piatrowski's voice:

"He's alive."

"Thank God," Kate breathed.

"This is extraordinary!" Russell uttered. "How could he have gotten in there?"

The cop came outside. "I'm going to have to ask you a few questions, Mr. Wright."

"Yes, yes, of course," Russell said.

The police were on their phones calling the paramedics. Kate had to sit down or else she would have fainted. It was then she noticed, amid the commotion, standing at the far side of the attic was Edgar Wright. He was smiling.

"It was a lady," Jimmy was crying, once the paramedics had revived him. His mother was trying to calm him. They had him strapped to a stretcher, his jeans and shirt sopped with sweat and piss. "It was a lady who chased me up here!"

"A lady?" Piatrowski asked. "What did she look like?"

The boy's eyes were wild, flying around the room, shaken by the sight of so many police officers. "She had

. . . long black hair . . . and a long black cape. . . . She was like a witch . . . a ghost . . ."

"I see," Piatrowski said.

"And then a man—a man who had no face—it was all ripped to shreds, and he had one eye that was gone— he was up here, and he put me in here, and locked the door—"

"A man with one eye and no face," Piatrowski repeated.

Russell smiled indulgently. "The town has long believed this house to be haunted, Officer," Russell said, almost as an aside to Piatrowski, a hint of a smile on his face.

"Yes." Piatrowski smiled back. "I remember the stories as a kid myself."

Russell narrowed his eyes at the boy. "And now that I recall, this is the young man who destroyed our rosebushes not long ago."

"*What?*" Mrs. Parsons asked sharply.

"You've seen him before?" Piatrowski queried, growing interested.

"Yes," Russell said. "We caught him, and his buddies, out in back. Go down and look what they did to our rosebushes."

Jimmy looked bleakly from Russell to his mother.

"Isn't that the same boy?" Russell asked Kate.

She felt complicit in something she wasn't entirely comfortable with. But yes, it was the same boy she'd watch destroy her roses, the same child Russell had pinned to the ground.

"Yes," Kate admitted. "That's the boy."

Piatrowski looked at her with her arm in its cast. "Are there any other women in the house besides Mrs. Wright?" he asked.

"Just Auntie Cee," Russell said. "My ninety-eight-year-old aunt."

Piatrowski nodded. "Of course. Miss Cee."

"And there's Mrs. Tynan, but she's only here during the day." Russell looked at Mrs. Parsons. "I believe she's a neighbor of yours. I doubt *she'd* chase Jimmy up the stairs."

"Of course not," Mrs. Parsons said, looking at her son.

"How about any one-eyed men?" Piatrowski asked. "You got any of them here?"

"No," Russell assured him. "There are no one-eyed men living here."

"Jimmy," the policeman asked, turning to the boy as he drank a bottle of water offered by the paramedics, "did you break into this house? Sean O'Brien said you did."

The boy wiped his mouth. "Yes," he admitted. "But still a lady chased me up the stairs and a guy with with one eye locked me in here."

Piatrowski sighed. He turned to the paramedics. "Okay, you can take him down to the hospital and check him out," he said. He looked over at Russell. "Are you going to want to press charges, Mr. Wright? Trespassing? Vandalism?"

"Charges!" Mrs. Parsons barked. "Charges against my boy! What about how he was locked in here!"

"Old doors have a way of getting stuck, Mrs. Parsons," Piatrowski informed her.

"No," Russell told him. "I don't want to press any charges. I'm just relieved the boy is safe and he's going to be okay."

"Then I think we can all go back downstairs," Officer Piatrowski said, and he closed his notepad.

"That was Bobby Shortridge, wasn't it?" Kate asked. She was staring at Russell. Everyone had left.

"The one-eyed man."

"Yes, I think it probably was," he said, sinking into an old chair in the parlor beneath the portrait of his great-grandfather.

Kate sat on the couch opposite him. "Why?" she asked. "How?"

"I don't know," Russell said, his thoughts dreamily going off to Rosalind, wherever she was. "He's never blamed her. He's become too simple, I guess. He was always asking for her. She told me she was going to go see him. She must have convinced him to go along with her. . . ."

"He could talk to the police then," Kate warned. "He could implicate Rosalind."

Russell shook his head. "He probably doesn't even realize what he did."

"Part of me wants to tell the police she did it. Why should we protect her when that boy could have been badly hurt, or killed?"

"I understand, Kate."

She sighed. "But we can't, can we? Not until we can find out what this house is doing to us. And to her."

Russell stood to look up into the eyes of Asa Wright.

"All of this is horrible, Russell," Kate said. "I feel just horrible."

"Rosalind *is* horrible." Russell closed his eyes. "But she did it for me, you have to understand. She takes care of me. She always has." A small smile crossed his face. "And I guess I have to accept the fact that she always will."

Erik, at Last

"Sweetie! Are you all right?"

"Yes," she told him. "But can you come up here? Please? Today?"

"Of course. I've been frantic about you. I was going to call the police when I couldn't reach you. I've been calling and calling, and Russell just kept telling me you weren't up to talking. . . ."

"I wasn't." She looked around to make sure Russell wasn't anywhere nearby. She still hadn't found her cell phone, and was talking on the phone in the kitchen. "We can talk when you get here, Erik. Just come. Let me give you directions. . . ."

"Kate, I know how to get there. I've *been* there. Didn't Russell tell you?"

She looked again over her shoulder. "No. No, he didn't."

"Yes, I was there looking for you, but you'd already left for New York."

"New York?"

"I rushed back here as soon as I could and I went to your old place, but you weren't there . . . and you never called me."

She tried to steady her voice. "I never went to New York, Erik."

"You didn't? But Russell said—"

"Russell and I have both been victims of some horrible mind games, Erik. I'll tell you more when you get here. Please, just hurry."

"I can be there in three hours."

"Thank God you're coming, Erik." She closed her eyes and breathed a little easier. "Thank God."

Up with Auntie Cee

Kate wasn't surprised at how easily the police had believed Russell's story. The morning's paper showed how influential the Wrights had once again become. The headline proclaimed: OLD TOWN DAY TO RETURN TO WRIGHTSBRIDGE.

Outside, the painters and carpenters went about their tasks, fixing up the exterior of the house. They laughed and called out to each other. It was as if nothing horrible had taken place here. Kate watched Russell as he dressed calmly, his face carefree, knotting his tie in the mirror, whistling a little tune. It was as if the events of last night had never happened, and his wife hadn't spent days bedridden, being slowly poisoned by his sister. No, Russell was in fine spirits, looking forward to his meeting with the mayor this morning in town, where they'd make final preparations for Old Town Day, now just a little over a week away. Kissing Kate on the cheek as he was leaving, he'd admonished her to eat the breakfast Mrs. Tynan made for her. "Get back your energy, darling," he said. "I want to be proud of you at my side on Old Town Day."

Kate had watched carefully as Mrs. Tynan prepared her poached eggs, and then she ate them ravenously. The nurse was pleased to see Kate up and feeling better. And feel better she did, at least physically. She couldn't wait to have the cast off her arm. She felt hindered by it, made more vulnerable than she wanted to be.

Oh, how much she looked forward to having Erik here.

She hadn't told Russell he was coming. Would Erik stay at Wrightsbridge? She wasn't sure. She had no idea even what she wanted Erik to do. Just be there. Just listen to her. Erik would know what to do.

She believed Russell when he said he didn't know what Rosalind was doing. She believed him when he said how sorry he was. She believed him when he said the forces in this house were responsible, not he. For how could she blame him? It would undermine everything she wanted so desperately to be true: that she had found a home and a family and a man to love. All day yesterday they'd just held each other, and he seemed once more every inch the man she had fallen in love with. Together they would fight the ghosts of this house. Together they'd triumph.

But she was smart enough to remain just a little bit wary. His untroubled demeanor this morning frightened her. He acted as if the horror were past, but Kate knew this house wasn't through with them yet.

After breakfast and a shower, she felt at loose ends. She knew she needed more information about the secrets of this house if she were to understand what was happening to both her and Russell. And for that, she knew she had to talk again with Auntie Cee.

During her illness a package had arrived, and Kate examined it now. It was from her old boss at the video store. Weeks ago she'd written to him, asking to borrow a couple of old silent movie videos for Auntie Cee. They weren't rented out that often, and her boss had kindly sent her three: *Broken Blossoms* with Lillian Gish, *Sparrows* with Mary Pickford, and *Queen Kelly* with Gloria Swanson. Kate clutched them to her chest with her good arm and hurried up the stairs.

The heat and humidity had reached a breaking point, and low, distant, ominous thunder threatened from the horizon. She found Mrs. Tynan and elicited her help. From Russell's old room—a place she found creepy just to enter—they dragged out a VCR and portable television set, Mrs. Tynan lugging them both up the stairs to the third floor. Kate tried to help but her cast made it impossible. Mrs. Tynan brushed off her attempts, saying they weren't heavy and besides, if it would make Miss Cecilia happy, she was glad to do it.

Kate found Auntie Cee in her usual place, staring out her large picture window down at the garden.

"Kate, dear. Are you feeling better?"

"Yes, I am, thank you, Auntie Cee."

"What is all that you have?"

Kate smiled as Mrs. Tynan connected the TV and the VCR and plugged them into the wall. "We are going to watch a movie. Didn't you say Gloria Swanson was your favorite?"

"Oh, I can scarcely believe it!"

"Well, enjoy your movies, you two," Mrs. Tynan said when she was finished. "I'm going to the market now. I'll be back in a few hours."

So they watched. It was a queer film, with lots of erotic undertones: Swanson as a young girl being whipped by a sadistic woman in satins and fur. But Auntie Cee seemed enthralled, even if the screen had to be positioned only a foot away so that she could read the titles, which she did, out loud, in a slow, halting voice. When the villain appeared, Kate looked over at the old woman and saw how caught up in the story she was: her hands clasped in front of her, her eyes wide. Kate was glad she could offer her this little pleasure.

Then the lights flickered, and the power went off. Gloria Swanson suddenly went dark.

"Oh, dear!" Auntie Cee said.

Thunder shook the house as Kate lit some candles.

"Thunder frightens me," the old woman admitted.

Kate smiled, sitting back beside Auntie Cee. "Really? That surprises me."

"I hear things in the thunder."

"What things?"

"Cries. People calling me."

"Who?"

"People who've gone before."

Kate felt a rush of cold, despite the oppressive heat. "You believe there are ghosts here, don't you? You've *heard* them. *Seen* them."

Auntie Cee turned her weary blue eyes to her. "Yes," she said. "Of course I do. I've lived too long not to."

"Why are they so unsettled? Why aren't they at peace? What do they want from us?"

Auntie Cee closed her eyes. "I heard Edgar today, just a while ago." She touched her hair, trying to find the wisp that had strayed from her bun and kept tickling her face. "I heard him up in the attic. Where she kept him. My poor brother."

"What caused him to go mad?"

"Inger said it must have been syphillis," Auntie Cee said matter-of-factly, opening her eyes. "He was often away from home, and he visited the whorehouses with regularity. Everyone knew about it. Inger hated him for it." She sighed. "But it was when he strayed closer to home that really caused the tragedy."

"What do you mean?"

"Poor Edgar. I wonder sometimes what came first. The madness or ..." She looked at Kate. "He must have been mad to do what he did."

"Setting fire to the house, you mean?"

"Oh, that was after. After Inger found out that her suspicions about the children were true."

Kate was confused. "What? What suspicions about the children?"

"Edgar must not have been in his right mind. That's the only way to explain it. He wouldn't have done what he did otherwise. I have to believe that." She sighed. "My brother wasn't a bad man. He was just weak ... and women were his greatest weakness. Sometimes he'd bring them home with him. Young girls he'd meet in town. Oh, how it enraged Inger. Edgar wasn't thinking right. That's the only way I can explain it."

"But to lock him in the attic! How barbaric! And no one told—"

The old woman looked pained. "I *told* her that. I told her it was inhuman. But she said they'd just lock Edgar up in an asylum. What would be the difference? It would actually be worse. And the *scandal*—Inger wouldn't stand for scandal. You see, Edgar and Inger were very prominent in town. You have to understand that."

"But there are treatments for syphillis. He wouldn't have needed to be locked away in an asylum. This wasn't the nineteenth century."

Auntie Cee moved her sad eyes off to the garden, where the rain now fell hard and furiously, tapping against the glass of the picture window. A crash of thunder, and she pulled back in her chair. Lightning lit up her face. "Inger didn't see it that way," she said. "She wanted revenge."

Kate shook her head. "Revenge for what?"

Auntie Cee was lost in the horrible memory of it all. "And she was so strong, like a bull, Inger was. She just kept pushing at him, pushing at him, right up the stairs, all the way to the attic, and locked him in that little room. I'd hear him cry from there, and I'd beg her to let him out. But I'd had my stroke, you see, and I couldn't leave my room. Inger said it was for the good of the children, so they would be safe from him. But it was just her revenge. Oh, my poor brother.''

"Why didn't his son do anything about it? Bernard?''

"Oh, Bernard was too drunk to do much of anything.''

"He didn't want to help his father? He didn't feel guilty?''

Auntie Cee widened her eyes. "Oh, he felt *terrible* guilt. Terrible shame. That's why he killed himself.''

Kate's mouth went dry. "How . . . how did he kill himself?''

"He hanged himself in the basement.''

Kate gasped. *The hanged man.*

He was Russell's father.

"What would you say if I told you I've seen them, too?'' She looked Auntie Cee deep in her eyes. "From the day I got here. Even before.''

The old woman nodded. "I believe you.''

Kate leaned in close to her. "I've *got* to understand. Why did Russell's grandmother treat them so cruelly? Why did Bernard hang himself? What was the secret they feared so much?''

"The children,'' the old woman said plainly, just as thunder shook the house again.

Kate looked at her. "Russell? And Rosalind?''

Auntie Cee nodded.

"But why? What about the children?''

"Inger couldn't forgive them.''

"Forgive them for what? Just for having a mother who was beneath their social standing?''

Auntie Cee looked at her with such sadness. "It wasn't the mother. It was the *father*."

"Bernard? But he was her own *son*."

Auntie Cee looked away. "Bernard wasn't the children's father."

"Who was?"

Auntie Cee had started to cry. The thunder came again, but farther away this time. The storm was moving away. The power flickered back to life.

"Please, Auntie Cee. I know this is all so painful for you. But I need to understand."

Suddenly Edgar Wright was screaming in the attic again. They both heard his cries, causing them to jump and gasp out loud. He banged at the door, even though Kate knew it had been forced from its hinges earlier this morning. It didn't matter. That door would always be locked for Edgar Wright.

"Please, stop!" Auntie Cee called out. "Why does he cry so often these days?"

"Because he knows she wants to hurt us," Kate told her. "Inger isn't through with her rage."

"Oh, please!" Auntie Cee covered her ears with her hands. "Oh, please, make him stop! Make him stop!" She was crying uncontrollably now, and Kate knew she could bear no more.

"It's okay, Auntie Cee," she said, wrapping her arms around her as the old man upstairs continued to wail. "Please. Just answer me one last question for now. Do you know the name Theresa?"

The old woman looked at her. Tears ran down from her ancient eyes. "No," she said softly, and truthfully, Kate believed. "I don't know that name."

Erik Returns

It didn't take long for Kate to find out who Theresa was.

"Russell's ... *wife?*" she asked, in disbelief, as Erik sat beside her, nodding.

They were sitting on the stone bench in the garden. Thunder continued to echo in from the distance and the sky had darkened, but the rain had not relieved the stifling heat and humidity. Erik had arrived, thankfully before Russell had gotten back, and Kate took him immediately to the garden. She felt safer talking outside the house.

"And she came to you?" Kate asked. "At a séance?"

"That's why I came up the first time to see you. I went to see my friend Professor Stokes at Yale. He's a very powerful medium. We were searching again for the little girl, but once more someone else showed up."

"Theresa," Kate said. "Around the same time she appeared to me."

"Yes. She told me you were in danger."

"But how do you know she was Russell's wife?"

"She told me her name was Theresa Wright." He took Kate's hands in his. "So afterward, I did some digging. I went to City Hall and discovered Russell had been married before. To a woman named Theresa Hill, who died of heart failure."

"Heart failure?" Kate asked.

Erik looked at her intently. "That was the official cause. But I spoke to the police officer who came out to the apartment. Russell had called to report Theresa's death. He told me Russell was very distraught, saying he'd just found her dead on their couch. The officer said she was thin and drawn, as if she hadn't eaten in days."

Kate kept her eyes on Erik, not wanting to think where he was going with this story.

"The officer told me that he suspected that she'd been poisoned, but there was no evidence to ever accuse Russell. But the hearts of young women with no previous history of heart trouble don't simply stop."

"Oh, Erik," Kate said, and started to cry. "She told me he thought she'd been cheating on him."

"Sweetie, you've got to come back with me to New York."

She considered it. She could just run upstairs, gather her things, and take off with Erik before Russell even got back. Because it all made sense: Theresa appeared to Erik just as Kate, too, was slowly being poisoned.

But it hadn't been Russell doing the poisoning. It had been Rosalind. And the ghosts.

"He must have somehow been influenced by the ghosts of this house then too," Kate declared. "Russell wouldn't simply kill his wife." The words caught in her throat, and she started to cry harder.

"Sweetie, you don't know that."

"And you don't know that he poisoned Theresa! That police officer could've been wrong!"

"But she admitted it to you! That's why she came to you! To warn you about him!"

"I can't abandon my husband," Kate said determinedly. "Not until I know for sure what's happening."

Erik sighed. "Kate, you're taking a great risk."

"Maybe I am." She looked at him. Her tears had stopped. "Will you help me?"

"I'll help *you*," he said. "I don't give a damn about Russell."

She filled him in on all of the terrible events that had occurred, and all of the family history that she had learned, and all of the ghosts she had witnessed. "I believe the spirit of the grandmother is behind all of this," Kate said. "And it's not just me in danger, but Russell, and Rosalind, too. She hates them as much as me. Maybe even more. Just why I'm still not fully sure. But it's the only explanation I can think of for why Rosalind would do the things she did."

Erik eyed her. "Don't you think it's a little bizarre that you still haven't met this sister?"

"Yes. Yes, I do. But I think it's because she's somehow in the grandmother's power. . . . I think Russell periodically breaks free, but I think Rosalind is completely enthralled."

"Possessed, you mean? You think she's possessed by the grandmother?"

Kate shrugged. "You're the expert, Erik. Maybe I'm using the wrong terminology."

"No, from what you describe, it sounds like a classic possession," he admitted.

"How else to explain what she did to me?" Kate asked. "Remember, Edgar Wright tried to warn me even before I got here. Inger doesn't want me in this house, just as she didn't want Russell's mother."

An idea suddenly came to her. "That's it!" Kate exclaimed. "We need to talk with Russell's mother! She can tell us what Auntie Cee can't!"

"Russell will be angry with you," Erik warned.

"What will Russell be angry about?"

They both looked up. Just as the rain came, just as a crack of thunder overhead signaled that the storm had returned, Russell stood in the doorway looking out at them, his black eyes shining.

Russell's Lies

He wasn't happy to see Erik, but he masked his displeasure well. This was the man who'd said he'd never liked him, right in Russell's own parlor, in Wrightsbridge, under Asa Wright's portrait. Russell had neither forgiven nor forgotten. But he showed none of what he was feeling. He shook Erik's hand and even managed a small smile.

Erik was here to help, Kate told him. Help? Russell wasn't sure anyone could help, let alone Erik.

When confronted, he didn't deny having lied to Erik, telling him that Kate had gone into New York. "I don't know why I said that to you," he mused, standing at the window, watching the rain pound the earth.

"I do," Kate offered. "She wanted you to say that."

"Who?" Russell asked, looking back at his wife.

"Your grandmother." She looked from Russell to Erik. "You see? This house tries to take power over us. It's made us *all* doubt our sanity."

Russell sighed. "Yes, Erik." He leveled his eyes at the

other man, who was sitting too close to Kate on the couch. "I've come to believe Kate when she talks about the ghosts of this house, and their power over us."

Kate noticed that the two men continued to eye each other skeptically. She felt Erik still harbored deep distrust of Russell. But she believed her husband. She'd seen the power of the dead here, and she'd begun to learn the depth of the tragedies that had taken place in this house.

"Well," Erik admitted, "it *is* true that a place that has been the scene of much tragedy, or injustice, or suffering, can sometimes trap that energy, and visit it upon future residents."

Russell offered him a sardonic little chuckle. "One cannot begin to fathom the suffering that took place in Wrightsbridge."

"Why did you ever want to come back here?" Erik snapped.

Russell shrugged, looking away. "I'm not sure anymore. My sister convinced me."

"Of course she did," Kate said. "She was doing the bidding of your grandmother. Russell, you've got to find Rosalind. We've got to help her."

"How?" he asked, suddenly animated. "How can we help Rosalind? Tell me."

Erik sighed, leaning back into the couch. "Well, if she truly *is* possessed, then we would need to attempt an exorcism."

"Could you do that?" Russell asked earnestly.

"I've never performed an exorcism." Erik closed his eyes. Clearly he was struggling with the idea. "It's against what I believe in so many ways. I've always tried to make peace with the dead first, rather than attempt any kind of violence against them."

Kate moved closer to Erik on the couch. "But the

dead have attempted violence against us. Against an innocent boy from the town."

"Well," Russell sniffed, pulling away, "he was *hardly* innocent."

"Pulling up our rosebushes hardly mandated the kind of punishment he was given," Kate scolded. "Erik, do you think you could perform an exorcism on this house? Drive the spirit of Inger Wright away? Would that free Rosalind—and the rest of us—from her power?"

"I don't know," he said.

Russell had fallen strangely silent, looking out into the darkness of the night.

"Let me try to explain something," Erik said. "The dead aren't much different from us. Yes, they can do things we can't, but we can also do things they are sometimes unable to do. Such as understand a wider picture. The dead are often confused, and that is why they remain in one place. I suspect your grandmother, Russell, still believes she must somehow 'protect' Wrightsbridge, as she did all her life."

"Protect is hardly the word for what she did," Russell said, not looking back.

"Well, then, she remains as misguided in death as she was in life." Erik seemed to resolve on something. "Perhaps I can reach her. Perhaps I can reason with her."

Russell just laughed.

"I don't think Inger Wright was a very reasonable person," Kate offered.

"Well, I'd rather try that first before attempting any kind of violence against her," Erik said.

"What exactly would you do then?" Kate asked.

"There are various ways," Erik told her. "I'll have some books of mine FedExed up from New York." He withdrew his cell phone, excusing himself as he walked into the kitchen to make a call.

Kate stood and embraced Russell from behind. "We'll get through this, Russell. I promise you that. We're stronger than she is."

"I hope so, darling," he said. "I truly hope so."

He bent down, taking her into his arms and kissing her. More passionately than he had in weeks.

The Séance

The next day, Erik determined that he needed to talk with Inger. Russell seemed skeptical, but kept his reservations to himself. At dusk, Erik arranged three chairs around a small oval table in the parlor. In the center of the table he lit a candle.

"All we're going to do is talk with her," he explained. "There's no reason for fear."

Kate wasn't so sure. "She can play with our minds, Erik. She's done that before."

"I'm going to approach her respectfully. I'm going to ask her not to play any tricks. To simply listen to what we have to say."

Russell just laughed again, shaking his head.

"Are you sure Auntie Cee is asleep?" Kate asked Russell.

"She's asleep," her husband assured her.

They settled down into the chairs. "Now," Erik said, "we will all hold hands and concentrate. Clear your mind of all other thoughts and just follow my words.

And do not break the circle. No matter what happens, remain seated and holding hands."

Russell let out a long sigh but did as Erik instructed.

Erik cleared his throat. He took Kate's hand first and then Russell's. Kate's was trembling slightly, but Russell's was cold and steady. Erik realized his own hands were damp and clammy. *Why am I frightened?* he asked himself. *I've spoken with the dead before. I'm a well-known author on the paranormal. I'm not scared of such simple things as talking to the dead.*

But he *was* scared. Maybe Russell had unnerved him. But usually he wasn't so easily rattled. No, it was this house. He'd felt the malevolence in this house from the moment he walked in. Inger Wright was not going to be easy to talk with. But he had to try. He couldn't simply assault her without any warning. It went against everything he believed, everything he wrote about.

They sat in darkness, alleviated only by the small, flickering candle that cast odd, dancing shadows across their faces. "Inger Johanssen Wright," Erik whispered. Then a little louder: "Inger Johanssen Wright. We wish to talk with you."

There was nothing. Erik listened. He felt Kate's hand grip his tightly. Russell's hand remained cold and impassive.

"Inger Wright," Erik called again. "We are here to ask you to move on. It is time for you to go. We wish you no harm, only that you leave us in peace."

A small sound, from somewhere in the house. It may have simply been the electricity. Or Auntie Cee, turning over in her bed.

"Inger Wright? Is that you?"

Silence again.

"There are others in this house, too. Others who

have departed this life. Others you are keeping here against their will. Let them move on. We beseech you, Inger Wright. Let them go. It is time for all of you to move on."

The candle was snuffed out, leaving them all in darkness. Kate gasped. Erik felt Russell attempt to break free of his grip. "Russell, do not break the circle," Erik commanded. For the first time Erik felt Russell's hand grow moist.

"Inger Wright, you are here with us. Appear to us. We are not afraid of you. We know your pain. We know of your loyalty to this house. But it is no longer yours. It belongs to your grandson and his wife. They are here to restore Wrightsbridge. They will take care of—"

Suddenly Erik was blinded by a white light. It consumed him. There was nothing but brightness replacing the dark, and in his ears a horrible, high-pitched whine threatened to overpower his senses. He was falling, free-falling through space. The parlor had disappeared; Kate and Russell were nowhere to be seen.

The high-pitched whine became laughter. A child's laughter. It seemed to come from all around him. It would drive him insane to listen to it for very long.

"Inger Wright!" he shouted. "You have no power over me!"

He was suddenly confronted by an image: an old man's face, horribly gaunt and whiskered, several teeth missing from his mouth, his eyes mad and yellow. Erik screamed. He tried to find his footing, to stop his falling, and when he managed to do so, he began to run—run down dark, cobwebbed corridors, turning this way and then that, lost as if in a maze. He began to sweat, to pant for breath, all the while being followed by that hideous, high-pitched laughter. And it was getting closer.

He had run as far as he could. He was up against a door. The laughter, accompanied now by footsteps, was nearly upon him. In a panic he opened the door in front of him. A man dangled there by a noose, his face black, his eyes bulging out. Erik screamed.

"Erik!"

He felt himself melting. The laughter engulfed him. He tried to place his hands over his ears but it did no good.

"Erik, talk to me!"

He felt hands on him. "No!" he cried. "Stay away!"

"Erik, it's Kate!"

He tried to open his eyes. In the blackness he saw a figure in the far distance. It spoke to him.

"There is no reasoning," it said.

"Erik, are you all right?"

He opened his eyes. It was indeed Kate hovering over him. He realized he was on the floor. The table had been overturned, and the lights were back on. Russell stood a few feet away, staring down at him with unreadable eyes.

"What—what happened?" Erik asked.

"You suddenly collapsed," Kate said. "And you began shouting. Was it her, Erik? Did you see her?"

"I—I'm not sure," he said. "I saw many things. Horrible things."

"Welcome to Wrightsbridge," Russell said sardonically.

Erik looked at Kate. "Your husband was right. This is not a spirit with whom we can reason."

She helped him to his feet. Erik sighed. "I'll call Professor Stokes at Yale. He's performed exorcisms before. I'll—I'll ask him what I need to do."

He didn't like it. He didn't like the idea of perpetrating such violence. Yet it appeared the only way. He had just witnessed the kind of violence Inger Wright was capable of perpetrating herself.

But why hadn't he seen her? And whose laughter had he heard? It was a child's laughter, not a grown woman's. He'd never be able to forget that horrible sound for as long as he lived.

The Exorcism

It wasn't until the next evening, again at dusk, that Erik was ready to perform the ritual. It was still just as hot as it had been the day before. The storm hadn't broken the heat wave. If anything, it had only gotten worse. The mercury had risen to 111 degrees that afternoon, and Russell worried Auntie Cee would have heatstroke. Earlier in the day Mrs. Tynan had driven him into town so he could purchase a window air-conditioning unit, and Erik had helped him lug the heavy machine up the three flights of stairs. By dinnertime Auntie Cee's room was cool and the old woman was breathing easier.

The steady whirr of the air conditioner would drown out any noise from below—a good thing, Kate thought. The poor old woman would only be frightened by the strange incantations Erik would recite from his book on exorcisms.

"I will need a forked stick," Erik told Kate, and they both traipsed out through the meadow into the edge of the woods.

They stepped through the torn and twisted remains of an old barbed-wire fence. "This was where Bobby Shortridge had his accident," Kate said, feeling faint. Russell had described the tragedy to her. Rosalind had been with him. Rosalind could have prevented it. There was no blaming the grandmother's spirit for that. Inger had been very much alive then. Rosalind had acted entirely on her own. . . .

"Kate?" Erik was calling. "Are you coming?"

"Yes," she said. "I'm coming."

In the woods, she located an old branch that Erik said would serve him well. He snapped off the outer ends of the dry wood until the branch looked like a Y.

He looked at Kate with utter seriousness. "If at any point I feel a sense of danger, of not being stronger than the ghost, then I will tell you," he said. "You must get out of the house immediately."

"What about Auntie Cee? She can't be moved."

"I don't think she will be in danger. It's *you* the grandmother doesn't want in the house."

Kate felt the sudden chill of the dead. She had immuned herself to it as a girl. It was the only way she could integrate her ability to see the dead with living a normal life. But now she felt the malevolent coldness that Inger Wright felt for her. Kate prayed Erik's exorcism could work. He believed that if they could banish Inger's spirit from the house, they'd all be free. Kate, Russell, and Rosalind, too. Even more than they, too: Erik believed Edgar and Bernard Wright would rest in peace as well.

Erik had studied the paranormal under many experts, worked with many parapsychologists in the course of his career. He used to tell Kate that he wasn't afraid of the dead: they were just like us, he'd say, except in a different form of existence. The dead were no more evil than the living: but also no more good. If they were evil in life, they would likely not be transformed after death. And Inger Wright, as they all had come to believe, had been very evil in life indeed.

But now, after the experience of the séance, Erik admitted to Kate he felt a little humbled. "I feel like a pacifist during World War Two," he said. "The ones who were so opposed to any form of warfare who, after seeing the atrocities the Nazis were committing, suddenly enlisted and marched off to fight."

Inger Wright would not be reasoned with. The only way to fight her was with force equal to her own.

Mrs. Tynan had left for the night. The sun was setting beyond the trees, suffusing the house with a pale golden glow. Russell paced anxiously in the parlor by the mantel under the portrait of Asa Wright. Kate sat on the couch with her hands in her lap. Erik positioned himself in the front hallway so that he could look up the stairs while still being seen from the parlor.

"Are you all set?" he called to Russell and Kate.

"Yes," Russell replied.

"Do I have permission to perform an exorcism in your home, Russell Wright?"

Kate turned to look at her husband. He swallowed, seeming to hesitate. Part of her worried the old, coldly rational man might resurface, the one who would have balked at such goings-on. She feared for a moment he'd put a stop to all this madness, as he'd have called it then. But he didn't. "Yes," Russell said finally. "Yes, you have my permission."

Erik fixed his gaze up the stairs. "Very well, then." He braced himself.

Kate wrapped her arms around herself on the couch.

"Inger Johanssen Wright!" Erik called. "Your time has come! You must face the reckoning of the living!"

He raised his forked stick, pointing it first up the

stairs, then moving it around in a circle to take in the whole house.

"I abjure thee, I repudiate your power! Your hold over this house is ended!"

There was nothing. No sound. Kate felt her palms dampen.

Erik raised his voice. "Inger Wright, odious and contemptuous spirit, I command you to depart! By the judge of the quick and the dead, by thy Maker and the Maker of all things, depart this house in haste! Thou restless spirit shall no longer hold power here!"

Suddenly there was an awesome wind from outside. Shutters began to bang against the house, and the portrait of Asa Wright fell from the wall, nearly hitting Russell. Kate gasped. Russell picked it up and looked down at it, staring hypnotically into the eyes of his ancestor.

"Hear me, Inger Wright!" Erik continued. "Tormenter of virtue! By thy Maker be cast back into the outer darkness!"

A terrible scream was heard from upstairs. Russell made a move forward, calling, "Auntie Cee!" But Kate held him back, telling him it wasn't Auntie Cee. It was *she*. The Grandmother.

The scream sounded again, closer this time. A shadow moved at the top of the stairs.

"Defiler of innocence!" Erik shouted. "I cast thee back into the darkness where your punishment awaits you!"

The house shook as if an earthquake had rumbled beneath its foundations. The power flicked off and then back on. The chandelier in the dining room trembled, its glass tinkling, threatening to fall and smash into a thousand pieces.

"Depart this house, Inger Wright! Leave your family in peace!"

"Family?" bellowed a voice, deep and horrible.

Russell cried out, covering his ears. "It's her! It's her!"

At that moment she appeared on the landing of the staircase. Kate drew back in horror. It was the same woman she'd seen before: big and strong, with broad shoulders and a large, flat face, with enormous hands that she held out in front of her. She wore a plain black dress. The dress she'd been cremated in.

"They are no family of mine!" she rasped.

Never had Kate seen a face so consumed by anger and hatred. She dared to look over at Russell. His face had been drained of all color, and he fell to his knees, covering his eyes.

"Begone!" Erik commanded. "Leave this house!"

The dead woman had stopped on the stairs. She opened her mouth to speak and her voice, deep and cold and toneless, seemed to arise from every corner of the house.

"Do you think by casting me out you will be free? Are you really such fools as that?"

Erik made a motion toward her. "Do not play your games of words with me, spirit! Begone from this house!"

"Fools!" she shrilled, even as she started to walk down the stairs again. *"Fools!"*

Erik stepped aside as the dead woman made her way through the foyer. Kate watched her in mute horror. Inger paused as she passed the parlor and glared in at Russell. Her grandson shrieked, "No!" and rolled over onto his side. Kate ran to him. He had fainted.

And then she was gone. The front door opened and she passed out into the gathering gloom. Kate peered out the window to watch as the dead woman continued her walk down the front path and disappeared into the shadows near the bridge. The wind stopped then, and suddenly there was a palpable sense of relief in the house. The pressure had lifted. Indeed, the very humidity that had so oppressed them for days was gone. In its place, a cool breeze blew from the windows.

"Is it possible?" Kate whispered.

Erik sat down on the couch, winded and exhausted. "She's gone. I think she's really gone."

Kate ran to her husband on the floor. "Russell! Darling! Wake up, Russell! We did it! We've won! She's gone! The house is ours!"

But just then they heard a small, high-pitched laugh. The laugh of a child. Kate and Erik looked up quickly. There, on the stairs, was the little girl with the one-legged Raggedy Ann doll. She was laughing at them.

"Fools," she echoed the grandmother.

Then, with spritely little steps, she turned and ran back up the stairs.

Temperatures Rising

Those last days of June were filled with the monotonous drone of the air conditioner from Auntie Cee's room, the heat and humidity having returned, and the low but heavy sighing that Russell would make, stretched out on his bed in his old room. He had been unexplainably depressed since the exorcism.

Erik told Kate such depression wasn't uncommon. "If his grandmother had even partial control over him, the sudden withdrawal of her spirit could indeed produce a feeling of abandonment. He'll recover, Kate. Give him time."

Kate wanted to believe it, but the appearance of the little girl dampened any exhilaration she might have felt about the exile of Inger's ghosts. Kate had tried asking Russell about the girl, but he insisted he hadn't seen her, and knew of no little girl who had died in this house.

"One thing is certain," Kate told Erik. "He might not know her, but she knows him. She followed us on our wedding night. We were off-base when we thought she was connected to that cottage. She is from *here*. Wrightsbridge."

Erik conceded it seemed likely. "But she could be just a mischievious spirit, trying to stir up trouble. Not really evil. I believed we exorcised the true evil of this house."

Kate hoped he was right. But there was something she couldn't remember—something about the little girl. Had she seen her here before? Kate had a vague but terrifying memory, from just before she fell ill. Had she seen the little girl? Had she done something to hurt her?

Russell reported he'd been unsuccessful in locating Rosalind. She was the focus right now of the worries of both Erik and Kate. No one knew how the exorcism of the grandmother's spirit may have affected her. If Russell was depressed and he'd only been partially under her control, who could say how Rosalind reacted? But Russell said it was hopeless to try to contact her; Rosalind only came back when she wanted to.

"And this time," Russell said, close to tears, "I'm afraid she may never come back."

Two days after the exorcism the mayor called to talk about Old Town Day, now just four days away. Kate had to tell him that Russell wasn't feeling well, that he wasn't up to coming to the phone. "But we need to get onto the property," the mayor insisted. "We need to start setting up the stalls and the stages."

Kate still despised the man. She hadn't forgotten the sloppy pass he'd made at her during the picnic. He was a repulsive man, but Russell had made an agreement with him, and she'd abide by it. "You have my permission to do whatever you need to do," she told the mayor. "Just please try to be as unobtrusive as you can. I don't want anything disturbing my husband."

"But we'll need Russell to welcome the people to the estate on the day of the event," Mayor Miller protested. "Just as his grandfather used to do."

How insensitive could this man be? "Mayor, I've just explained my husband is ill. Let's hope he's better in time."

Maybe he would be. Kate hoped that by the Fourth of July, the excitement Russell had been feeling about the festivities would return. Maybe hearing the workmen hammering away on their temporary structures would rouse him out of his depression.

It was with some reluctance that Erik left to return to New York. He had a series of lectures to give, but he would have canceled them if Kate had wanted him to. She insisted that was nonsense. "It's a different place now," Kate said. "I can feel that."

"Let me know if you see the little girl. Don't hesitate to call me."

"You're probably right, Erik. She's just a little trouble-maker. Nothing to worry about."

She withheld from Erik the knowledge that she was still frightened by the girl, as frightened by her as she had been on her wedding night. No need to worry him further; he'd already done so much.

They embraced on the front porch just as the town trucks were pulling up and employees from the department of public works were carrying sawhorses over the bridge.

"Call me if anything seems out of place, sweetheart."

"I promise, Erik. Thank you again. For everything."

He smiled. "I love you, Kate. If I were straight—"

She laughed. "I know. And if I were a gay man—"

She felt like crying as she saw him cross the bridge and get into his rental car. But she blinked back the tears to greet the town workers. "Set up whatever you need, wherever you want," she told them, suddenly very aware of her status as mistress of Wrightsbridge. "Just don't disturb the garden."

The garden. She'd managed to replant some of the rosebushes, but didn't know if they'd take. Most of the spring flowers were gone, and in their place had sprouted white daisies and pink cosmos. Kate looked forward to some semblance of normality returning, getting back out into the yard, tending the garden.

But would it ever be the same between her and Russell again? She hoped that the horror of what they'd been through would only draw them closer together. Despite everything, she still loved him . . . though she had yet to forget the terror she'd felt toward him while he'd kept her confined to her bed.

He was under Inger's control then, Kate reminded herself. Both he and Rosalind had succumbed to their grandmother's control, just as they had as children. He couldn't be held responsible for his actions. The power their dead grandmother had wielded was considerable. *Look how she gave me those blackouts, removing whole portions of my mind. . . .*

Yet she couldn't shake the lurking feelings of fear she still had toward her husband, especially now with Erik gone.

She looked in on him. He was sleeping quietly on his bed. She walked up gently and sat down beside him, stroking his hair. How handsome he was. How innocent he seemed, sleeping here.

His eyes flickered open.

"Hello, darling," he whispered.

"Hello, Russell. May I get you anything?"

"Just sit with me a bit."

She did, holding his hand as he fell back asleep. *We*

have our whole lives ahead of us, Russell. We can put all this behind us. We've won.

She had to believe that.

When he was sound asleep again, she walked out into the garden. Beyond her in the meadow she could hear the workmen laughing to each other. The buzz of an electric saw burned through the air, once again growing humid and stale.

The sun had burned the grass, giving the garden a sickly pallor. She sighed, thinking she ought to haul out the watering can, when she was distracted by a ringing sound, something from the workmen in the meadow—

But it was Auntie Cee, ringing *her* bell, and Kate was standing in the doorway to her room.

No!

She was inside the house, when only seconds before she had been in the garden. Seconds—or hours—or days—

It can't be happening again!

Inger is gone!

Kate closed her eyes and pressed her fingers hard into her temples. When she opened her eyes again she was back in the garden, the workmen still laughing and banging their hammers, and the oppressive heat was still beating down upon her.

It was just the heat. Just my imagination. I've got to keep my head on right. I've got to stay clear.

But the ringing sound continued, and she forced herself to focus on it, find it among her thoughts. And then she realized it was the telephone, ringing from the kitchen.

"Russell?" she called, remembering as soon as she said his name that Russell was immobile, unable and perhaps unwilling, to move off his sweat-soaked bed. Kate ran back into the house to grab the phone from its cradle—

"Hello?" she rasped, out of breath.

"May I speak with Kate Wright please?"

"This is—"

"Mrs. Wright, this is Officer Piatrowski. I was there at your house the other night."

"Yes, of course, Officer. What can I do for you?"

"An Erik Narducci asked me to call. He's had a slight accident. He's been transferred to the county hospital."

"Dear God, no!"

"He's all right, ma'am. He was crossing the street to the train station when a car hit him. The ambulance took him up to the hospital, but I think his injuries were minor."

It's not over, Kate realized.

"Thank you, Officer. I'll—I'll call the hospital now."

It's not over, Kate thought again.

Of course, it *could* have been just an accident. But somehow she didn't think so. And she suspected Erik didn't either. She called the hospital and didn't learn anything. She couldn't drive Mrs. Tynan's car with one arm in a cast, so she called a cab. Russell was still asleep, for which she was glad. She didn't feel like explaining it to him.

When she got to the hospital, her suspicions were confirmed. Erik was being treated for lacerations and a sprained ankle, but his injuries weren't the cause of Kate's horror.

"It was the little girl," he told her. "I was crossing the street and I saw her. At first I didn't recognize her, just thought she was some kid in the way of the oncoming car. But at the last minute I realized it was her. The same ponytail, the same doll, the same evil little smile on her face. Of course she disappeared just as the car came barreling past, knocking me down."

"We've *got* to find out who she is," Kate said.

Erik nodded. "I think now we went after the wrong ghost, Kate. I think this little kid, whoever she is, is a whole hell of a lot worse than Inger Wright."

Family Values

The address in the phone book was 44B Morning Glory Circle. Kate found an old map of the town in the drawer of a desk in the parlor, but such a street was not named. Of course not. The map had been printed in 1955.

She walked into town, leaving the sound of hammering and sawing behind her. She had taken over all the planning for Old Town Day, giving her okay for the Ladies Guild to come out later this afternoon and set up the tents. She'd spoken to the amusements company to arrange the Ferris wheel, and to old Farmer Paulsen about bringing out his ponies. Russell remained depressed, just lying on his childhood bed, grunting replies to her questions and shrugging whenever she'd keep him apprised of the plans.

She *had* to get to the bottom of this. She had a feeling Russell wouldn't snap out of it until she had.

Thankfully, the day was warm, but not too humid. She stopped at the gas station on the corner of Main

Street. It was an old Texaco, with two pumps out front, and no quickie food mart inside. Instead, there was just a dirty oily desk with a cash register. Against the wall stood a rusty cigarette machine.

"Excuse me," Kate called inside.

A rotund man in an oil-stained T-shirt poked his head from the door that led into the garage. The T-shirt was so tight the man's nipples poked through, and a concave indentation announced his navel. "Can I help ya?" he asked cheerfully.

"I'm looking for Morning Glory Circle. Do you know where that is?"

"The trailer park?"

The words caught her short. "I don't know," Kate managed to say. "All I have is an address."

"Well, Morning Glory Circle's the trailer park. That and Honeysuckle Terrace. They named all them streets after flowers. Forsythia Lane, too. Tried to make it pretty for the folks, you know."

Kate smiled.

"It's at the other end of Main Street, out by where the river bends around," the man said. "You can't miss the trailer park if you walk past Town Hall and then under the railroad bridge toward the river."

"Thank you," Kate said, turning to leave.

"Hey, aren't you Russell Wright's wife?"

"Yes," Kate said, cautiously.

"Well, it's the same river that slivers down into the brook around Wrightsbridge, only it doubles back toward town after it cuts through the woods," the man said. Kate smiled, then turned to leave again.

The man followed her a ways. "You aren't going out to the trailer park to find old Molly Wright, are you?" he asked, rubbing a rag over his grimy hands.

Kate was about to tell him it wasn't any of his business,

then asked herself, what would be the point? "As a matter of fact," she responded, "I am."

"Jeezis," the man grimaced. "Good luck."

Kate chose not to pursue it further. She thanked the man and left.

They tried to make it pretty for the folks.

Well, they failed.

Morning Glory Circle was off Forsythia Lane, right after the slash in the sand that was Petunia Drive. Some of the trailers were up on concrete blocks, ruling over tiny patches of dusty earth, with scattered crabgrass and dandelions the only green in sight. A few homes had occupants who had given more care to their appearance—window boxes with flowers, a lamppost out front, a meager attempt at new grass. But most were rotting pieces of tin and wood, and the stench of cabbage was everywhere.

44B was behind number 44, a smaller trailer than the rest, covered with a pale green aluminum siding. It was obviously garbage day: all of the homes had set barrels of trash out at the end of the path. Inside the can for 44B, Kate noticed empty bottles of whiskey.

She knocked on the door.

There was, as she had begun to hope, no answer. She began to feel it had been a mistake to come out here, to interfere in Russell's past, to try and engineer a reconciliation that she hoped might make things better. It could in fact just make things worse. But at the very least, Kate *had* to meet her. She was her mother-in-law, after all.

Then the door opened, and she saw her.

"Yeah, what d'ya want?"

She'd seen her before. It was the woman from the post office.

People die there, she'd said.

"Oh, it's you," Molly Wright was saying, her penciled eyebrows arching.

Kate swallowed. "You're—"

She grinned. "That's right. I'm Molly Wright." From behind the screen door she looked even uglier than Kate remembered from that day in the post office: deep-set brown eyes like Russell's, but with dark circles under them and a nose blotched with veins. She wore screamingly red lipstick. "What can I do for ya?"

"Mrs. Wright." She could hardly say it. "Mrs. Wright. I'd like—I'd like to talk with you about—Russell."

"He send you here?"

"No, ma'am."

"He hasn't had nothing to say to me for twenty-five years. That's just the way it is."

"Mrs. Wright, I need to know the way it is. Please tell me."

The woman behind the screen door was obviously drunk. Kate could smell the whiskey even outside.

"He's a Wright," she snarled. "That's the problem."

Kate tried again. "He's going through a hard time, Mrs. Wright. I was hoping—"

"What? That Momma would come and make things all better? Oh, honey, things are long since past that bein' possible."

"I just thought—well, maybe you and I could talk . . ."

Molly Wright looked at Kate for several seconds. Then she exhaled some cigarette smoke and opened the screen door to allow her to come inside. "I'll give ya five minutes," she said.

"Thank you," Kate said.

She stepped inside the trailer and almost gagged. It smelled of cigarettes and whiskey, bacon grease and garlic, a heavy, choking, smoky odor. Ashtrays over-flowed with butts on the coffee table in front of the small plaid love seat. There was a flask of whiskey in the sink, and a plate with a half-eaten cheese sandwich on the floor. On the television, *The Price is Right* blared into the room: "Anna Maria Markowitz—come on down!"

Molly flicked off the set with the remote control, and gestured for Kate to sit on the love seat. The kitchen-living area was no more than four yards deep, and at its end a door presumably led to a bathroom and a tiny bedroom. A closet behind the TV set was half open, revealing flower-print dresses and overcoats crammed inside. On the wall to her right Kate noticed a plastic plaque, on which read: LIFE IS A BANQUET, AND MOST POOR SONS OF BITCHES ARE STARVING TO DEATH.

That's right, she remembered: *Auntie Mame.*

"So what about my son?" Molly asked.

"Things have been happening in that house, things I hoped maybe you could help me understand."

Molly lit a cigarette and inhaled deeply, letting the smoke out before she answered. "What the hell did you two ever come back here for? Why didn't you just stay in New York?"

"Auntie Cee needed care," Kate told her.

"So? Russell's got enough money to pay a full-time nurse."

"He loves Auntie Cee. He felt he owed it to her to be here himself."

"Ha!" Molly Wright stood and began pacing the small room, waving her cigarette. "He doesn't owe that old bitch a thing! What good was she to him? She didn't protect him from that horrible woman. I called Cee once, after I left, and tried to get her to sneak the kids out of the house. But she was too fearful of Inger." She made a sound of disgust. "Russell doesn't owe her a thing!"

Kate studied her. "Why did you never try to get custody?"

Molly spat into the sink. "Oh, I talked to people downtown about it. Don't think that I didn't. But Inger Wright was a very powerful woman. She made it known to everyone that I was an unfit mother." She looked at Kate squarely. "She was ready to use any and all information against me if I tried to get my kids."

"What kind of information?"

She was staring at Kate, then looked away. "I couldn't have taken them here," she said, her voice losing some of its edge. "Look at this place. I've been here for nineteen years, since the park was new. It wasn't so bad back then." She blew smoke up into the air. "It really is a sad thing how it all worked out. How much he hates me."

"Mrs. Wright, if the two of you could just talk, maybe—"

"What else he tell ya? About me?"

"Not much."

She squinted at Kate, drawing in a drag from her cigarette. "What did he say about his father?"

"At first, nothing. Just that he died. He lied and said a car accident. I only recently learned that he . . . hanged himself."

"Oh, *Bernard*—he told you about Bernard." She exhaled. "Of course."

Kate braced herself. "I know Bernard wasn't his real father. Does Russell know that?"

Molly squinted at her. "How'd *you* find out? The old lady?"

"Yes. Auntie Cee told me."

"I don't know what Russell knows."

Kate steeled herself. "Mrs. Wright, I'm Russell's wife. I'm concerned about him. He's depressed. I want to understand everything I can about him. Please. Tell me who his father was."

Molly looked at her, a naughty little smirk playing with her lips. "What if I told you—I didn't know?"

Kate folded her hands in her lap. "I'd believe you."

"Bah!" The older woman sat back down. "I know who it was. There was only one it *could* be. It sure couldn't have been Bernard. I don't think Bernard ever liked the ladies—*if* you get my drift."

"Why did he marry you then?"

She shrugged. "We were both drunk. I think he just wanted to piss off his parents. You know, rebellious little rich boy picks up the local tramp."

"Mrs. Wright, I know you loved your children. And still do."

Molly looked away. "I don't want to talk anymore. I want you to leave."

"Please, Mrs. Wright. Tell me what I need to know."

"The twins' daddy? Is that what you want to know?"

"Yes," Kate said.

Molly Wright stood, her face a mask of rage and grief. "It was Edgar Wright! Are you so thick that you haven't figured that out? Why Inger hated us all? Why she took revenge against all of us, even the children?"

"Edgar!" Kate gasped. "His grandfather!"

The tears were falling down Molly's leathery face. "No, not his grandfather! His *father!* Do you understand? Me and Edgar! Shall I act it out for ya?"

"No, please!" Kate stood. "I'm sorry, I'm just—"

"Just what? Shocked? Repulsed?" Molly laughed, dragging on her cigarette again and exhaling the smoke in Kate's face. "Not as shocked or repulsed as Bernard. Though it took the damn fool five years before he hanged himself."

Suddenly Inger Wright's evil seemed to come from somewhere; still inexcusable, but maybe—at least partially—explainable. "She lost her husband *and* her son," Kate mused.

"Don't you go feeling sorry for her!" Molly shouted, coming forward at Kate as the younger woman backed up toward the door. "Not after what she did."

"Mrs. Wright, please! I love your son. I know you do, too. Maybe he can somehow be helped by a reconciliation with you. Actually, it might help both of them. Russell *and* your daughter—"

Something seemed to twist behind Molly Wright's eyes.

"My *daughter*? Whadya bringin' up my *daughter* for?"

"Well, she—"

"Don't talk about my daughter!" she bellowed. "It's bad enough you comin' in here talkin' about my *son*, but don't mention my daughter!"

"I'm sorry," Kate managed.

"Go on, get outta here," she said, stubborn now. "Your five minutes are up. Way past up!"

"Fine." Kate turned to leave. "I don't think you'd be any comfort to him anyway."

"Tell him—" She had reached out and grabbed Kate's arm, preventing her from leaving. "Ah, forget it. Jeezis. It ain't my fault what they did to him. They did it to me, too, to all of us. We all got lousy lives because of that old witch—and even more because of that crazy old man. He was even scarier than she was. Don't let the old sob sister on the third floor fool you. Inger may have done something monstrous to him, but Edgar Wright was the real monster. Don't ever forget that."

She let go of Kate's arm. Her face was tight, and she stubbed her cigarette out in the sink. Kate watched her, fascinated. "Family ain't what it's cracked up to be, let me tell *you*, young lady," Molly said. "These frigging politicians and their talk about 'family values.' Makes me *puke*. Family's about hounding ya, and condemning ya, and trying to make ya be somebody ya ain't. They never liked me, never liked me from the start. My father was a bartender, an Irishman, a Catholic, for Chrissakes! Well, I'll tell you: *they* weren't good enough for *me!*"

Kate closed the screen door behind her as she left. In the still afternoon, Molly Wright's sobs echoed all the way through the trailer park.

Kate was still thinking about her, about how tragic Molly's life had turned out, when she began crossing the little footbridge leading up to the great house.

Her hand brushed the head of Michael the archangel.

But even before she'd made it across the bridge she knew something was wrong. Something was different. One of the angels on the other side looked different.

It was moving.

"Dear God," she whispered.

Lucifer stood from his crouched position and turned to face her. The angel with the broken wing. He was not stone, but pulsing flesh. He grinned, a mouthful of fangs, and lifted his talons as he bore down upon her.

She screamed.

And suddenly she was back in her room, writing in her journal at her desk. She gasped.

It's happened again.

She stood up quickly, her heart still thudding in her chest. No demon angel threatened her. It had been a hallucination.

This house hadn't finished playing with her mind.

She moved over to the window. The sun was setting.

I missed the rest of the day. Dear God, please no! It can't be happening all over again!

But it was. She looked out the window and saw not the garden, but a cemetery. A lone grave digger was stabbing the earth with a spade. There was a coffin waiting to be buried. Whose?

It's worse now! I'm losing my mind!

She was drawn back to her journal to see what she'd been writing.

Over and over again, three pages worth, she'd scrawled: *RW, RW, RW, RW, RW.*

And then finally, at the bottom of the last page, in handwriting not her own: *My name is Rosalind Wright.*

The Eve of the Fourth

When he was a little boy, Erik was telling them, he used to catch fireflies in a glass jelly jar with the label scraped off. Then he would set the jar in his room at night and watch them glow, a soft, pulsing light that made him feel happy, especially when his mother was in the hospital, which was all the time, it seemed.

"Of course," Erik said, "I'd poke holes in the top of the jar so they could breathe, and I'd put in a little water and some grass. And I'd always let them go in the morning."

Russell watched them, Kate and Erik, such dear old friends, sitting there knee to knee in the garden. Erik's crutch was propped beside him and his face was bruised from his car accident; Kate's arm was still in its cast. They looked like survivors of a cataclysm: Russell supposed in a way they were. They were talking about New York, about people he didn't know—names he'd heard before but whose faces were unknown: Clay and Marisa and Tomas and some old guy named Mr. Bell.

Oh, how they laughed, the two of them. How outside their little world Russell felt. He listened with interest to Kate's description of yet another blackout, of the vision of a cemetery here in the garden, but he made no comment. He listened to Erik pretend to offer explanations, hypotheses for the continued haunting of Wrightsbridge. But mostly he listened to their banter, their easy embrace of each other's friendship, and he was jealous. He sat away from them, his eyes on the sun setting behind the trees. He was close enough to respond when the scattered comment or question was tossed his way. But he kept his distance, watching them.

She kept secrets from me, he was thinking. *And now look at her with Erik. He says he's gay, but look how he touches her. The way he looks at her.*

Russell had not forgotten Erik's words to him: *I never liked you.*

Well, the feeling was mutual. Russell glowered at Erik. He more than disliked Erik. He *hated* him. Hated him as much as he'd hated Bobby Shortridge. For it was Erik who made Rosalind go away.

When the fireflies first appeared, hovering over the blueberry bushes, Erik had clapped his hands together like some little country boy and told his tender little story of catching them in the jar. And then Kate had turned and asked Russell if he'd ever caught fireflies as a boy.

"No," he said. "But my sister used to catch butterflies."

He looked back at the setting sun.

And it was glorious. Tomorrow was the Fourth of July, but no fireworks that the town would host could match the intensity and vibrancy of the colors now lighting up the sky. It was as if some frustrated painter had simply tossed all of his hues against his canvas, not caring where or how they might land, and then stood back, in astonishment, to admire this accidental beauty.

The Fourth of July. At long last, the Old Town Day festivities would return to Wrightsbridge. Russell looked out at the scaffolding and tents set up in the meadow. Pennants flapped in the warm night breeze; the smell of sawdust was everywhere.

Are you pleased, Grandmother? Are you proud?

But Grandmother, like Rosalind, was gone.

Because of them. Kate and Erik. *They drove my family away, and now they sit so comfortably, so smugly, as if Wrightsbridge belonged to them.*

He felt cold all of a sudden, and he heard an angry buzzing near his ear. He swatted away a firefly. "It's getting chilly," he said, standing over them. "I'm going inside."

"All right." Kate nodded, and she watched Russell walk across the garden and through the back door, the flip-flops on his feet adding incongruously snappy punctuation to his lethargic stride.

"He's still depressed," Kate said, almost apologizing, to Erik.

"Tomorrow, after the festivities are over, you've got to talk with him," Erik scolded.

She sighed. "I know. I just haven't had the heart."

"Sweetie, if he did indeed poison his first wife—"

Kate shivered. "If he did, it was the grandmother—"

Erik looked angry. "Stop making excuses. He was in New York then, not in this house."

"The evil followed him," she said defensively.

"We exorcised Inger Wright's spirit from this house, but still the evil remains." Erik looked at her intently. "Have you ever stopped to think the evil might be within Russell himself?"

Kate wouldn't look at him. "I love my husband."

Erik ran his hand through his hair. "Oh, sweetie . . ."

"There's been so much pain in his life. After talking with his mother—"

"Which you haven't told him about."

Kate shook her head. "Oh, I couldn't. Not yet."

"I wish you'd come back to New York with me tomorrow night."

"No. I need to try to find Rosalind. She's key to all of this. Why else would I write what I did in my journal?"

"I don't know," Erik said. "Somehow I don't think this sister will be found unless she wants to be found."

Kate looked up the side of the house. She saw a hand at a window—the same window from which she'd spied Rosalind before.

"Maybe," Kate said, "maybe she isn't so far away after all."

The Cemetery

At five A.M. the first of the trucks arrived, hauling the ponies from Farmer Paulsen's farm. The mechanics from the amusement company were next, testing the creaking iron gears of the Ferris wheel set up in the road. By six the Ladies Guild had arrived with their pies, dozens of them, and men in overalls began setting up the wheels of fortune that would win for some lucky soul Mrs. Tyrwhit's blueberry pie (fresh this time) or Barbara Lacey's cinnamon-apple crisp.

From the window in his room, Russell watched them all arrive. He saw Kate and Erik greet them, give them instructions on where everything went. There was Kate signing some form, as if she were mistress of the house. Russell drew back his lips, feeling them go white. He had to get out. He had to be free of all of them.

He had to find Rosalind.

He slipped out through the rarely used side entrance, which led only a few feet away into the woods. One could so easily sneak in or out of the house from this spot. Russell could hear the eager, excited chatter of the ladies setting out their pies. Barbara Lacey was saying it looked as if it would be a spectacular day.

"We'll see about that," Russell whispered to himself.

He wanted to go swimming. He'd head out to the old swimming hole, and he'd swim in the nude. He wanted to feel that cool, muddy water all over his body.

Rosalind had always loved to skinny-dip in the old swimming hole.

Pushing his way through the woods, he felt like a kid, as if it were 1975 all over again. He had with him his comic books, and he was going to lie on a rock and catch some tadpoles and maybe go for a swim. He saw the slit of water ahead of him, heard the gentle babbling of the creek that wound its way through the dry, crunchy leaves of the woods. He smelled the moist earth here in the deepest, darkest part of the trees, where the sun only intruded in patches, in startling spotlights of brightness. He could crawl up on a rock and lie back to gaze directly into the sun's rays, burning his eyes so much that when he closed them, he'd still see the sun, in a dazzling whiteness surrounded by a rainbow of reds, blues, and greens.

On one such rock, next to the pond, there remained, even now, the faint outline of a long-ago deed, something that made him sad to remember it. It was shaped like a comma, no bigger than the kind made by an old-fashioned typewriter, and probably no one else in the whole world could discern it but Russell. Yet there, on the rock lit up by the sun, was the mark of the dead tadpole, the tadpole he'd killed that long ago day when he was fourteen. He'd fished it out of the pond intending to bring it home, to watch it grow into a frog. But something possessed him that day, and he scooped the little squiggly creature out of his pail with his hand, and laid it down upon the rock. It shook a few times in the glare of the noonday sun, as bright then as it was now, and then it was still. The rock was hot, and the tadpole just a slithery comma. And it was as if that poor creature was now permanently etched into the surface of the stone, as if the rock itself had absorbed its tiny little life, preserving it like some obscene fossil to remind Russell, to taunt him, all the rest of his days.

It was not like Russell to do something like that. It was more like Rosalind. But by then Rosalind was—

Suddenly he heard a laugh from somewhere out in the woods—that familiar musical, cascading laugh, that laugh like a waterfall, like a hose of water turned directly at you on the hottest day of the summer. It startled him, but did not surprise him.

"Rosalind," he whispered.

But she was playing with him; she remained hidden. First he heard her laugh from somewhere in front of him; then, with a rustling of leaves, her laughter came from behind. He turned slowly in a semicircle, his eyes intent.

"Rosalind," he said again.

He began to run, his feet crunching through the leaves, snapping twigs. He ran through the shadows and through the patches of light, and he knew where he was heading, but not why. He knew Rosalind would follow, because she always did. He pulled off his shirt as he ran, heavy with sweat now. He let it fly behind him, and he imagined it getting caught in a web of dead limbs, a flag of surrender, dirty laundry hung out to dry.

He stopped as he entered the small cemetery on the other side of the woods, where the maples and the oaks and the elms gave ground to a forest of pines and blue spruces. Here the ground was soft and slippery with needles, and here old stones, dating back to the eighteenth century, protruded from among the saplings, forgotten graves of forgotten families, dead two hundred years or more.

Here was where those demon children had met in their secret clubhouse, where Rosalind had listened to them, found out their secrets. And here was where the Wrights were buried, where someday Russell's flesh, too, would rot.

Rosalind was leaning against the tall marble obelisk in the center of the graveyard, as he knew she'd be.

"Beat you, baby brother," she called to him. "I always *was* faster than you."

As he approached, he watched her long black hair wave in the air. She didn't seem winded from the run, just a bit flushed, her cheeks rosy and her skin just slightly raised with a few drops of sweat. Her arms were bare: her red lace blouse was sleeveless, tucked loosely into her tight jeans. She was looking down with her hands clasped, and he joined her by her side.

"Just paying my respects," she said with her usual little smirk.

He looked down at the inscription below the obelisk, and he read the names out loud:

EDGAR CLAPP WRIGHT MARCH 18, 1899–AUGUST
13, 1977
HIS WIFE
INGER JOHANSSEN WRIGHT JANUARY 3,
1920–SEPTEMBER 15, 1992
THEIR CHILDREN
JOSEPH CLAPP WRIGHT FEBRUARY 20,
1939–FEBRUARY 23, 1939
FRANCES MARY WRIGHT OCTOBER 2,
1940–OCTOBER 3, 1940
ELIZABETH ANNA WRIGHT JULY 14, 1942–JULY 14,
1942

GEORGE ASA WRIGHT March 11, 1943–March 19,
1943
HORACE JOHN WRIGHT May 5, 1945–May 7, 1945
IN SPECIAL REMEMBRANCE
THEIR SON
BERNARD EDGAR WRIGHT April 20, 1947–June 3,
1976
May God Have Mercy on His Soul

"May God have mercy on his soul," Rosalind said
bitterly.

Russell hadn't been out here since he'd come home.
He let his eyes survey the old cemetery, a place that had
fascinated him as a child, but that terrified him now.
He saw, not ten feet away, the Wright mausoleum, where
their great founder Asa Wright and his sad, pathetic
wife—Auntie Cee's parents—were interred. He saw the
angel and the devil battling for their lives, carved into
the fresco over the crypt's door. And he saw the word
in large, raised letters:

WRIGHT.

"Rosalind," he said, finally turning to look at her,
"we need to talk."

"About what?" she asked, not looking up from the
grave.

"About what you did to that boy."

"It all turned out fine, didn't it?" she asked.

"Fortunately. But what else is going to happen, Rosalind? I knew you'd come back."

She faced him. "You tell *me*, baby brother. What do
you think should happen?"

"I don't know."

"Kate's going to leave you, isn't she? She's going to

go back to New York with that friend of hers. You'll be alone."

"*You'll* be here," he said, in a low, frightened voice, the voice of the boy who killed that tadpole, sizzling it on a hot rock in the noonday sun.

"Oh, be real, baby brother. For once, be real." She resumed looking at the grave. "Isn't it interesting how they gave Bernard special billing, over all the dead babies?"

She threw her head back and laughed, and it terrified him more than he had been in a long time.

"Come along, children," Grandmother had demanded, her voice rough and thick.

They were trudging through the woods on a crisp autumn afternoon, when the colors were just beginning to fade. Everything seemed yellow: yellow sun, yellow leaves, yellow grass. Russell didn't like going to the cemetery. It usually put Grandmother into a particularly foul mood afterward. But to refuse to go would have meant a beating, or worse.

"Pick up the pace," his grandmother barked back at him. Rosalind turned and looked at him and made crazy eyes. He suppressed a smile.

"Rosalind, you go and pick some chrysanthemums around the mausoleum," Grandmother said. "We should leave some flowers."

Rosalind skipped ahead of them, whistling.

Russell followed Grandmother into the clearing, where the pine trees guarded the ancient stones. Work had just been finished on the tall obelisk and the ground surrounding it would need to be reseeded in the spring. But the magnificent grave was now complete, and Grandmother had wanted to come and admire the work she had paid so dearly for.

Russell had watched her face as she surveyed the stone from head to foot, noticing how diminished she appeared—how, just for a fleeting instant, when she looked upon the inscription, he felt sorry for her. *So many babies*, he thought. It was as if he could read her mind.

"May God have mercy on his soul," she read quietly.

Rosalind had come up behind them and was busy placing clusters of chrysanthemums beside the grave. "No, *no*," Grandmother suddenly harped, bending down and pushing Rosalind out of the way, arranging the yellow and orange flowers in a pattern she considered neater, more appropriate. "Stupid girl," she said.

Russell watched Rosalind retreat, and he waited for some reaction. But there was none. She just stood back and kept her eyes focused straight ahead, avoiding his.

Grandmother stood up. She was crying. Not noisily, and her voice was calm and even, but there were tears in her eyes. "Sometimes I think I should lose you both out here in the woods," she said, not looking at them. "You mean nothing to me. You're not my blood. You're the reason Bernard did what he did. My only son."

She said it so calmly, as if she were reading a prepared script. It didn't seem to disturb Rosalind, but Russell felt weak-kneed. When Grandmother spoke like this, it usually was a prelude to a beating. He tried to steel himself, but he felt too weak, too frightened. He was terrified of being lost in these woods. What if Grandmother made good her threat?

He looked around the cemetery, surrounded by the graves of his family. And he realized then that he had no family. Even Auntie Cee, trapped on the third floor, could not protect him. He was here, among the dead, vulnerable to his grandmother's wrath, and only his sister—his cunning, cruel, and yet much beloved sister—could save him.

"I look at you," Grandmother said, turning to Rosa-

lind, "and I see your white trash whore of a mother."
She turned to Russell. "And you—I see that bastard of
a father, that twisted beast who spawned you."

"But he was your son," Russell dared, regretting the
words immediately.

She hit him across the face with the back of her hand.
"You little bastard!" His face stung, and he cried out
in shock, gripping his face with both hands. He saw
Rosalind's face darken, her eyes glow with hate for the
old woman, but she didn't move. Not yet.

Grandmother had rushed off into the woods, leaving
them there, the evil stepmother hoping Hansel and
Gretel would be captured by the witch. But they followed
her, keeping several yards behind her, all the way back
to Wrightsbridge.

Now, standing in the same place, Russell turned to
his sister and said: "Don't leave me, Rosalind. Please
don't leave me again. I was desperate without you."

She was placing some daisies in front of the obelisk.

"Poor Bernard," Rosalind said quietly. "Our poor
brother."

"Our brother," Russell echoed, and he looked down
upon the grave of the man he had long tried to believe
was his father, but who had been, instead, his brother—
a revelation that had led poor Bernard Wright, so long
ago, to hang himself from a beam in the basement.

"Let's go swimming," Rosalind said, all at once, jumping to her feet.

"I—I don't have my suit," Russell protested.

"Oh, baby brother, I know what you look like naked."
She grabbed his hand and pulled him along with her,
back into the woods toward the swimming hole.

Russell was happy.

Kate and Auntie Cee, Part Three

"Auntie Cee," Kate said, "I wanted to introduce you to my friend, Erik Narducci."

"Oh, hello!" The old woman clasped Erik's hand. "Have you come for Old Town Day?"

"Yes, ma'am," Erik said, smiling and looking over at Kate. "It seems like it's shaping up to be quite the day."

"Yes! I can see all the people arriving down there now. It's just like it used to be!"

"You have a prime vantage point from up here," Erik said.

She nodded. "Oh, yes. I can see the pony rides and the cakewalk, and look! The clowns have arrived with their balloons!"

It was quite the show. The third floor offered a near panoramic view of the garden and the meadow. It was like a sky box at a sports arena. Auntie Cee wouldn't miss a thing, and everyone who came would be able to look up at her and wave.

Kate smiled. "The gates don't open until eleven A.M., but already there are people lining up in the street."

Auntie Cee beamed. "Oh, how wonderful it is to see people back on the estate. Just like it was before—before all the troubles started."

Kate sat down next to her, motioning Erik to sit as well.

"Could we just talk to you for a moment, Auntie Cee?" Kate asked softly.

The old woman turned knowing eyes to her. "It's Russell, isn't it?"

Kate nodded. "I'm worried about him. So I need to ask you a question." She paused. "Do you know where his sister is?"

Auntie Cee began to tremble.

"Does Rosalind frighten you, Auntie Cee?"

The old woman looked at her with terrified eyes. "She's come back, hasn't she?"

"I don't know. But I need to talk to her."

"No, no. You mustn't."

Kate took her old hands into her own. "Tell me, Auntie Cee. What power does Rosalind hold?"

"Where is Russell now?"

Kate shrugged. "I don't know. I've just been looking for him." She paused. "I think he's with her."

"Oh, dear. Oh, dear." It seemed as if for a moment that old woman tried to stand up, but then she calmed herself and continued, looking over steadily at Kate and Erik. "And on such a day, too. I should have known we couldn't bring happiness back to this place. Something always gets in the way."

"Please, Auntie Cee. Tell me about Rosalind."

The old woman sighed. "When Inger shut her up in that room in the attic, the girl was like a demon. Oh, how she fought! She was like a possessed *thing*. I heard the commotion. I heard the screaming. I saw Inger fall down the stairs and Rosalind leap upon her, like a tiger, like a lioness going after her prey. She beat at her face, clawed at her hair. And I screamed and called for her, but she just lifted her eyes to me like some wild animal, and I covered my face with my hands. The hatred in her eyes! For *me!*"

She was crying now, and Kate, for a second, wanted to stop her, afraid of where this might lead her. But she let her go on.

"But Inger managed. She got her up into the attic and locked her in there. What a cruel thing to do to a little girl."

"How old was Rosalind then?" Erik asked.

"Just fourteen." Auntie Cee looked hard at Kate. "She wasn't born bad. Please believe that. It's what happened here in this house that turned her that way. It was the only way she knew how to survive!"

"Mrs. Wright?"

Kate turned, startled. It was Mrs. Tynan in the doorway.

"I'm sorry to disturb you, but the mayor and his wife are here. And I can't seem to find Mr. Russell anywhere."

"All right," Kate said. "I'll be right down."

"We'll talk more later," Erik said to Auntie Cee.

The old woman just nodded.

"Auntie Cee," Kate said, standing and kissing her on her aged forehead. "I'm sorry if we upset you. Try to enjoy the day. This *will* be a happy day. I'll see to that."

Suddenly the old woman spun on her. Her eyes were red and bulging from her face. Her teeth suddenly elongated into sharp fangs.

"You will find no happiness here!" she bellowed in the angry, deep, cracking voice of a demon awakened after a long sleep. *"You will find no happiness here!"*

Kate screamed.

Old Town Day

"Kate?" Erik was asking. "Are you all right?"

They were in the garden. Music was playing. Flags were flapping. She saw Mrs. Tyrwhit carrying a platter of pies.

"Erik," she whispered, grabbing on to his arm, her heart pounding in her ears.

"What's the matter, sweetie? You just started shaking all of a sudden."

She looked at him. "It's getting worse."

"What happened?"

She was still shaking so badly she had to sit down on the stone bench. "The hallucinations. I don't think I can trust myself to get through the day."

Just then they were approached by Mayor Miller. He was wearing a white T-shirt that read OLD TOWN DAY in neon-green letters, tucked into absurdly multicolored bermuda shorts cinched together with a black belt. "Ah, there you are, Mrs. Wright," he intoned, his gravelly voice once again immediately having the same effect as fingernails on a blackboard. "I want you to meet my wife."

Kate looked up at them, trying to regain her composure. Her terror subsided before her dislike of the mayor. She clasped the hand of his poor wife.

"I'm Mae Miller," the woman told her. She was small, thin, and bespectacled, her little face dwarfed by the enormous yellow wide-brimmed sun hat she wore. Did she know about her husband's passes at other women? Just how much had he forced her to endure? Kate felt enormously sorry for the little lady standing in front of her.

"Pleased to meet you, Mrs. Miller," she managed to say, standing up to greet her.

Erik took Kate's arm. "Mrs. Wright just had a dizzy spell," he explained. "Are you feeling all right now, Kate?"

"Yes, yes," she said. "I'm fine. Mayor and Mrs. Miller, this is a friend of mine from New York. Erik Narducci."

The mayor shook Erik's hand, eyeing him suspiciously. "And where is your *husband*, Mrs. Wright? Our esteemed host?"

"I'm sure he'll be back momentarily," Kate said, not sure at all.

The mayor was beaming out across the fairgrounds. "Ah, what a fine day. What a glorious moment to see Old Town Day returned to where it started. The school parking lot just never quite cut it." He hooked his fingers into his belt and threw his shoulders back. "I so well remember those wonderful celebrations Edgar Wright gave the town. Do you remember, Mae, the year he brought in those circus animals? What a show!"

"I think that must have been Mildred or Pauline, George," his wife said, her eyebrows inching above her cat's-eye glasses.

"Oh," he said, caught again. "It was so long ago."

"I *do* remember the last year it was held here, though," Mae Miller said, looking over at Kate. "I remember Edgar wasn't well. It seemed all the joy had gone out of the celebration. Inger said how worried she was about his health. And it was right after that—"

"That's all right, dear," the mayor said, cutting her off. "No need to dwell on unpleasant things. The fact is Old Town Day has returned to Wrightsbridge, and I'm sure good old Edgar, wherever he is, is delighted!"

Edgar Wright was the real monster.

Molly's voice.

"If you'll excuse me," Kate said, "I want to see if Russell's back."

"Yes, of course," the mayor said. "Only an hour till showtime. We'll wander through and do a little glad-handing. Election Day's not all that far away, you know." He laughed in that horrible laugh of his. Kate couldn't wait to get away from him.

Inside the kitchen, Kate grabbed Erik's hand. "Something's wrong," she said. "Where is Russell? I'm frightened."

Erik gave her a sympathetic look. "I'll stick by you, sweetie. If you have a hallucination, I'll be there to watch over you."

Kate moved to the front window and pushed aside the curtain. "That's not the only reason I'm frightened," she told him. Her eyes took in the sight of some three hundred people waiting to be let onto the estate, and more were arriving all the time. "Something's going to happen. It's not just us in danger anymore, Erik. It's everyone who steps foot onto the grounds of Wrightsbridge."

Russell Returns

Russell returned just as the gates were opened and the citizens of the town flooded into the meadow behind the great house. There was much cheering and excited chatter, and Russell stopped in his tracks. Suddenly he felt the blood pumping feverishly through his veins.

It had happened!

It was Old Town Day!

Wrightsbridge had been returned to its old glory!

He leaped up onto a raised platform and began waving his arms, beaming like a proud father. "Welcome to Wrightsbridge!" he shouted. "Welcome, one and all, to Wrightsbridge!"

Kate watched him from some yards away. She turned to Erik.

"He's changed again," she said. "I can tell."

"Well, he's not depressed anymore. That's a good thing, isn't it? Isn't this what you hoped—that the day would galvanize him?"

Kate shivered. "Look at his eyes. They're not his."
She looked up at Erik. "He's seen Rosalind. She's back."

Erik put his arm around her shoulder. "We'll keep
an eye on him."

"I don't know what good that will do." She looked
back at Russell. "We've got to find Rosalind. She's here
somewhere. I know it. He's like this whenever she's
here."

She looked up at the house. Somewhere inside, Rosalind lurked. She had to find her.

"Welcome to Wrightsbridge!" Russell was calling out
to the incoming crowds. Some of them cheered up at
him, giving him thumbs-up signs and blowing him kisses.

Kate knew all at once that this was what Edgar Wright
had done, welcoming the townsfolk. In fact, as she
watched Russell, he seemed to fade in and out, becoming one moment the old man with his white beard and
jodhpurs, and the next moment himself again. Russell
had truly become the master of Wrightsbridge.

Their eyes caught. Kate tried to wave but his eyes
terrified her. She braced herself. Yes, she knew even as
it happened that she was hallucinating, but such knowledge didn't make the forked tongue that snaked out of
Russell's mouth any less terrifying, any less repugnant.
She just told herself it wasn't real, and it went away. But
she remained cold with terror, for whoever had the
power to do these things to her had the power to do
much, much more.

That's when she spotted her among the crowd. At
first she was just another child among the dozens that
passed by the entrance booth, happy little children carrying balloons and stuffed animals, excited little faces
eager for a day of fun and play. But among them she
stood out, her movements slower, more deliberate, her
smile not one of exuberance or joy but of deviance and

hate. There was nothing innocent about this little girl, whose legless doll she carried underneath her arm.

She's out there, among them, Kate realized. *There's nothing I can do to stop her.*

An Unexpected Visitor

"Can you believe it?" Russell asked, bursting into Grandmother's room. "All these people! Here, once more, on the grounds of Wrightsbridge!"

Rosalind was stretched out on the chaise longue as usual. "You did it, baby brother," she said. "You've returned the glory to Wrightsbridge!"

He beamed. "You *must* come outside, Rosalind. Meet the mayor! The members of the Common Council. The way Grandmother once did."

She smiled mischievously at him. "Isn't that your little wife's job?"

Russell snorted. "I'm embarrassed by her. She has no class. You were right, Rosalind. As always, you were right."

"Maybe next time you'll just listen to me, instead of always fighting with me?"

"I promise, Rosalind!"

She sat up, stretching in a long, catlike yawn. "Had you only finished what you'd started, Russell," she said wearily, "you'd be free of her by now. And it could have been me standing beside you out there. *Me*."

She stood languidly to move slowly, stealthily, across the room to admire herself in the free-standing mirror. Russell watched as her silken hair moved as she walked, the curve of her thighs, the cleavage of her small breasts beneath her red lace blouse.

"I'm sorry, Rosalind. I just didn't know what to do. I was confused." He moved up behind her and placed his hands on her shoulders. They were exactly the same height and had the same build. He kissed her neck. "I'm always confused when you go away."

She laughed, shrugging him off. She moved over to the window, parting the curtains just enough to peer down at the festivities. The music filtered through the walls; the shouts of happy children reached their ears.

"Look, Russell," Rosalind said. "Look at the little children riding the ponies. Do you remember when we rode the ponies?"

He peered over her shoulder. "Yes. I was terrified. But you reassured me."

"Of course I did. And you were frightened of the clowns, too. The *clowns!* Oh, Russell, what a scared little child you were. Thank God you had me."

He looked at her with utter devotion. "I had no one else."

Rosalind grew quiet. Her body stiffened. She began making a low growling sound in her throat.

"What's wrong?" Russell asked.

She was staring down at something on the grounds below. Russell noticed she began clenching and unclenching her fists, just as she would do when they were children and something would anger her, arouse her, offend her sensibilities.

"What is it, Rosalind?" he asked. "What do you see?"

Her voice escaped her throat in a long hiss, like the

sound of a faulty radiator. "She *dares* to step foot on the grounds of Wrightsbridge."

Russell followed his sister's gaze. He saw the reason for her anger.

She was out there.

With Kate.

"*Mother,*" Rosalind seethed.

"*Mother,*" Russell echoed.

Molly's Revelation

Molly Wright was drunk. Well before noon and she was already soused. Kate tried to escort her into the house, but she wouldn't budge.

"You're not gonna hide me away," she said, surly and belligerent. "I came to Old Town Day because I have the *right* to. I'm a citizen of this town just like anybody else."

"Of course you have a right to be here," Kate said, her terror only mounting. This was the recipe for disaster. She didn't want Russell to see his mother.

"So *you're* the great mistress of the house now," Molly was saying, and a few passersby looked askance at her. Kate noticed Mrs. Tyrwhit turn her nose up at her and move away quickly. The mayor kept glancing over at them, looking stern and disapproving.

Kate wanted to get Molly as far away from the crowd as possible. "Why don't we sit down over there in the garden, Mrs. Wright, and we'll have a cup of lemonade?"

Erik offered to get them each a cup. Molly reluctantly agreed to be led off to a quiet spot in the garden, among the remnants of the rosebushes.

"It's been a long, long time since I've been to this house," Molly was saying.

"Why don't we just sit here and enjoy the sun?"

Molly plopped herself down on a stone bench and lit a cigarette. From this angle they could see the Ferris wheel spinning around and around from the front of the house, and hear the delighted shrieks of its passengers. The sun was now directly above them in an unbroken vibrant blue sky. It was warm without being humid. A perfect day.

A butterfly landed on a nearby bush. Kate watched Molly's bloodshot eyes follow as the insect danced from one blossom to another, then fluttered off into the air beyond them. The older woman suddenly started to cry.

"I don't know why I came," she said. "It's just that everybody was coming. Everybody was talking about Old Town Day and going back to Wrightsbridge. The whole trailer park. The whole town. I'd have been the only one not here."

Kate felt compassion for her. She reached over and took her hand.

Molly's swollen eyes found hers. "I remember the last one of these things. The children were so small. Bernard put them on the ponies and I watched. Oh, Russell was so scared of them. He was always so scared of things." She paused, and her eyes became hard once again. "Who could blame him, growing up in that house?"

Erik had returned, bringing them their lemonade. Molly accepted it without thanks, and just held it in her hands, not drinking it.

"But Rosalind," Molly continued, the smallest of smiles creeping across her face, "*she* wasn't frightened.

Oh, no. *Nothing* frightened that girl. That's why Inger had it in for her. That's why Inger did what she did."

"What did she do?" Kate asked.

Her eyes moved past Molly, up the side of the house. She saw her clearly then, for the first time: Rosalind, in the window of Grandmother's room, watching them. Rosalind, a tall, beautiful, dark-haired woman in a red blouse. Kate's breath caught in her throat.

"She locked her in that room," Molly was saying, the tears falling from her face, unaware of her daughter watching them. "And they blamed me, I know! The children blamed *me*, hated *me*, for not taking them! But I *couldn't!* Inger wouldn't have allowed it. The scandal— that the children's grandfather was really their father! She'd never have allowed it!"

Erik had stooped down beside Molly. "Mrs. Wright, I'm a friend of Kate's. You can trust me."

She looked at him. "I trust no one."

"Try trusting me," he said, taking her lemonade and setting it on the ground. He took her hands in his. "Look into my eyes, Mrs. Wright. Look there and tell me if you trust me."

Kate watched Molly look into Erik's eyes. Erik was very good at hypnosis. He was obviously going to try to gain whatever information he could from Molly. "Look deep into the center of my eyes," Erik was saying. "Find the center."

She just stared into his eyes, saying nothing.

"Have you found the center, Mrs. Wright?" Erik's voice was low and soothing. "Keep looking. Keep looking for the center of my eyes."

"The center . . ."

"That's right. The center. The deepest part of my eyes . . ."

"The deepest part . . ."

"Yes. Find the center. Have you found it, Mrs. Wright?"

"Yes," she said dreamily.

"Do you trust me, Mrs. Wright?"

"Yes," Molly said at last. "I trust you."

"Tell us what happened when Inger put Rosalind in that room," he said.

Molly just began to cry harder, but she continued staring into Erik's eyes.

"They never told anyone, but I knew," she said brokenly. "I found out the truth."

"You can trust me," Erik assured her. "Tell us what happened to Rosalind."

Molly stood, her eyes wild. "She *died!* She died in that room!"

Erik took her gently by the shoulders so she wouldn't fall but she kept on wailing.

"They found her body! Inger killed her! *Inger killed Rosalind!*"

Kate's eyes darted back up the side of the house. Rosalind suddenly moved away from the window, the curtains falling back into place.

"Are you *sure?*" Kate asked Molly. "Rosalind is— *dead?*"

"Yes, yes! They killed my daughter! *They killed her!*"

"I was starting to suspect that," Erik admitted.

Kate stood up. "Stay with her, Erik."

"Where are you going?"

"I've got to go inside," she said.

"It's not safe!"

She looked at him intently. "I *have* to do it. I have to confront Rosalind!"

* * *

From the kitchen inside, the house was quiet. Only the hum of the refrigerator and the muffled sounds of music and merriment from the meadow.

Kate steadied herself against the wall. Rosalind was dead. Had it been a ghost at the window then?

She tried desperately to make sense of it all. Did Russell know she was dead? He *had* to. But he had *seen* her; she had *been* here. She had picked lilacs for the house; she had called Kate *trash*. So often had Russell talked about her . . . sleeping with men . . . traveling through Europe . . . poisoning Kate under the influence of this house! Had Russell in fact been living with a ghost all these years?

Maybe he *didn't* know . . . maybe . . .

A hand suddenly appeared from behind her, clamping its sweaty palm over her mouth. She tried to scream, but there was a voice in her ear.

"I've wanted you from the first time I saw you."

That voice. Slurred with alcohol. It was Mayor Miller. She struggled to throw him off.

He released his grip and moved his obnoxious face in front of her. "Mae's off with the girls," he said, the ice in his cocktail clinking in its glass. "How about taking a little walk with me?"

Kate's eyes moved past him. In the parlor beyond them stood the little girl. Kate gasped.

The mayor drew closer. She could smell his breath. "How about it, babe? We could have such fun."

"All right," she said, in a voice not her own. She could feel a grin twist her features against her will. "Just give me a minute."

She kissed him. Hard, passionately. He reacted with surprise but quickly recovered to slip his cold thick tongue into her mouth.

Kate recoiled, pushing him away.

The little girl was laughing.

And now Kate was in the parlor and the mayor was gone. Had it been real? Another hallucination? But she could still taste his horrid tongue in her mouth. The danger she faced had been ratcheted up several degrees. Whoever was haunting her had now progressed beyond inducing hallucinations into taking over her personality. Kate felt sheer terror threaten to seize control.

She turned in time to see Rosalind, long dark hair and red lace, moving through the shadows up the stairs.

Bobby's Instructions

Bobby Shortridge knew people looked at him, but he never really understood why. He didn't understand a lot of things. He thought he did once, a long time ago, before the snowmobiles. But he couldn't really remember. So when people looked at him he just looked back. Usually that made them run away.

When he'd gotten to the fair he remembered where she'd told him to meet her. Oh, she was so pretty. Just like he always pictured her in his dreams. So tall, with that long black hair, and those big black eyes. She promised he could kiss her if he did one more thing for her. Bobby couldn't wait for that.

She had told him to come through the side door. She'd shown him where it was the last time, when she had him play that joke on that boy. It had been a funny joke. Bobby laughed about it all night, but when he tried to tell his father about it, he'd just told him to shut up. His father was always telling him to shut up.

Bobby walked through the crowd. People were pointing at him but he paid them no attention. He walked off through the yard around to the side of the house. It was close to the woods. No one was over there. Just as Rosalind had promised. He opened the door and stepped inside.

The house was very quiet. He could hear somebody in the kitchen. He thought maybe it was the mayor, but he couldn't be sure. Besides, Rosalind had told him to come straight upstairs, to meet her in the room with the old-fashioned record player. So he went directly there and waited for her.

It wasn't long before she slipped inside quietly and sat herself down on the funny-looking couch.

"Okay, Bobby," she purred, "she's in the house."

He nodded.

"It's time we play another little joke. This time on Mrs. Wright. Kate Wright. You sure you know who she is?"

He nodded again.

"Good," Rosalind said. "She's heading up the stairs now."

"I getta kith?" Bobby inquired, his misshapen hands entreating.

She smiled. "Yes, Bobby. You'll get a kiss."

Kate and Auntie Cee, Part Four

"Oh, isn't it just wonderful!" Auntie Cee was exclaiming, looking out her window from her chair. "All of the people! There must be five hundred!"

Kate couldn't indulge her. There wasn't time. "Please, Auntie Cee. It's not wonderful, and I think you know that."

The old woman's eyes met hers. "She's here, isn't she?"

"You've got to tell me what happened. How Rosalind *died.*"

Auntie Cee put a hand to her mouth. "It was an accident. Truly it was. But they'd never believe the truth. That's why we had to lie."

"Even to Russell?"

She trembled. "Oh, I can't . . . I can't remember that. No, please . . ."

"You *must!*"

She looked away. "I think I hear Samuel . . . I think Samuel is home from the war . . ."

"No!" Kate stood above her, taking hold of her by her frail shoulders. "Please, Auntie Cee! You can't retreat into the past! I *need* you! *Russell* needs you!"

"Russell . . . ?"

"Help him now, the way you couldn't before." Kate sat down beside her. "Look at me. Tell me how Rosalind died."

The old woman's eyes flickered over to hers once more. They seemed to focus, to settle on the inevitability of truth. "It was an accident," she said slowly. "Rosalind was in there for three days, and she didn't stop screaming and cursing, banging on the walls. Oh, such words coming from a fourteen-year-old girl. But then the noise stopped. Inger thought she'd just shouted herself hoarse, and decided to let her stay in there another six hours, just to teach her a lesson."

The tears ran down her old parchment face.

"When she unlocked the door next morning, Rosalind wasn't there. But the old Murphy bed—it was *up*, not down. Folded back into the wall on its springs. Inger pulled it down and discovered Rosalind's little broken body inside. She'd suffocated to death. Somehow the bed must have sprung up, while she was on it—she weighed so little—"

Suffocated. She suffocated to death.

"I want to see a picture of her," Kate said.

Auntie Cee sighed. "There is only one picture left of Rosalind. All the rest are gone. One day, in one of her moods, she decided that the family would have no more pictures of her. Without our knowing, she stole each and every one of her photographs from all the albums and burned them." She shivered briefly. "She was such a willful girl." Auntie Cee looked over at Kate and smiled sadly. "But I had one she didn't know about."

The old woman reached into her blouse, knotty fingers slipping beneath the soft cloth. She pulled out a gold locket that hung around her neck. "Here," she said, holding it out to Kate as she unsnapped its lid. "This is Rosalind."

And what Kate saw in the small oval was an angel: a dark-eyed, dark-haired angel. She was what Russell would have looked liked as a girl, a girl of maybe ten, a girl with a smile so sweet—and in her arms she held a Raggedy Ann doll.

A doll that was missing one leg.

Near Death
Experience

She had to find Russell. She needed to confront him with this information.

The little girl was . . . Rosalind?

It couldn't wait, not even with all those people out there. Maybe even *because* all those people were out there. More and more the feeling was mounting inside her that something bad was about to happen, something terrible—

And she knew now the source of the evil.

It was Rosalind.

She heard a sound as she stepped off the staircase from the third floor into the second-floor corridor. A figure in the shadows in the closed-off east wing.

"Russell?" she called.

But not Russell. The figure lumbered toward her, and sunlight caught its face.

Or rather the twisted, pulpy flesh that had once been a face.

Bobby Shortridge's one bulbous eye gleamed at her. Kate screamed.

He was on her in a second, clamping his deformed hand over her mouth. She felt his long arms pick her up, throw her over his shoulder like a doll. She tried to kick, to break free, but it was impossible. With only one arm she was even more defenseless than she might otherwise have been. He carried her off into the darkness of the shuttered wing.

He threw her down onto a bed in one of the unused rooms. It was very dark, with only the slightest spears of sunlight making their way through the slats that covered the windows. The dust was thick and choking. The sounds from outside—the raucous band, the laughter of children from the Ferris wheel—seemed impossibly far away. All Kate could concentrate on was the heavy breathing of Bobby Shortridge looming over her.

"Bobby! Keep away from me! You don't want to do anything that would hurt me! That would get you in trouble!"

He just grinned, a revolting contortion of exposed facial muscles.

"Let me go, Bobby! Whoever told you to bring me here was wrong! They just want you to get into trouble!"

He moved closer to her. His hands reached out in an attempt to touch her breasts.

Kate managed to roll off the bed and position herself beside a table. With her good arm she lifted a lamp, holding it out at Bobby.

He backed up. He grunted, as if remembering this wasn't part of his instructions. Kate suddenly intuited that all he'd been told was to bring her here, that someone else would arrive soon. And she had a good idea who'd given him his instructions, and who her visitor would be.

Bobby turned and rushed out of the room, locking the door behind him.

It's just what he did to little Jimmy Parsons, Kate realized. *Except I don't think I'm meant to get out of here alive.*

But maybe Jimmy hadn't been intended to live either. Kate felt certain now that Russell had been in on that scheme with Rosalind—with whatever Rosalind was. But he had broken free of her somehow. He had had second thoughts—a conscience—and he'd found a way to set Jimmy free.

She could hear footsteps coming down the corridor. Strong, steady footsteps, not like the shuffling Bobby Shortridge.

She drew close to the door. "Russell?" she whispered. "Russell, is that you?"

The footsteps came to a stop on the other side of the door.

"Russell, listen to me. I am your wife. I love you!"

She heard the key insert itself into the lock.

"Russell, before you open that door, think about what's happening here. Think about the dreams we had! We can still be happy together! We can still win, if we fight her off together!"

The key began to turn.

"Russell!" Kate called, crying now, desperate. "I know Rosalind is dead! She's the little girl! It's she who's been terrorizing us! It's been a ghost you've been dealing with, Russell! *A dead woman!*"

She waited for the doorknob to turn, but it didn't.

"She's *dead*, Russell! And I'm *alive!* Rosalind's dead and I'm alive! *I* love you, Russell. She doesn't! Not if she makes you do these things!"

Footsteps again, faster this time, running away from the room back down the corridor.

Kate tried the door. It opened. She hurried into the hallway but saw no one.

"Russell!" she called after him. "Russell!"

Russell's Choice

Damn her. Damn her lies.

He sat in the darkness of one of the unused rooms. It had been Bernard's room once, he realized now. Bernard. His brother.

Where was Rosalind? He needed her now. Needed her to make sense of Kate's lies. "She's a whore!" he called into the darkness. "You were right, Rosalind! She's a whore!"

He had seen Kate kiss Mayor Miller. She was just as bad as Theresa. He remembered finding the scraps of paper with the phone numbers on them, tracking the men down, finding Theresa in their arms, just as Rosalind predicted he would. Theresa had cheated on him, lied to him, kept secrets from him, and now Kate had too. Rosalind was right.

Rosalind was always right.

The whir of the Ferris wheel and the music from the meadow made him feel only a little wistful. Oh, it could have been so different. He'd wanted it to be different.

He'd tried to start a new life, first with Theresa and then with Kate. But he hadn't been successful. He'd tried to get away, but here he was, cowering in the shadows of Wrightsbridge as he had done as a young boy, and out in the meadow Old Town Day was in full swing.

How had he managed to find his way back here?

He let his mind return to the train—to his freedom train that had once taken him away from this place. It was just an old commuter train, running along the Connecticut shoreline, making its hourly journey into the city. He sat beside businessmen on their way to work, routinely reading their *New York Times,* their sport coats neatly folded and hoisted up onto the overhead rack. They would return at the end of the day, return to their homes and their families and their lives—as would the wealthy Greenwich housewives who clustered together in the front of the car, on their way into Manhattan for a day of shopping. But Russell would *not* return, not for eleven years. He had with him only one small bag, and he didn't know where he was going, but he was getting away from Wrightsbridge.

The train passed through the backyards of suburban, lower-middle-class homes. Watching out the window, Russell felt like a voyeur, seeing parts of people's lives he wasn't supposed to see. Yet instead of guilt, he felt privileged to have such a glimpse: the backyard swing set, the garbage cans, the broken flowerpots, and the rusting toolsheds. This was *real* life, the way people *really* lived, not the manicured facade presented by their front yards. Backyards, however, offered to strangers a glimpse into the *real* lives of people, littered with bikes missing wheels, forgotten toys, and composts.

Russell remembered, even now, the little boy he'd spotted in one backyard, swinging idly on an old rusty swing set behind a one-story house. The boy had seemed lost in thought, oblivious to his surroundings, unenthusiastic about his swinging. He didn't even look up as the train whizzed past his house. It must have become so routine for him: the clatter of the tracks, the blowing of the horn. He didn't raise his eyes in excitement at the approach of the train, as most children would: it was something he heard every day, several times a day, and it brought him no joy.

Oh, how Russell had wanted to call out to him, to tell him to look up, to hop onto the train with him: "It can take you away, too," he wanted to shout out at him. "It can save your life, too."

But as the train got closer to New York, passing through the Bronx, his hope had turned to fear. For here, seeing into the hundreds of windows of decaying brownstone apartment buildings, he saw even more despair than he'd seen on the face of the little boy. He could smell the poverty, even in the security of the train that whisked them cleanly in and out of the ghetto without stopping, carrying its businessmen and Greenwich housewives. He saw no human beings among the tenements, just empty, monstrous brownstone apartments, dozens of them, scratching at the overcast sky.

Then, in one window, a flowerpot caught his eye, a flash of red geranium. It had made him want to cry, this meager attempt at beauty, this momentary grasp of life amid death. Yet it made him happy, in some small way, and the hope returned.

You can make your own beauty, your own joy. You can find your own happiness.

Who had said that? Theresa? Kate? He wasn't sure. But there was no joy—could never be any joy for him—without Rosalind.

Oh, how he hated Grandmother for lying to him. Telling him she'd sent Rosalind away to boarding school in Europe. Oh, he'd believed her at first, and he would cry himself to sleep imagining his sister walking the streets of Paris, carefree and gay, laughing with an entourage of beaus, flirting outrageously. Why did she never write him? Had she forgotten him? Abandoned him to survive the horrors of Wrightsbridge on his own?

But then he'd come to realize that Grandmother had been lying. Rosalind had never gone away. Rosalind was still there, with him. As always.

"Don't ever leave me, Rosalind," he'd cried, after a beating with a hairbrush that had left welts on his legs and rump. Rosalind had been beaten, too, but she didn't cry, not like her sissy brother Russell. No, she just staggered back into her room and found her Raggedy Ann doll in her toy chest, and without saying a word, pulled off one of its legs.

"Please, Rosalind!" he begged. "Don't ever leave me!"

"Not if you never leave me," she'd snarled back at him.

He looked up now into the darkness. He knew this was the end. There was only her way now.

The door opened from the hallway, and light sliced its way into the darkness. Rosalind stood there, waiting for him.

"Are you ready, baby brother?" she called to him.

He took one last breath, letting it out slowly.

"Yes, Rosalind," he answered. "I'm ready."

Russell's Room

"Kate!" Erik called. "Are you all right?"

He had just come up the stairs and saw her staggering down the hallway. She nearly cried when she saw him. She fell into his arms.

"Oh, Erik!"

"Your cast," he said, examining her arm. "It's been damaged."

"Never mind that now. We've got to find Russell."

"What happened?"

The tears came but they didn't stop her from walking. "He tried to kill me. He had Bobby Shortridge abduct me."

"Dear God! I knew when you didn't come back outside something was going on! Let me get the police!"

"No!" she snapped. "There's more."

She quickly filled him in on the little girl and Rosalind. She made her way down the corridor to Russell's old room and pushed open the door.

"He may be dangerous," Erik warned.

"Russell!" she called.

He didn't appear to be in here either. Kate let out a long sigh. "What I don't understand," she said, opening Russell's boyhood closet, "is if Rosalind died at age fourteen, why have I seen her both at that age *and* as an adult woman?"

"That *is* strange," Erik admitted. "Are you sure it was her you saw at the window and on the stairs?"

"Yes. And I've had glimpses of her as an adult before today as well." She made a face in confusion. "But she never *lived* to be an adult. How is it possible then to see her that way?"

Erik shook his head. "That's apparently how Russell has been seeing her too."

"But Russell isn't the only one who's seen her as an adult!" Kate said suddenly. "Jimmy Parsons saw her! He said it was a lady who chased him up the stairs. And she coerced Bobby Shortridge into doing her dirty work for her!"

Kate peered into the darkness of the closet. A stack of old comic books, each carefully sealed in plastic, slid over into a mess at her feet. *Nothing there,* she told herself, *no one hiding inside.* Where could Russell be?

She leaned against the door while Erik continued looking inside the closet. "It was *Rosalind* who didn't want me here. *Rosalind.* She's jealous of me, Erik. She doesn't want Russell with any woman."

"Like Theresa," Erik reminded her.

Kate felt as if she might cry. "She made Russell kill Theresa."

Erik sighed. "I've never known a ghost to do such a thing. Kate, I'm sorry to say this, but we can't absolve Russell of responsibility here. In his own mind—"

He stopped.

"What is it, Erik?"

"Look," he said softly.

Kate turned her eyes. There, in the back of the closet, hanging behind an old tweed jacket, was a red lace blouse. Erik stooped down and retrieved something else.

It was a long black wig.

Auntie Cee and Rosalind

Finally, they left the room, those nosy intruders. She slipped back into Russell's room as soon as they were out of earshot. She'd deal with them.

They'd left her clothes where she'd hung them. Had they seen them? She didn't care, not anymore. It was too late to care.

Yes, she'd deal with Kate and Erik. Russell was counting on her to deal with them.

But first things first, she told herself as she slipped her red lace blouse over her head. First she had to pay a call on Auntie Cee.

She had yet to see the dear old girl. All this time back in Wrightsbridge and not once had she gone up to the third floor to say hello to her aunt. To look down at her and thank her—for all she did to protect her and Russell.

Thanks for nothing, if truth be known.

Her footsteps echoed dully up the stairs and then

down the old wooden floorboards of the third-floor hallway.

Auntie Cee was watching the festivities below through her picture window. The band was playing "Happy Days Are Here Again." Laughter and merriment wafted up through the window. The sun filled the room.

She walked up behind the old woman without being heard.

"Hello, Auntie Cee."

She turned around in her chair. Her ancient eyes lifted and then grew wide.

"Oh, dear," she said, her hands trembling as she moved them to her face.

She smiled as she came ever closer. "Aren't you glad to see me, Auntie Cee?"

"Oh, dear," Auntie Cee said. "Oh, dear dear dear dear dear . . ."

The Mayor

Old Mayor Miller was certainly winded from three flights of stairs, but he had waited long enough for that tasty little wife of Russell's. It had been nearly an hour now since she'd planted that smacker on his lips, and he'd been waiting eagerly for her to come back downstairs. But no sign of her. She must be playing with him. Bad little girl . . .

Hey, the way she'd kissed him, he *knew* she wanted more. He might not have the body and looks he once had, back when he was the star quarterback of the county high school football team, but he *was* the mayor after all, and women went weak in the knees in the presence of a little power. He smiled to himself. He liked nothing better than the idea of porking Russell Wright's wife right here in Wrightsbridge while her husband was outside well-wishing the guests who were still streaming onto his lawn.

He took another sip of his whiskey. Mae was already starting to nag him that he'd had enough, but he paid her no mind. A little whiskey gave him the balls to do what he had to do.

Which was to find Kate Wright.

God, she had tasted *good*. He hadn't had any chicken that young and sweet in a long, long time.

Maybe the old lady knew where she was. All day long people had been waving up at her sitting there in her chair on the third floor. He'd pay her a courtesy call. Nothing wrong in that. He was the goddamn mayor, after all. He could do what he liked, go where he pleased. He'd find out from the old bitch where that tasty little treat Kate was hiding out, and then track her down.

But as the mayor approached Auntie Cee's room, it seemed dark.

He tapped lightly on the door, which was ajar.

"Miss Cee?"

The curtains had been drawn. Maybe the old lady was taking a nap.

But then he detected motion. He peered in through the darkness.

"Miss Cee?" he called again.

In the dimness he made out a figure. It was a woman. Red lace.

She put on red lace for me. . . .

He felt a leap in his pants. Taking a few steps inside, he smelled talcum powder and something else. Something heavy like incense. A kind of perfume, he thought. Maybe they'd moved the old woman to another room. Maybe this was where Kate planned their rendezvous. . . . Kinky, he thought, but he liked it.

Suddenly the door behind him slammed shut.

"Hey?" he called out. "Kate?"

"Over here," came a whisper.

"Put on the light," he said. "I can't see."

She laughed at him.

"You're a naughty girl," he said, feeling the grin push against his cheeks, "but you sure have me going."

He bumped into something and his drink fell from his hand.

"Shit!" He looked around blindly. "Where are you?"

Without warning the curtains were suddenly pulled open and bright sunlight returned to the room. He blinked against it, then looked down at what he had bumped into.

It was the lifeless body of Auntie Cee in her chair, her eyes and mouth open in terror.

"Sweet Jesus!" he screamed, then turned to see the thing that was approaching him.

"No!" he shouted. "Stay away from me!"

The thing advanced.

"Stay away—"

The mayor backed up toward the picture window.

Another Death at Wrightsbridge

Below, in the garden, Mrs. Tyrwhit was talking with the Lacey sisters, and they were in a heated discussion over whose pie ought to be auctioned off as part of the raffle. Beatrice Lacey had just said something mildly insulting about Mrs. Tyrwhit's crust, and the old dowager was getting ready to storm off in a huff, when they heard the crash overhead.

At first Mrs. Tyrwhit thought someone had thrown a stone at her.

But it was glass.

In the rain shower of glass that followed, all three women would sustain injuries, Mrs. Tyrwhit eventually losing an eye because of it. But they counted themselves lucky: for had they been standing only a few feet to their left, the body of the mayor would have come crashing down upon them, and certainly they'd be dead. As dead as he was.

No one at that year's Old Town Day celebration would ever be able to forget the harrowing scream or the thuddering crash that the mayor made as he fell three stories into the garden. His head actually separated from his body, rolling some twenty feet away from the scene to come to rest at the foot of a clown.

The screaming started then.

Panic and the Police

Kate had seen him fall, smashing out of Auntie Cee's window. She had returned to the garden to sit with Molly Wright, and she'd stood in horror, unable to make any sound. Molly had sat there watching as well, unmoving, unblinking, as if she weren't in the least bit surprised to see such tragedy once again unfold at Wrightsbridge.

It's just a hallucination, Kate told herself, *just another of those horrible hallucinations.* But no, this was real: this was happening. The sudden rush of people, the screaming, the sirens all at once filling the air.

She looked around for Erik. In the crush of people, she couldn't find him. Cries of terror now bounced off the walls of the great old house, replacing the laughter and cheers of just minutes before. The on-duty police guards had called in more officers, who now swarmed onto the estate in large numbers, ordering people back. Kate hurried to the scene, spotting Officer Piatrowski.

"What's happened?" she cried.

"Mrs. Wright! Where's your husband?"

"I don't know. What's happened?"

"The mayor's dead," Piatrowski told her.

She looked into the garden. The garden she had once tried to restore, tending so carefully, with such hope and so many dreams. There was never any beauty there, she realized. It was useless to try to create any. The mayor's blood now covered the daisies and the daylilies, and his headless body was twisted in an obscene position, embedded into the earth.

"Auntie Cee," Kate whispered, looking up at the shattered window above.

Piatrowski escorted her into the house, where policemen were already tracking muddy footprints across the kitchen and into the parlor. Mrs. Tynan stood at the foot of the steps, her face white.

"She's dead!" she cried when she saw Kate. "Miss Cecilia is dead!"

Kate grabbed her by the shoulders. "What do you mean?"

The nurse was distraught. "I should have known from the moment I took this job! I saw the ghosts! I saw the misery! I should have known this kind of tragedy would happen!"

Mrs. Tynan burst into tears and ran from the house. Kate looked after her for just a second, then raced up the stairs, following the army of policemen.

She found Auntie Cee still in her chair, a look of terror on her dead face. Kate knelt down in front of her and took her hand in hers, pressing it up against her face. She began to cry. Gently she reached up with her good arm and closed the old woman's eyelids. "Sleep well, Auntie Cee," she whispered. She was with her beloved Samuel now. "The nightmare is over for you."

But not for the rest of them.

Piatrowski was conferring with a few of the officers and then turned to Kate. "We're getting the coroner up here, but it looks as if Miss Cee died of a heart attack," he told her. "Maybe the mayor found her and was startled—"

Kate looked up at him. She knew the truth was much more fearful than that. She stood, walking over to the shattered window. Here Auntie Cee had looked down upon the garden for decades. Quiet decades, but she had known the horrors had never really left Wrightsbridge. She'd known they'd come back.

"Look at this," one of the policemen said. Kate turned. He had observed a glass on the floor. A spilled drink. "The mayor was pretty drunk," the officer was saying. "Lots of folks saw him stumbling around, and this glass here sure smells like whiskey."

"He was toasted," another policeman concurred. "That explains it. He freaked when he found the old lady dead and fell out the window."

But Kate knew it was much more than that.

"Mrs. Wright?" Officer Piatrowski had come up behind her. "We're going to need to question both you and your husband. Any idea where he is?"

She just shook her head slowly. She looked again at the terrified face of Auntie Cee.

What had she seen in the moment before her death?

Molly Returns

The crowd was being evacuated from the estate but Molly Wright slipped into the house, allowed to enter by a policeman who recognized her as one of the family, even if she hadn't been part of it in years. They were stringing yellow police tape around the house now. A crime scene. *It's been so for years,* Molly thought.

She wasn't heading to the old lady's room. What was there for her to see? She'd heard that Cee was dead, but she would shed no tears for her. She could've helped those children more than she did. *She could've helped me,* Molly thought bitterly to herself.

She climbed the stairs slowly, one at a time, as policemen thudded past her in both directions. *Look at all the mud they've tracked in, Inger,* Molly laughed to herself. *Your precious Wrightsbridge, overrun with us common folk.*

She was looking for her son. She didn't know if his wife was right—that somehow she could help him. But she thought maybe she wanted to try. Ever since Kate had come to see her, she couldn't stop thinking about

Russell—about that scared little boy who had cried as she was leaving, his little hands imploring her to take him with her.

Oh, if only I could have, Russell. Everything might have been different. . . .

Molly couldn't imagine what she could do for Russell now. She knew he'd hated her all these years. The one time she'd seen him, when he was a teenager, she'd tried to approach him on the street, but he'd cut her dead. "We don't talk to trash," he'd said.

Molly had always wondered about that "we." Why did she have the sense he meant himself and Rosalind? But Rosalind had been dead by that time.

She entered Russell's room. Once, years ago, she'd tucked him into bed in this room, sung him lullabies . . .

You're being a damn fool, she chided herself. *A damn drunken old fool.*

On his bed she noticed a pair of khaki shorts, a T-shirt, and men's underwear, all hastily clumped in a pile, as if the wearer had taken them off in a hurry. She turned to leave, and noticed a jar of perfume on top of the bureau. A jar she recognized. She sniffed it. It took her back years, to the early days of her marriage to Bernard, when the children were babies. A heavy, tangy Indian fragrance that she used to wear all the time. What was it doing in Russell's room?

"What am I doing in this house?" she said, starting to cry a little.

And then she knew where she had to go.

Molly continued up the stairs to the third floor. She paused only briefly on the third floor, peering into Auntie Cee's room to glimpse the police officers questioning Kate. *That'll keep them occupied for a while,* she thought.

She pulled open the door to the attic steps. It creaked, and she turned around to make sure she hadn't been heard. The coast was clear. She walked up the narrow steps.

The attic was hot and the air was stale. She coughed a little from all the dust. In the dim light she made out the room. How she had hated coming up here, bringing that old monster his meals. Slipping them through that little grate on the door. How he'd bang at the door, plead to be let out.

"I hope you rot in there," Molly had spat.

He had, of course. When the paper printed Edgar Wright's obituary, it made it seem as if the old man had died peacefully in his bed, surrounded by his loving family. Molly knew he'd died up here, alone, his mind and body eaten up with disease and guilt.

In the same cell where her daughter would also die. Her Rosalind.

She stood looking into the little room. Its door had been forced from its hinges, and it hung at an odd angle. She peered inside, recoiling for a moment from the stench of urine.

"Oh, my baby," she said softly.

She *did* come back for them. She *did* try. She had saved some money, and she snuck into the house one day when she knew Inger was in town. The children would be in school, and she knew it would just be Auntie Cee on the third floor. She snuck in and surprised her and told her she was there for the children. Would Cee help? Would she tell the children to meet her at the bridge that night? *Please, Cee, will you help them escape?*

But that's when the old woman had started crying. Rosalind was dead, she told Molly. Just a few nights previous. She was too late. Rosalind was dead.

Here, in this room.

Where her monstrous father had gone mad and died himself.

Molly stood over the rusted Murphy dead. She ran

her fingers across its musty, moldy mattress. She began to cry. She sat down and covered her face in her hands.

"Mother."

She looked up.

A little girl, with dark hair and dark eyes, holding a doll.

"Rosalind?"

The girl approached her.

"Have you come back, Mother? Have you come back for me?"

Molly didn't feel fear. Maybe it was just one of her drunken hallucinations. But she didn't care. It was her daughter, and she was there with her. She held out her arms to the child.

The little girl fell into them.

"Will you take us away from here, Mother? Will you take us away?"

"Yes," Molly said dreamily. "Yes. You and Russell. We'll go away . . ."

"Oh, my Rosalind, my sweet little Rosalind."

She heard a sound. The creak of a floorboard. She looked up over the little girl's shoulder. In the doorway now stood another figure. A horrible figure. A man with no face shuffled toward her.

She stood, terrified. The little girl in her arms had disappeared.

Then she noticed someone else behind the faceless creature. It was dark, but she could make out the face.

"Russell," she said softly.

"Hello, Mother."

She looked at him as he too began approaching her.

"Russell," she asked, "why are you dressed that way?"

Fireworks

They could see them explode over the trees, a combustion of gunpowder that sent angry little spirals of green twirling through the night sky. Crazy blue rockets shattered into a hundred droplets of red and gold that rained down all around them like acid rain.

But Erik and Kate paid no attention to the fireworks. They sat in the parlor exhausted, the last police officer finally departing only minutes before. A cruiser remained parked out in the street, in case Russell was spotted. They still hadn't found him. A search party had gone off into the woods, and the house and grounds were still cordoned off. Until Russell was found, they couldn't officially declare the mayor's death an accident. The disappearance of the master of Wrightsbridge left open the possibility that the old man had been pushed.

"I can't imagine a motive Russell might have had to do such a thing," Kate had said.

Officer Piatrowski had nodded. "I'm sure it was an accident, Mrs. Wright. But where could he have gone?"

They'd searched the house. They'd found nothing, not in the basement, not in any of the rooms, not in the attic. It was as if Russell had just disappeared into the essence of the house itself.

And maybe that wasn't so far from the truth.

"It's changed," Kate whispered at last to Erik.

"What do you mean, it's changed?"

"The house. I no longer feel any presence here. It's as if it's been sated, had its fill, gotten what it wanted." She paused. "Russell."

Erik had to admit he felt the same lack of presence. "It's how I felt right after the exorcism," he said. He looked over at Kate. "But the evil came back then. It could still return."

She sighed.

"Let's go back to New York tonight, Kate," he said. "Put Wrightsbridge behind us."

She frowned. "That would look awfully suspicious, don't you think? A man dies here and then we take off, just like Russell?"

"We'll tell the police where they can find you," Erik said. "We'll keep them fully informed."

She stood up, pacing across the room. "No. Auntie Cee's funeral won't be for several days yet. I can't leave." She looked at Erik. "Besides, I'm not leaving without Russell. He's my husband. I've got to find him. It's not too late to help him. It's still not too late."

Erik ran a hand through his hair in exasperation. "She's *got* him, Kate. You need to accept that. You can't fight her."

"I'm not so sure."

Erik sighed. "She's gone, anyway. And likely taken Russell with her."

"*Where* has she gone?"

He smirked. "Gone where the goblins go. I don't know, Kate. I just don't want her to come back."

"She's just a little girl," Kate said, imploring him to understand. "Anything she did was out of her own fear, her own sense of loss, her own tragedy."

Erik made a face and began ticking off items on his fingers. "Let's see now. Both alive and dead, Rosalind caused Bobby Shortridge to lose his mind and his face. She caused Russell to kill Theresa. She may have scared Auntie Cee to death and she likely caused the mayor to fall out that window. She's also tried to kill a little boy from town—and wait! Oh, yes! She tried to kill both you and me, too." He gave her a look. "So I'm sorry if I find it rather hard to view Rosalind sympathetically."

They sat up late into the night, not speaking much, just being together. It was getting close to morning when Kate said she might try to sleep for a bit. "We can talk more in the morning," she said.

"Sweetie," Erik said, taking her hand, "it's just that I want this nightmare to be over for you."

She looked at him with weary eyes. "It will never be, not until I can find Russell."

She said good night and walked up the stairs as the sound of scattered fireworks still ripped through the quiet of the night.

Erik settled back against the couch. He couldn't sleep. Never had he known a day like this. Or a house like this. He'd already begun planning a book about it. With Kate's permission, of course. It wouldn't be like any of his others, that was for sure. This was no *How to Make Friends with Ghosts*. No, sirree.

He heard a footstep on the stairs.

"Kate?" he called. "Decided against sleep? I don't blame you, sweetie, I—"

He looked up.

It wasn't Kate standing in front him.

"Dear God!" he managed to shout just as the knife bore down and pierced the flesh of his chest.

A Discovery in Kate's Room

There was someone in her bed.

"Russell?" she asked hopefully, flipping the light on.

But the light failed to illuminate the room. She looked up. Someone had removed the bulb.

"Russell?"

She approached the bed. Whoever was there didn't stir.

Kate braced herself.

She pulled back the covers.

A firework outside her window suddenly filled the room with fleeting, shimmering, pink light.

There, in Kate's bed, was the body of Molly Wright. Her face was blue.

Kate screamed just at the moment Erik screamed downstairs. Then the celebration in the night sky was over and Kate was left in darkness.

The Chase

She quickly composed herself, hurrying back into the hallway.

"Erik?" she called.

Had he screamed? Had something happened?

She heard footsteps running down the corridor. She knew they weren't Erik's. They were heavy, lumbering. Bobby Shortridge appeared from the darkness of the east wing. She turned and ran.

Up the next flight of stairs she went, hearing Bobby's footsteps behind her grow faster and harder. She almost made it to the third floor, but Bobby tackled her. She came crashing down on her cast, and found it didn't hurt nearly as much as she thought. In fact, she was able to move her right arm swiftly and elbow Bobby firmly in the stomach. She managed to slip out from his grasp and ran to the top of the stairs. But he took hold of her ankle and she came toppling down again.

The misshapen creature stood over her, his one eye telegraphing his thoughts.

"Kith," he rasped.

"Bobby, no . . ."

His tongue snaked out of his mouth as he bent down over her.

Instinctively she thrust out her feet, landing them smack in the center of Bobby's torso. Standing on the top step of the stairs, he lost his balance, and fell backward down to the landing, his head smashing into the stained-glass window of St. Sebastian. He let out a wild howl as he fell, and then did not stir.

Kate struggled to her feet. She hadn't meant to harm him. But he was going to rape her. She felt sure of that.

She felt her arm. Had it healed so fast? She took a couple of steps down the stairs. She had to check on Bobby. She prayed that he wasn't dead. He was just a pawn in this terrible game, a pawn of Rosalind's. . . .

That's when she saw the shadow creeping up from the second floor.

New footsteps. And they weren't Erik's.

The shadow grew larger as Kate backed up the stairs. The shadow of a woman. Long hair. And Kate could already smell the heavy Indian perfume.

"Russell . . ." she said in a tiny voice.

But the shadow continued moving. She saw a hand on the banister just before reaching the landing.

The attic, she thought to herself. *He's afraid of the attic.*

She hurried around the corner of the staircase to the door to the attic. She pulled the door closed behind her and raced up the steep, narrow stairs. Her arrival into the dusty space disturbed the bats, which suddenly swooped at her, flapping their hideous wings. But they didn't scare her nearly as much as that thing behind the attic door.

The thing she'd once called her husband.

"You wouldn't dare come up here, Russell," she

called, hearing his footsteps stop outside the door. "Your grandfather is here. Banging at his cell . . ."

There was no sound outside the door.

"Go away, Russell! We can still win! We can still beat the evil of this house! Go to your room and stay there! Take off those clothes and you'll be safe, Russell. Stay in your room and I'll come for you."

There was still silence.

Maybe he *had* gone away.

But then the doorknob began slowly to turn.

"Russell, stay away!" Kate commanded.

She heard him laugh. Except, it wasn't quite his laugh. She saw the figure open the door and begin its ascent up the stairs. It was Russell's shape, but hardly his walk.

She watched in wide-eyed horror.

She'd known, of course. Ever since they'd found that blouse and wig in Russell's closet.

But seeing it took her breath away.

Russell, in a long black wig and tight black jeans, and a red lace blouse. Russell as he imagined Rosalind would have looked, had she lived to grow into a woman.

Kate knew at that moment that the Rosalind that lived in Russell's mind was a far more determined— and dangerous—adversary than even the ghost of the little girl.

The thing in the black wig spoke to her in a voice that sent chills to her soul. "You made the mistake in thinking it was Russell running after you. But it was *me*. It was *Russell* who was frightened of the attic. *I* never was. *I* was never frightened of anything."

"Russell, listen to me. Your sister is dead and her ghost is gone. Whatever took place here today ended her power. Listen to me! *You're Russell Wright and I'm your wife!*"

He threw back his head and laughed. He looked so

absurdly frightening in that wig and that blouse. "Ended her power? Oh, my dear, you deceive yourself."

Kate wouldn't back down. "Rosalind always had a blood lust, ever since what she did to Bobby Shortridge. Even before that, Russell. Remember what she did to the butterflies!"

Something flickered behind his eyes.

"It wasn't her fault, Russell. This house made her that way. But *you* survived differently. You survived by being gentle. By being *good.* Today Rosalind sated her thirst. There's been death all around. You can be *free* of her now, Russell! *Free!*"

Her husband stopped in his approach. He suddenly looked uneasy and defiant. "You made her go away before," he said. "You won't be able to do it again."

"Your mother is downstairs in my bed," Kate shouted. "Maybe that's why Rosalind went away. Maybe that's all she needed! To know her mother came back! That she loved her! As she loved you, Russell!"

"*Noooooo!*" Russell screamed, throwing his hands into the air, the wig toppling off of his head. "She didn't love us! All we had was each other!"

He lunged at Kate, his cold hands closing around her throat. Kate struggled to free herself but he was gripped with the power of madness. She tried to kick, scream, push—but she was overcome. She fell to her knees as Russell bore down upon her.

She gripped his hands trying to pry them from her throat. She looked into his eyes. They were red, wild. Nothing familiar there. There was no way she couldn't get through to him. She had lost. She felt herself begin to lose consciousness as the breath was choked out of her—

"Russell."

He looked up at the sound of the voice, keeping his hands tight around Kate's throat.

"Russell."

Kate managed to move her eyes. There was someone in the attic with them.

"Russell, no."

Theresa. She stood there ethereally at the far end of the room, just watching. Russell's grip loosened somewhat and Kate gasped for air. Russell keep looking at the spirit of his dead wife, and finally dropped Kate to the floor.

"Theresa," he said.

"Not again, Russell. Not again."

He looked from her down at Kate, who was wheezing on the floor below him.

"Not again," he said in a soft, small voice. "Not again, Rosalind. I can't do it again."

Kate watched him. It was as if he were two people simultaneously. One second he was speaking in his own voice, the next he was speaking in hers.

"You puny little fool!" Rosalind spat from his mouth. His eyes suddenly danced with fire. "You're nothing but a weakling. Oh, Grandmother would be so ashamed of what you've become, Russell!"

"No, no more!" he shouted, in his own voice again.

The ghost of Theresa had disappeared. Russell looked down at Kate.

"No more," he whispered.

"Russell?"

With a trembling hand he reached down and stroked Kate's hair. "I did love you. I did want us to be happy. Remember that, Kate. But it's not possible for me. Nothing's possible for me without Rosalind."

She braced herself to fight him, anticipating the return of his hands around her throat. But instead he just kept looking at her, with the saddest and yet most peaceful expression she had ever seen on his face. Then he stood, gracefully, and ran back down the stairs.

Kate stumbled to her feet and followed.

She caught sight of him as he rounded the corner into Auntie Cee's room. From the shattered window, the wind blew fiercely. Only a few flimsy boards had been rudimentarily nailed across it by the police.

When Kate got to the doorway she saw Russell in front of the window, clearly in agony. His hands were in his hair and his face was contorted, the two halves of him at war. How pathetic he looked in his red lace blouse.

His eyes made one last contact with Kate's. Then he jumped, throwing his shoulder against the wood that had been meant to prevent just such a tragedy from occurring again. It snapped easily against the impact, and his body hurtled out into the night.

Kate screamed and ran to the window.

"Russell! Russell! Russell!"

On the other side of the house, the sun was rising. The pink fingers of dawn revealed his body not far from the spot where the mayor had died.

"Kate."

Hands were on her shoulders, comforting her. Bloody hands.

She turned.

It was Erik. He was bleeding from his chest, but he'd managed to tie his shirt around the wound, stopping the blood as best as he could.

"Oh, Erik!" she cried, embracing him. "Oh, Erik!"

"Sweetie," he said.

"Russell's dead," she sobbed. "Russell's dead."

"Maybe he thought that was the only way."

She touched his wound delicately. "Are you all right?"

"I think so." He winced a little. "Can't say the same about Bobby Shortridge."

"Is he dead, too?"

Erik nodded.

"So much death. So much tragedy."

"Let's get out here, Kate. Before any more tragedy occurs."

She glanced down at the body of her husband in the garden below. The sun was now sending low rays of gold across the meadow. The purple shadows of the night retreated.

"Look," she said softly, pointing to the ground below, the tears dripping off her face.

Erik followed her gaze.

A small smile crossed Kate's face. "I think the tragedies of this house are over forever."

Below, in the gathering light of dawn, a mother was walking from the garden out into the meadow, holding the hands of two happy little children, a girl and a boy.

She had come back for them. At long last, their mother was taking them away from Wrightsbridge.

Mistress of the House

The funerals had been over for a couple of weeks. The window had been repaired and all the questions answered satisfactorily to the police. The day was warm and the sun was bright. In the garden black-eyed Susans had opened their bright golden petals for the first time this season.

"Are you sure you won't come back with me to New York? Even for just a little while?" Erik asked her as they stood on the bridge.

Kate smiled, idly allowing her hand to fall and caress Lucifer's restored wing. "Oh, I have so much to do here. I've really begun knocking pages out for my novel, and there's lots to be done getting the garden ready for next year." She winked at him. "Wait till you see the roses next year. There's a contest in town. I'm going to enter it!"

He looked at her. "Sweetie, are you sure you're okay?"

She nodded. "My place is here, Erik. It's my house now."

He embraced her. He flinched a little, the wound in his chest still tender. The stitches would come out in a week. Kate caressed his face gently, her own arm free at last of her cast. The doctor had been astounded by how quickly she had healed. He'd never seen anything like it.

"I love you, sweetie."

She touched his face. "I know. If you were straight—"

He smiled. "I'll be back soon."

"Well, we expect frequent visits. It's only a short train ride."

He promised. His eyes flickered back up to the house. "Tell them . . . tell them I said good-bye."

"I will."

He kissed her cheek. Kate watched him walk across the rest of the bridge to his rental car, where he stopped and waved once more. She watched him drive off, tooting his horn as he passed out of view. She let out a long sigh, patted her belly, and then walked back up to Wrightsbridge.

The fresh coat of paint had done wonders. And the new trim, a light blue gingerbread, gave the house a whole new ambience. So much more inviting upon first view, she thought. All the shutters on the east wing had been opened, fresh air blowing through their rooms. Kate smiled, looking up at her house.

She was mistress of Wrightsbridge.

She walked back into the house. Not a speck of dust anywhere to be found. Surfaces gleamed brightly, and from the landing on the staircase St. George and his dragon were aglow with bright primary colors, the sun lighting the stained glass from behind.

"My home," she said to herself.

She had never had a home. Never had a family. Not until coming here.

She patted her belly again. She did that quite a bit these days.

"Kate?" came a voice from the parlor.

She stepped into the room. She'd had a new portrait commissioned and it now hung over the mantel. Russell—back-framed by the cables of the Brooklyn Bridge, the wind in his hair, the lights of Manhattan behind him. That's how she liked to remember him.

"Kate, did Erik leave?"

She looked down at the young woman sitting on the couch. Such a pretty girl, younger than Kate, in her ankle-length taffeta dress and high-button shoes.

"Yes, Cee," she told her. "He's gone back to New York."

"Such a *nice* man," Cee said. "I hope he visits often."

"Yes," agreed the young man beside her, resplendent in his army uniform, decorated with ribbons and medals for bravery. "I thought he was one fine chap."

Kate smiled. "Well, he said to tell you both good-bye. Even if he never *could* see you." She settled herself in the recently restuffed armchair. "And really, Samuel, you should feel free to take Cee and move on anytime. I'm fine here now. Really I am."

"Oh, we're not going anywhere for a while, are we, Samuel?" Cee asked, reaching over and patting his leg. "We just want to make sure you're acclimated, that's all."

Kate looked over at them. "How very kind you are."

"Besides," Cee said, a little smile stretching across her face, "there's a little event I want to witness—oh, about eight months from now. . . ."

Kate smiled. She had never had a family. Until coming to Wrightsbridge.

"Well, if you'll excuse me," she said, standing, "I

have a manuscript waiting upstairs." She offered them a saucy little grin. "My heroine has just moved into a house cloaked in shadows and intrigue . . ."

"With its share of resident ghosts, I presume?" Cee asked, a twinkle in her girlish eyes.

"But of course," Kate told her.

She left them in the parlor. Kate ascended the stairs, feeling the sun on her face as it poured through the stained-glass window. Russell's child would know a far different Wrightsbridge than he ever did. There would be laughter and joy, family and friends. No more tragedy, no more pain.

She continued walking upstairs into the bright warmth of the sun.

Look for
Robert Ross's
next novel

DON'T CLOSE YOUR EYES

Coming soon from
Pinnacle Books!

Here's a sneak preview. . . .

Something sinister is happening to the citizens of
Falls Church, Massachusetts,
a tiny fishing village on Cape Cod. Something from
the town's long-buried past has awakened—
and it is spreading to everyone, one by one, like a
terrifying cancer. Soon all will know
firsthand the wicked, dark secret of Fall's Church.

Wednesday, May 3, 3:15 A.M.

"Mommy!"

Josh McKenzie's sheets are damp, and his little heart
races like the Road Runner.

"Mommy!"

He bolts upright. Across his bed the moonlight paints
a white stripe through the darkness, illuminating his
Barney pajamas and the stuffed rabbit who always sleeps
beside him.

"Mom-eeeeeeeeee!"

Suddenly there's light overhead, orange and stark.
His mother blinks her eyes in the doorway. "I'm right
here, baby," she's saying. "I'm right here."

Her yellow hair sticks up crazily from yesterday's
mousse. Her flannel nightgown clings to her right breast
in static electricity.

"Mommy, Mommy," Josh chirps, his voice funny, as if it's not his own. "I had a nightmare."

"It's okay, babe," his mother assures him. "I'm here now."

She sits down on the side of his bed the way she's done before. Gently she pulls him into her warmth, his face pushing into her flannel, his heart thudding in her embrace. But it does little good. Josh remains afraid, his little body still hiccuping in terror. He doesn't understand. Usually this would be the end of his nightmares: in his mother's arms, they would recede into the dim memory of sleep. The smell of his mother's powder, her hair gel, her cigarettes, would counteract his terror, dissolving it like soap in bathtub suds.

But not this time.

"He's *here*, Mommy," Josh tells her, one eye peering over the crook of her elbow. "He's *here.*"

"Who's here, Josh? There's no one here."

"He *is*, Mommy. He's here." He pulls from her embrace, glances around his room.

Everything looks just the same as it did when he went to sleep. The Pokemon balls on his desk, the Game Boy on the floor, the Power Rangers poster on the wall, the picture of him and Mommy and Grandpa hanging slightly crooked opposite his bed.

"Baby, no one's here." His mother stands up and walks across the room. "See, baby? Just you and me." She slides open the closet door. Josh shrinks back in his bed. "Nothing. See? Just your clothes and Pikachu."

He pulls his stuffed rabbit closer. "But I got to tell you, Mommy," Josh says. "I gotta tell you the dream."

She smiles wearily. "Why don't you just try to forget it, baby? It wasn't real. There's nobody—"

"If I tell you, it will go away," he says. His body still

shakes. Sweat still beads his brow. The terror hasn't let go.

His mother frowns in concern, placing her hand on his forehead. "Baby, you're burning up. Let me get you some asp—"

"No, Mommy, please! Please just let me tell you my dream."

She looks down at him. "Okay, Josh. Go ahead. Tell me the dream."

She sits down beside him again and takes him into her arms. The words come rushing out of his small frame against her bosom.

"There was this man," he says. "In a tall hat. I was sitting on the sidewalk in front of our house and he was walking toward me. He was far, far away at first, but he just kept on walking, closer and closer, and I just kept watching him. You know how you tell me all the time that I shouldn't talk to strangers? How if any man ever comes up to me and asks me to go with him, I should run far away as fast as I can? Well, I was thinking that in my dream but I couldn't run. I saw him coming but I couldn't move. He just kept getting closer and closer and I knew he was coming to get me. He finally got right up next to me and . . . and then . . . he smiled!"

His mother grins a little herself. "That's not so scary, baby."

"But, Mommy—he had worm's in his mouth!"

She manages a little laugh and pulls him closer. "Well, yuck."

"They were like—coming through his teeth and—" He pauses, looking up at her. The terror is gone. He feels a sudden relief, like the kind when he's finally gone pee after holding it all the way home from Grandpa's. The relief settles across him like a warm comforting blanket. "And I guess that's it," he says. "I knew I'd feel better if I told you."

His mother places her hand on his head. "And you've gotten cool again. Still, I'm going to get you some children's aspirin and a cold cloth." She moves to stand. "Is it okay if I go now, just to get you the aspirin?"

"Yeah, it's okay now, Mommy. I'm not scared anymore."

She smiles. When she returns with the two chewable tablets in her hand and a wet facecloth draped over her arm, Josh has already fallen back to sleep.

Kathy McKenzie has had a long day. She had just drifted off to sleep when Josh's cries awakened her. She hadn't gotten into bed until nearly one o'clock, finally finishing the laundry that had been piling up all week. She'd had no clean underwear left in her drawer, and Josh had used the last towel in the bathroom getting washed up before bed. She did four loads, the whites carefully sorted from the colors, lugging the plastic basket up the wooden steps from the basement each time. She'd folded Josh's T-shirts and underpants and placed them outside his door, not wanting to wake him. When she was finally finished, Kathy desperately craved a cigarette, but successfully fought off the urge. She just flopped down exhausted onto her bed.

Sleep hadn't come easily. Each time she began to nod off she'd wake up, the burning in her chest stronger. *I won't give in,* Kathy told herself, forcing herself to shut her eyes and not look over at her purse on the table, where inside was concealed one last pack of smokes, in case of emergency. *It's not that bad. I can fight it off. If I give in now, everything's lost.*

Of course then Josh had cried out, and any hope of

getting some real sleep this night was shattered. Josh isn't the kind to have nightmares very often, but when he does they're usually doozies. He's a resilient boy, for which Kathy is thankful. It isn't easy growing up in a small town where everyone knows your whole life story. Josh has already heard the whispers about his father, and Kathy has tried to be as honest as possible with him. "What matters," she has said to him, time and again, "is not what other people say, but what you *know*. And you know that you are very loved. By me, and by your grandpa, and by all your true friends."

How much does Josh remember of his father? He was just two when Kathy had finally called the cops that last time, crawling on her hands and knees up those very same wooden basement steps, She had pulled herself up, step by step, dragging one useless arm beside her, dripping blood between the spaces of the steps—plop, plop, plop onto the concrete floor below. Sly had pushed her down the stairs; she'd later learned her left arm and two ribs were broken, and her right knee was splintered. How long she lay there, crumpled at the foot of the stairs like a burlap sack of potatoes, she didn't know. She woke up hearing Josh crying upstairs; her first thought was that Sly had hit him, too. She had no clue as to her own injuries; the pain was a general thing, from head to foot. She had no choice but to crawl, dragging herself step by step. Her baby needed her; he might be hurt, worse than she.

He wasn't: Josh was just hungry, standing in his crib, his face red and bloated from tears and frustration. She couldn't stand, couldn't take him in her arms to console him, and that was far worse than anything else. She could only try to reassure him from the floor, but it did no good, just made him scream harder. Sly had ripped the phone out of the wall, but—stupid crack head that he was—he'd forgotten the cell phone in the bedroom. Kathy pulled herself with her right arm across the linoleum kitchen floor, making a horrible squeaking sound, and then down the hardwood of the hallway. She was in luck: the cell phone was under the bed, where Kathy often stashed it. She pressed 911.

Her knee aches suddenly. *Stop dwelling on the past,* she scolds herself. She sits down on her stool in front of her vanity and rubs her knee. *He's gone. Secure behind iron bars and concrete walls for at least another three years. Josh doesn't remember him. Never speaks of him. Grandpa is enough Dad for him, even if he lives an hour away.*

Still, Kathy worries—worries Sly will get out, that he'll come for Josh. She has indeed told her son many times that if any man ever approaches him and tries to take him away, he is to run with all his might as far as possible in the opposite direction. Maybe she's frightened him. But better that he be frightened than fall into Sly's hands.

Looking into her mirror she sees the circles under her eyes. She'd worked a double shift today; Berniece had called in sick, and so Kathy had stuck around for supper hour as well. Old Mr. Lamphere had been particularly ornery tonight, sending his cheese rarebit back to the kitchen. Kathy made him a peanut butter and jelly sandwich as replacement. She'd been annoyed at having to give up her break to do it, but she really didn't blame Mr. Lamphere. She's not sure she could eat that processed orange cheese goop over toast and bacon either.

Worst thing was missing dinner with Josh. Usually her job at Barnstable Convalescent allows her to be here and waiting when Josh gets home from school at three. Her shift is normally six-thirty to two-thirty. She gets Josh up at six, makes him a quick breakfast of oatmeal and toast, then drops him by Pat Crawford's on her way to work. He waits with Pat's son Kyle until seven-thirty when the bus picks them up. It's a routine that has worked—so long as no crisis erupts to knock it off course. If Josh gets sick, she has to call in sick; Berniece has filled in for her a number of times. So Kathy feels duty-bound to stick in there for the supper shift, calling Pat and asking her to keep Josh until she gets home at seven.

"And could he eat with you all, too? I hate to ask. If it's too much trouble, I can pick up a pizza from Gerry's on my way—"

"No, no, Kathy. Don't worry about it. Of course, Josh can eat with us. I'm sure a good meal of meat, potatoes, and vegetables would do him some good."

Kathy slides back into bed now and turns off the light, trying once again to ignore her craving. She quit smoking a week ago, and so far is very proud of her accomplishment. But remembering Pat Crawford's superior tone pisses her off. Like she doesn't feed her son balanced meals! Okay, so they do eat pizza a lot, and sometimes they drive down to Wendy's in Orleans— hey, where else can they get those damned Pokemon balls? Pat Crawford's just a privileged bitch who can afford to sit around on her butt all day because her husband is a fucking real estate agent who's selling off this town bit by bit and making himself rich from it. . . .

Kathy feels her eyes closing against her thoughts. *Don't put out such negative energy,* she can hear Berniece telling her. *What you put out comes back to you, sweetie.*

Off in the distance the foghorn calls, low and sorrowful. It usually soothes her, as it has all her life. But tonight, in that moment just before sleep, she feels it's a warning that comes too late.

* * *

She opens her eyes suddenly. It's daylight. She looks up. There's a man standing over her. A man in a tall black top hat.

She's sitting on the sidewalk in front of their house. She can still hear the foghorn.

Dear God, she thinks, looking at the man. *Don't let him open his mouth.*

She knows what's behind his thin red lips, and she can't bear to see it. He keeps his mouth closed, in a tight straight line. He beckons with his hand to follow him.

She does, although she'd prefer not to. She keeps trying to stop, or at least slow down, but he always turns back and looks at her. She's terrified that he'll open his mouth, and she figures if she just follows him she won't have to see what's inside.

They go out to the beach. "No, please," she says, but it's like talking underwater. Her voice sounds strange to her ears. She hears the motorcycle on the boardwalk. She turns and sees Sly, with a bundle tied to the back of his bike. Something's kicking from inside the bundle. She knows it's Josh.

"Let him go!" she screams, but it's no use. Her voice is still muffled, and since when did Sly listen to her anyway? The Harley roars off down the boardwalk, the way it used to when she was sixteen, gripping Sly from behind, the wind in her hair.

"No! No! No!" she screams.

"Yes, yes, yes," comes the voice of the man in the tall hat behind her. She spins around and looks at him. She can see the worms now, slipping and slithering around on his tongue, between the gaps in his rotting teeth, over his thin dry lips. He comes closer. She can smell him. She has a weird, intrusive thought: *I've never smelled anything before in a dream.* But this is fierce and unavoidable: a wet, musty, wormy smell, like the driveway after a heavy rain. The man leans in and kisses her hard. The worms wiggle inside her mouth. She tries to scream, but only manages to swallow the worms, one after one after slimy one.

"Well, good morning, Josh," calls Mr. Silva, the postman. "No school today?"

Josh looks up at him with tired eyes. "My mother's not feelin' so good."

"Sorry to hear that." Mr. Silva reaches around in his bag and pulls out a bill from ComElectric. "Sorry all I got for her today is this. Afraid it won't do much cheering."

Josh takes the letter. His eyes look different to Mr. Silva, as if he'd gotten no sleep in weeks.

"You feelin' okay yourself, son? You don't look so good neither."

Josh shrugs. He's sitting on the front step, moving a toy race car back and forth on his leg.

"Looks like it's gonna rain again," Mr. Silva observes. "Feels like spring won't ever get here. Still so cold and damp. But it'll come around. Spring always does, and then summer. You lookin' forward to summer vacation, Josh?"

The boy just shrugs again.

"Well, tell your mom I hope she feels better," the postman says.

"Mr. Silva."

The postman looks up. Behind the screen door stands Kathy McKenzie. Her face looks weird, distorted through the screen.

"Well, howdy, Kathy. Josh here tells me you're not up to snuff today."

"Mr. Silva, could I possibly . . . just for a minute . . . possibly talk to you?"

Her voice is trembling. Hiram Silva steps forward to look up at her. He knows all about the tough breaks Kathy McKenzie has had. He and his wife Betty have often remarked that they feel really sorry for Kathy, having to raise that boy all alone out here in the low-income housing on Cranberry Terrace. She's from such a good old local family, too: Betty and Hiram have known Eddie and Delores McKenzie for years. They have thanked God that Kathy's miserable ex-husband Sly Sankner is locked away in state prison, and that Kathy can finally rest easily. She's a hardy one, that Kathy McKenzie, a real survivor. Everyone says so.

"What's wrong, Kathy?" Hiram asks her. "Are you okay?"

"Please, Mr. Silva . . . please . . ." She sounds so pathetic. She disappears back inside the house.

The postman looks down at Josh sitting on the step. "I better go in and see if she's okay," he says awkwardly, stepping past him and opening the screen door. Josh doesn't respond, just keeps running his race car down his leg and over his knee.

Inside the McKenzie house Mr. Silva notices a strange smell. Almost like . . . *a locker room,* he thinks. Sweat. Steam. The couple times he's been inside the house before, it has always been so fresh and clean-smelling. Now he walks down a hallway strewn with cigarette butts. "Kathy?" he calls. "You okay? Where are—?"

He spots her sitting at the kitchen table, leaning on her elbows, looking down, her hands in her hair. On the table are dozen of cigarette butts, overflowing from a small tin ashtray. "Kathy," he says, approaching her.

On the wall the cuckoo clock suddenly chirps ten times. It startles him. Kathy doesn't look up.

"I had a dream," she says.

"A dream?" he asks.

She shifts a little in her seat. Her hair, dyed blond, nearly white, sticks up in stiff clumps. The back is matted to her head. "I've got to tell it to you . . . please . . . just let me tell you the dream and it'll be okay."

He rests his hand on her shoulder. She's burning up. He can feel her shaking.

"Maybe I should call a doctor," he offers weakly.

"No," she says. "Please. Just let me tell you my dream."

Hiram Silva is not a young man. Next year he's set to retire after forty years with the post office. He's a good man, well liked. Everyone in town knows his story, too. He and Betty had a daughter, Rose, who would have been Kathy McKenzie's age if she had lived. But Rose died of leukemia when she was eight. Everyone came to her funeral, including Kathy McKenzie's parents. Nearly everyone had come back to the Silva's little house on Pearl Street afterward, bringing their casseroles and fruitcakes and linguica, the Portuguese sausage. Hiram had eaten linguica for weeks after Rose's funeral. He can't bring himself to touch the stuff anymore.

Funny how he thinks of Rose now, as he bends down beside Kathy McKenzie, stroking her hair.

"All right, Kathy," he says. "Go ahead. Tell me the dream."

"There was a man," she breathes. "A man in a tall hat . . ."

And so she tells him . . . about following him to the beach, about Sly on his Harley, about Josh in the sack, about how the man kissed her, about the worms . . .

Hiram Silva feels terribly uncomfortable listening to it all, especially about the kissing and the worms down the throat. He's sure Betty would say it was a sexual thing; she reads a lot of books and says all dreams are sexual. Hiram's not sure, but as much as he wants to help poor Kathy McKenzie, all he wants to do right now is get out of there, back to his route.

Kathy does seem to brighten. "Oh, dear God," Kathy says. "I do feel better." She looks up at Mr. Silva. "Thank you. You must think me crazy."

"I'd still call a doctor if I were you," he advises, but already, even though he's no longer touching her, he can feel the temperature in the room dropping. The sweaty smell seems to be dissipating, too.

For the rest of the day, Hiram Silva delivers the mail with his usual promptness and efficiency, even when the rains come again, heavy and drenching. He pulls on his old blue, post office–issued slicker, and runs from his truck up each and every walk, belying his sixty-three years.

Yet many of the citizens of Fall's Church comment that day how distracted Mr. Silva seems, how distant. There's little of the usual chitchat with the women on their front porches, no exchange of town news when he stops in at Clem's Diner. That night, Betty Silva notices her husband eats very little of her pot roast and boiled potatoes, and questions why he's still awake, at eleven-thirty, defiant in his plaid La-Z-Boy recliner, forcing his bleary eyes to stay open for Jay Leno.

"You don't even like him, Hiram. Come to bed."

"I'm just not very tired," he lies to her—the first lie he's told her in forty-two years of marriage.

He can't have told her why he was procastinating. He isn't even fully aware of it himself. There is just a sense of being on the edge, cautious, careful.

Yet after about ten minutes he gives in, catching his chin thudding against his chest, and climbs into bed beside his wife. He looks once of the photograph of Rose they keep beside their bed, running his finger along the outline of her face, then turns off the light and pulls the sheets tightly up to his chin. He falls asleep a few minutes after he hears the clock in the living room softly chime twelve.

That's when he sees the man in the tall black hat with the worms living in his teeth.

ABOUT THE AUTHOR

Robert Ross lives in Massachusetts and is currently working on his next novel. He loves to hear from readers; you may write to him c/o Pinnacle Books. Please include a self-addressed, stamped envelope if you wish to receive a response. You may also e-mail him at RobertRossAuthor@aol.com.

Feel the Seduction of Pinnacle Horror